THE POSSE

The Posse

Lyn Horner
Frank Kelso
cj petterson
Charlene Raddon
Chimp Robertson
JS Stroud
Chuck Tyrell

THE POSSE

An Intellect Publishing Book

Copyright 2017 Intellect Publishing, LLC

ISBN: 978-1-945190-18-6

Cover design and artwork by Charlene Raddon

Edited by
Ellie Locket

First edition: 2017
PBF8MA

Visit the web Site: www.ThePosseBook.com

Intellect Publishing, LLC
6581 County Road 32, Suite 1195
Point Clear, AL 36564
www.IntellectPublishing.com
For inquiries: info@IntellectPublishing.com

From the publisher

It is not often that you get to do something you are passionate about (like publishing), and be proud of what you've done. This book accomplishes both.

From the time I can remember, I loved western stories—from Louis L'Amour to Zane Gray—and I lived for shows like Gunsmoke, Wagon Train, and of course, Have Gun, Will Travel featuring Richard Boone as Paladin.

These eight stories take you on thrilling western adventures, all written by professionals who love their craft, and realize that they are writing for you, the reader. I am so proud to be able to bring them to you.

Sit back and dive into each one, knowing that you are in for a true western adventure ... and I hope to continue bringing you more of these western tales every year.

John O'Melveny Woods

THE POSSE

Table of Contents

Find more author info and story excerpts at:
http://facebook.com/thepossebook.1
And also at: http://thepossebook.com/

The Posse

ONE WAY OR ANOTHER
Frank Kelso

Willie Little regretted not listening to his foreman's advice that morning. Instead, Willie ordered all of his ranch hands, even the cook, onto the Nueces plains of south Texas to finish the fall round-up in a final push today. No one expected his ornery neighbor to come calling.

"Listen to me, ya snot-nosed runt." Brad Buxton's ham-sized fist gripped Willie's blue flannel shirt collar, shaking him like a puppy who'd peed on the carpet. Spittle flew from Buxton's thick lips as he shouted. "Yer pa and me shared the water in the Nueces valley. He intended me to get his water rights when he died—he told me his-self. Ya done betrayed me."

Willie struggled to keep upright after Buxton tossed him aside.

"Don't know who told you what, Mr. Buxton, but my father left a signed and witnessed will. The county judge held probate court, declaring me the Muleshoe's sole owner. You have no say in it—it's the law." Willie took after his ma's family: slim, five-feet-ten, with her steel-gray eyes, fair complexion, and sandy hair.

Taller and heavier, Buxton shoved Willie again, sending him sprawling on his butt. The big man spat a gob of chewing tobacco between Willie's legs. Never a handsome man, Buxton's heavy brow ridge, squinty black eyes, and flattened nose fit his pugnacious bearing.

Willie glanced up to find Buxton had stepped close to shove the muzzle of his re-chambered 1861 Remington pistol a foot from Willie's face.

"This here's the law on the Nueces strip." Buxton cocked the hammer.

"Boss," a rider behind Buxton called, "His crew'll be here 'fore ya can get mounted."

Pounding hoofs grew into thunder as ten riders raced into the Muleshoe's front yard.

Buxton kicked dirt on Willie, as he lay sprawled on the ground. "Don't think this settles nothing. I'll get my water, one way—or another."

Dust swirled as the Muleshoe's riders reined in their horses across from Buxton's cowhands. Riders on each side laid a hand on their pistols. Four of Willie's crew carried rifles resting across their thighs. The horses snorted, shuffling their hooves, as nervous and agitated as their riders.

While Buxton toed a stirrup to mount, Willie climbed to his feet, slapping the dirt from his pants with his hat. "Mr. Buxton, my father respected you. You two shared the Nueces water for the last fifteen years. We can put this spat behind us. Let's continue as good neighbors."

With repeated jabs of his finger, Buxton shouted, "I'll show ya good neighbors—stay off *my* land. Don't ya or yer riders even use *my* road into Uvalde."

Willie glanced away, drawing a deep breath, before peering up at Buxton. "I studied law when East at college. The San Antonio to El Paso mail coach uses the road across your land, which makes it a public thoroughfare. You can't stop others from using the mail road—it's the law." He swept his arm in an arc from west to east. "Tomorrow, my crew will push your beef from my land. If necessary, I'll fence the boundary to keep your beeves off my grass."

"Ya can't cut me off from the water." Buxton had his old Remington half out of its holster again when the Muleshoe's *segundo* , Theo Tuttle, fired a rifle round into the dirt beneath Buxton's feisty stallion.

The frightened black horse scooted sideways, squealing as it danced.

Buxton needed both hands on the reins to stay mounted while settling the unruly black beast. The disruption stirred his heated anger, shading his face a deep scarlet.

"I warned yer pa not to build that damned lake. He started all this."

"The lake's half full already," Willie said. "By spring, it'll be full from winter rain and snow runoff. Encina Creek will flow from my valley to your land, like always." Willie shifted to leave.

Buxton shook his fist at Willie. "My grass is thinning 'cause *ya* are stealing all the water."

"The hell I am." Willie spun, pointing his finger. "You run too many cows. Overgrazing causes your poor grass, not lack of water. My father offered to build the dam astride Encina Creek with access for both of our properties, but you didn't want to spend the money."

"Why ya mealy-mouthed bookworm, what do *ya* know about cattle?"

"You're right, I'm not near the cattleman my father was, but I'm learning. Today, I learned not to ride this land unarmed. I won't let you push me around again. Now, get off *my* land."

Buxton touched his holstered Remington before glancing around to realize the futility of a fight when the Muleshoe's crew outnumbered him two-to-one. His hand slid away.

"This ain't over." He spat tobacco juice toward Willie before he and his crew wheeled their horses around to gallop away.

Tuttle, a grizzled Civil War veteran and a seasoned cattleman, dismounted with a casual ease. Astride a horse from the age of five, the bowlegged man wobbled side to side.

"Hope ya didn't bite off sump'n ya cain't swaller, Boss. Don't git me wrong—I'm mighty glad ya done it." Tall, with lean ropey muscles, Theo had been the Muleshoe's *segundo*, or foreman, for the past fifteen years, except during the War years.

"I out grew the habit of carrying a pistol while at college. I don't think about it now."

While he listened to his boss, Theo rolled a cigarette, licked the paper's edge, and stuck it in the corner of his mouth. With his thumbnail, he snapped a Lucifer, lighting it, as the match's sulfurous odor mingled with his exhaled smoke.

"That said ol' son, when were the last time ya handled yer Colt? Buxton ain't no gun hand, but he needn't be, if'n ya cain't hit a bull in the butt. Ya get out yer ol' .38 Navy Colt, an' clean it. Get to wearing it ever' time ya go outside." Exhaling smoke, he asked, "Can ya hit anything?"

"You taught me to shoot long before I went East. I wrote you Yale has a pistol team. They elected me captain in my senior year. I'm not afraid of him … I'd hoped to settle it peacefully."

"Them peaceable days is gone. Draw up a plan an' let us help. We'll fight for the Muleshoe."

"Don't want a range war if we can avoid it. He needed to vent some steam. After he cools off, maybe we can talk again.

Tell our men to keep off his land. Have them use the mail road."

The winter months struck hard as 1869 rolled in. A sleety rain, followed by snow, blew down from the high plains. The range crew bunched cattle in the sheltered coves of Encina Canyon's lower meadows, the Muleshoe's prime land. Man and beast hunkered down, waiting for spring.

After years of torment during the corrupt Reconstruction Era, Texans found relief when cattle prices soared on the eastern markets and in the western gold fields. Charlie Goodnight drove cattle west along the Pecos into New Mexico before turning north to Colorado. Meanwhile, cattle drives up Chisholm's Trail to Kansas allowed the vast Texas ranches to produce needed income, leading Texas to a financial recovery after the disastrous War Between the States.

With the changing cattle markets in mind, Willie rode the mail coach to San Antonio. He needed allies and money to fend off Buxton's malevolent threats to take down the Muleshoe.

A cattleman *must* stay at the Menger Hotel in San Antonio, or else it led to gossip hinting recovery had passed him by. Such gossip often led to tightened credit when a rancher needed it.

While Willie registered at the desk, he shot the clerk a scowl. "Why do you want my brand?"

"Cattlemen know brands. It seems to me they remember brands better than a man's name." The clerk wrote a small horseshoe symbol with an "m" inside instead of writing "Muleshoe."

At supper that evening, four older men, for whom Willie had a vague recollection from boyhood, stopped at his table.

Each expressed his condolence for his father's passing and, of course, asked about his plans for the Muleshoe.

Jack Harding, a man he remembered well, asked about Buxton. "Story's going 'round ol' Buxton's trying to squeeze ya—don't ya let him. Whatever ya do, don't ya sell him the Muleshoe. Come see me at the Rocker-H if ya decide to sell."

The notion that Texas cattlemen were worse gossips than old women at a quilting-bee flitted through his mind while he strolled the long hallway between the dining rooms and the Menger's ornate, high-ceilinged front lobby. Billiards clacking caused him to glance above when he passed through an atrium with wide, carpeted stairs leading upstairs to the smoking and gaming rooms.

A raven-haired young woman, still in her teens, attracted his eye, but what brought him to a halt wasn't only her beauty. She tugged on Brad Buxton's arm, urging him down the stairs. Well-dressed in a cultured fashion, she bore no resemblance to the "chippies" Buxton frequented in Uvalde's bawdy houses. *The old bachelor is living it up. But, why at the Menger?* While all eyes followed the young lady's antics, Willie used the time to slip away unnoticed.

The next morning, Willie decided to enjoy breakfast at his leisure in the main dining room. The South had suffered in the War and in Reconstruction, but the Menger maintained tradition. The hotel offered formal meals on a white tablecloth with a full silver service at each table.

By happenstance, the maitre d' seated Willie one table away from Buxton's young woman, chaperoned by an older woman dressed in black. Her youthful complexion, cascading jet curls, and stunning violet eyes attracted his attention. Noting Buxton guarded her with an old dueña, he wondered if she might be high Spanish given her pale skin and colorful eyes. To his surprise, the two women conversed in French when they passed his table upon their departure.

Over the next week, Willie busied himself conducting the ranch's business interests. He didn't dine at the Menger often, which resulted in infrequent glimpses of the mysterious and alluring young French woman. He failed to imagine Buxton courting her. *Why is she with him?* He snorted, shaking his head. *It's none of my concern. I need to tend to my own business.*

At week's end, he paid a porter to carry his traveling bag to the stagecoach station for the ride west to Uvalde. The stage station lay eight blocks west along Commerce Street beside the old Spanish Governor's Palace. Before the coach's departure, he strolled across the wide street to the Mexican outdoor market, or Mercado.

He glanced at the station door with surprise. The attractive French woman exited the station dressed in plain gray traveling clothes, topped by a beige duster, and a hat. He didn't notice the *dueña* with her, which caused him to search with care. Buxton's bulky form strutted through the station's wide door. *Damn and double damn—Buxton's taking the El Paso stage back to Uvalde.*

Willie waited in the shade of a twisted mesquite tree near the Mercado Plaza entrance. Buxton treated the young woman formally, not the touching and whispering of lovers, or even close friends. Willie couldn't fathom their relationship. He waited until the last minute to board.

"Was ready to leave ya—don't be expectin' me to wait on ya." The *jehu* (driver) shouted from habit, even when stopped at the station. Shouting while under way became a necessity so all passengers could hear him over the coach and team's noise.

"All right if I ride on top?" Willie asked.

9

"It ain't comfy up here. Gets right dusty. Don't want no complainin'," came the loud reply.

Buxton leaned forward to scowl at him through the coach's open windows.

The coach stopped for the night at the relay station in Hondo, the small hamlet's largest building. Weary from the rocking ride on top, Willie tottered like a drunk when he climbed from the coach. The stagecoach line provided sparse comforts for its first-class passengers: a fatty, beef-and-potato hash served on pie tins with a square of hot cornbread for supper. The sleeping accommodations consisted of a dusty, windowless adobe room with four well-used cots. The wood-frame cots with rope webbing held worn ticking filled with Spanish moss and bedbugs.

Willie couldn't tell which offended the young woman more, the sleeping arrangements or the food. She'd kept a perfumed hanky under her nose since she stepped from the coach.

Buxton glared at him, daring him to enter the sleeping room.

"I'll sleep in the coach, since I didn't get to use the seat cushions today," Willie said.

The next morning, Willie awoke to fresh coffee and frying bacon scenting the air. He hadn't noticed this many men inside a relay station before. The young woman's appearance brought the men to their feet when she entered the main room. They'd been waiting to gaze upon her.

The young woman glanced about the room, taking a small step back when confronted by the assembled men. She acted hesitant, unsure if she should move to the table. This morning, she had abandoned the perfumed hanky. In an unexpected move, she glanced at Willie and smiled.

"Papa has been so rude. He said you are our neighbor, but he failed to conduct a proper introduction. I'm MarieClare d'Iberville from Mobile. No doubt you have heard of the Mobile d'Iberville's?" She tilted her head to one side before raising an eyebrow in expectation.

Willie blinked twice. *Papa? Buxton?* "I'm at a loss, mademoiselle. I don't know the name."

"They are *quelqu'une quelqu'une* ... how do you say ... something special in Mobile. Well, I'm from Mobile ... but not from those d'Iberville's." She giggled, flapping her hand when she said "those."

Her slight French accent beguiled Willie, and probably the rest of the men in the station.

She pushed her chin forward, raising an eyebrow again, as if she expected something.

"I told you my name. I expected you to say yours."

"Willie Little, mademoiselle. *Enchanté.*" Willie grew concerned, because behind her, Buxton stood puffing his cheeks, growing as red as an over-stoked boiler ready to explode.

"*Vous parlé français? Tres bein.*" She glanced at her father, who stepped closer to her.

"*Un petite peu.*" Willie held his thumb and forefinger close together. "A little."

"*Voila.* You are a Little." Her dimples winked as she giggled.

It took Willie a heartbeat before he caught her pun. "*Oui, mademoiselle, un peu.*" The twinkle in her eyes led him to suspect she flirted only to get a rise from her papa. It certainly worked; Buxton shook with anger.

"Let us not speak *le français* around Papa. He fears we are being naughty," she said.

The light fragrance of her perfume reminded him of oleanders.

"Allow me to lead you to the table, mademoiselle," Willie said, offering her an arm.

She placed her delicate hand on his forearm.

After seating her, he sat on the table's other side but not directly across from MarieClare. He had no need to provoke Buxton any more than he already had.

At MarieClare's insistence, Willie rode inside the coach. She chattered like a squirrel teasing the baying hounds. She didn't run out of topics for which she had an opinion. At first, Buxton glared and tapped his holstered Remington pistol, but as the day wore on, her non-stop chatter became annoying. Buxton often rolled his eyes as if exasperated. Willie agreed.

Even with her father seated next to her, and covered by a travelling duster and hat, she radiated a sensual charge that attracted men like a dark wool suit attracts lint. Willie tried not to let his gaze fall on her sculpted porcelain face with her Cupid's bow mouth, but she sat across from him, smiling at him while encouraging his attention to her conversation.

The stagecoach arrived in Uvalde near dusk, too late for Willie to ride safely for the two hours to reach the Muleshoe. He glanced at Buxton. "There's only one hotel and one decent place to eat. Can we agree to be civil around your daughter until I ride out in the morning?"

"Ya stay away from her—she's too young to understand." Buxton's jowls quivered.

"I didn't even know you had a daughter. Am I supposed to ignore her, when she speaks to me? There's no need to be rude."

"There's a difference 'tween being polite and taking advantage of her. Don't ya be coming around while she's visiting. Stay off my land." Buxton spun on a heel, stomping away.

After Buxton jerked open the hotel's door, allowing his daughter to enter, Willie decided he'd have an early supper. Striding past the hotel, he headed toward the Cactus Café, where the aroma of frying beef beckoned.

When he stepped to the boardwalk upon leaving the Café, Buxton approached escorting MarieClare along the narrow, wooden walkway.

"Willie, I thought you went away without a farewell. Please, join us for supper," she said.

"I'd love to, mademoiselle, but I've finished eating. Perhaps, I'll see you at the hotel."

Willie tipped his hat to her before stepping aside as Buxton stomped past. While Willie strolled away, Buxton snarled angry words at her. His remark, "stay away," rang clear.

The days passed and spring lifted winter's siege. Life on the Muleshoe held disappointments and surprises. His dad had introduced sheep and goats into the rugged highland slopes where cattle couldn't graze. To his delight, their wool and mohair produced a healthy profit from the spring shearing. Even better, this spring's lambs and kids doubled the size of their flocks.

The disappointment came after moving cattle herds between the pastures upstream along the northern Nueces plains. Too many cows with new spring calves had gone missing. Someone must have raided the pastures, taking a few cows south across the Nueces each night.

"I'd say we've done lost more than twenty cows an' their calves," Tuttle drawled.

"I can't lose three thousand dollars. I'd expected to lose a few head this winter, but not twenty. Any chance of tracking them? Or finding somebody herding them south?" Willie asked.

"Slim to none on both. Too much territory to hunt tracks if they're in small groups. It's too easy to hide cattle in a swale or a deep arroyo. Ya wouldn't see 'em 'til ya rode into 'em."

"What do we do? Move the herd? Send out night riders to patrol along the Nueces?"

"Too much good grass beside the Nueces to move the herd to the Encina's meadows. If we do, they'll graze the meadows bare before fall. Don't like it, but we need a night watch."

"I'll ride to town in the morning to alert the county sheriff," Willie said. "Not much he can do now, but I want to know if rustlers are sniping all along the Nueces, or if they've singled us out. While I'm there, I'll spread the word we're hiring punchers to ride the night watch."

Willie turned toward the ranch house, but glanced over his shoulder. "What about the herd on the plateau?"

"Sent a rider up there 'fore I come to report on the plain's herd. While we're palavering, we ought to notch ears before branding the calves on the plateau—not waiting for the roundup." Theo scratched his salt-and-pepper stubble. "If'n ya ride the buckboard to town, buy more trail grub, sump'n a puncher can carry along. Let 'em hole up an' catch who's raiding our land."

"Sounds like we'll need a half-dozen punchers. It'll cost, but we don't have a choice."

In Uvalde the next day, Willie reported the rustling to the county sheriff, who responded with a shrug.

"You ranchmen got to know the Nueces might as well be the Rio Grande. Ain't nothing south of the Nueces but rustlers, bandits, and thieves and half of 'em are Mexicans or renegade Lipan Apaches." He stood hip-shot beside his cluttered desk

14

before he lifted his sagging holster belt. "There ain't much I can do, short of an army, to drive 'em across the Rio."

"Are other ranches reporting losses?" Willie asked before he glanced around. The office stunk of rancid tobacco juice left to ripen in open spit-cans placed around the room.

Sheriff Lancaster wiped his ruddy nose with a ragged bandana. "You're the only one complaining. The other ranchmen are sucking it up." The string-bean sheriff got his job from his brother-in-law, the county judge, when the Federal Reconstruction Law appointed new judges.

Willie didn't know a lot of Texas law, but he figured judges frowned on shooting a sheriff, no matter how stupid or corrupt. Muttering under his breath, he strode across the dusty street to Black's General Store in hopes they had filled his order, loading it in his buckboard. He threw open the store's door, almost striking MarieClare, who stood nearby with a woven reed basket.

She retreated a step before shaking herself all over, like a hen shaking off dust. "*Tiens.* You gave me a start," she squeaked in alarm while she scooted away. Her pale lavender dress had darker purple trim accenting the color of her eyes. The scent of lavender lingered after she moved away.

"I thought you didn't care. Now you rush in breathless to greet me. People will talk."

Willie half expected her to bat her eyelids after such a comment.

"MarieClare, your father has enough reasons to shoot me. Let's not give him a new one."

"Papa is not here. Perhaps you might offer to dine in your quaint café, *s'il vous plaît?*"

"Oh, *c'est bon.* Stop playing the coquette. You may be the most beautiful woman west of the Mississippi, but you're going to get men killed before you return to Mobile without a care."

"I'm not going back to … did Papa tell you?" She covered her lips with one hand. "Oh, he intends to send me back to the Convent." Deflated, her head drooped as she turned away.

To relieve his guilt, he touched her arm. "Okay, I'll take you to dinner, but only if you stop being a ninny. I'd like to learn more about you. Can we speak without all the silly flirting?"

"*Oui, monsieur*," she whispered before placing a hand on his proffered elbow.

While strolling across the wide street to the Cactus Café, he said, "You know someone is riding to your father's ranch to report this, as I speak? I hope I don't get you into more trouble."

"Papa is not at the house. He took men to …," she mimicked a stern face, affecting a man's voice, "'scour the south plains.' He's angry about missing cattle. He thinks I'm a silly goose."

"He's missing cattle? You must understand. He'll kill men over missing cattle. If some no-account rascals are taking advantage of Buxton's and my disagreement, they may try to keep us fighting each other while they steal our cattle. Please, tell your father I'm losing cattle, too. Ask him if we can work together to stop the rustling, instead of suspecting each other."

"I will ask, but he is very angry with you. He's also upset with me for speaking with you."

The Cactus Café offered a simple western fare, beefsteak pan-fried with sliced potatoes, served with overcooked seasonal vegetables and a basket of cornpones. After seating her, he ordered their dinner before returning to their earlier conversation. "I'm sorry you're in the middle of this. Your father gets angry every time he sees me. I don't want to fight him."

"It's not you. I thought he'd shoot one of his ranch hands when he caught us chatting in the barn. Papa doesn't understand. I have no social life. There's no one with whom I can talk. I might as well be back in the Convent—I'm lonely out there without another woman."

"You've mentioned a convent twice. What do you mean?"

"Now you embarrass me." She covered her face with her hands. "I've acted like the goose Papa thinks I am, but I'm lost out here. I never expected his ranch to be so desolate."

"I don't understand. You've changed the subject." Willie scratched his temple.

"Not really. I want no pretense between us. I don't know what to do or how to act. I know it's bold, but can we be friends? A friend to talk with or explain things. I've so many questions."

"I thought we were friends. I know your father and I don't get along, but why can't we be friends, talking like reasonable people? What is life like in Mobile? Tell me about yourself."

After a deep breath, MarieClare released it with an audible sigh. She decided if she told a version of her mother's story, it'd be easier than lying to him. She decided to see how he reacted.

"I'd never say this to polite company in Mobile. I … I am a love child." She dropped her gaze, almost losing her courage. "Mama's family denied her marriage to Papa. They said marrying him was a greater shame than bearing the child. Mama raised me in the garçonnière, a private cottage, at the plantation's edge."

"I beg your pardon. I've no right to intrude into your personal affairs. Please accept my humble apology. Society here is forgiving, but don't tell others hereabouts. They may not be that forgiving." He set his napkin on his lap. "To tread safer ground, why did you leave Mobile?"

"The LeCercq family lost their plantation after the war ended—carpetbaggers swooped in. They died soon after. Mama gave me the d'Iberville name to mock her family. Then she got the coughing sickness. It forced her to send me to the Little Sisters Convent in Mobile. Mama wrote to Papa for help. He would visit or send her money. After she died, he contacted the Little Sisters asking about me. The Sisters sent me to meet Papa at … the Convent house in New Orleans."

"I'm sorry this is so upsetting for you." He reached across the table, taking her hand, as she bowed her head to hide the tears.

"Of course," she whispered, squeezing his hand before gazing into his eyes.

"I'm mesmerized. Your eyes are so beautiful. Are they violet? I've never seen such color."

"Oh, *c'est bon*. Now who's flirting?" She beamed a dimpled smile before giggling.

Their dinner continued for three hours before Willie escorted her to her buggy, where a Mexican lad waited. "MarieClare, please ask your father to meet with me. Together we can stop the rustling. If we can meet as reasoned men, I'll ask if I can call on you."

She patted her cheek, wide-eyed. "Why Mr. Little, whatever do you mean?" Then she laughed. "I'll try to sweet-talk him. I don't want to go back to … the Convent. I like it here."

Willie washed at the pump after unsaddling his horse when he returned from town. Theo Tuttle joined him for supper, as he often did. They discussed the usual ranch activities before

Theo cleared his throat. "It ain't my business, Boss, an' a young feller gets his urges, but ain't it risky making eyes with Buxton's daughter with all this going on?"

"I see the moccasin telegraph still works between town and the ranches," Willie said.

"Ya know a puncher rides from town along the stage road. He talks to the next puncher an' the story spreads. Ain't much to do out there, an' gossip about the *jefes,* sure passes the time."

"You're right, about the risk and my urges. I can't stop thinking about her."

"S'pose I ought'nt say, but our punchers have seen her ride that fancy pinto mare into the cottonwoods by the waterfall pool where the Encina drops off the last upland meadow. They ain't spying exactly, but she wades in the pool barefoot, splashing and playing like a youngster."

"She told me Buxton has lost cows, too. He took a crew south of the Nueces today. I want her to ask her father to discuss joining forces to stop the rustling. I know I thought he instigated the thefts, but if he's losing cattle, someone else is diddling both of us."

"Ya are playing a risky game, ol' son. Hear tell she steals yer breath when she smiles at ya."

"That's only the half of it, but I got your warning, and thanks. You're right about it, though. I need to keep a clear head."

The days flew past while the Muleshoe's night watch chased away a few riders attempting to cross the Nueces at different places. With the watch, the rustling appeared to stop. Muleshoe riders roamed the Nueces's northwest plain searching for ground signs of driven cattle or finding beeves bunched together for driving at night. The riders spent long hours in the saddle.

Willie did his share of scouting the land. One sunny spring afternoon, he noticed a pinto grazing among the cottonwoods on Buxton's side of the Encina. By next week, the budding cottonwoods would hide anyone waiting by the pool. He rode closer to inspect, tying his sorrel gelding, Chico, in the trees. As quiet as a stalking cat, Willie eased toward the secluded pool.

~~~~~~

MarieClare waded, her back to him, her skirt hem tucked under her belt, which exposed her legs to the knees. Carefree, she sang a lovely melody in French. With her curly hair undone, she splashed water on her face and arms. The singing ended when she glanced over her shoulder.

"Willie? Are you a Peeping Tom? And I thought you a gentleman. Calling '*allô*' would have been polite." MarieClare turned, exposing her … wet cotton blouse clinging to her bare skin.

"What color are my eyes?" she asked in a husky, soft voice, but followed her question with a throaty chuckle. Shaking her hair with an alluring wiggle, she reached for his hand.

He stopped at the water's edge. "You're Bathsheba at her bath tempting David." He shucked his boots before wading into the pool with her, his gaze unwavering.

She tossed her hair. "The question is, Willie, do you have more wisdom than King David?"

Mouth agape, Willie struggled to meet her eye, his gaze dropping to her clinging, wet blouse.

"I love saying your name." She tilted her head toward her right shoulder. "Will he?" she asked, pushing the clinging wet material forward. She tilted her head the other way. "Or won't he?" she questioned as she pushed the right side forward, presenting a rosy bud. "Will he?

Willie splashed forward, embracing her. He kissed her mouth, and then her exposed neck.

She yanked his hair to pull his mouth away. "Slow down, we have all afternoon. Papa is away counting his herd." She glanced at his waist. "Are you going to get that big thing wet?"

Then, she tugged at his gun belt buckle. "You're blushing. Oh, Willie, you're such fun." *She must be careful, she can't be too bold, but she needed to get him doing something—and soon.*

~~~~~~

Willie stepped away, removing his gun belt, tossing it on the bank beside his boots. He renewed his embrace, but before he could kiss her again, she placed a hand over his mouth.

"Business before pleasure, *ma cher*. I came here hoping we'd meet." She pushed him backwards, standing on the sandy bank of the Muleshoe's side of the creek.

"Meet? Did your father agree to work with me on the rustling?"

"Papa isn't sure he wants to meet—he thinks you're behind the rustling. He doesn't trust you like he trusted your papa, so don't come calling yet." She tousled his hair. "He says he'll send me back to Mobile next month, or sooner, if the troubles continue." She pressed her hips to his while she held his face, gazing into his eyes. "I can't go back ... to the Convent. What'll we do?"

Willie moved her hand from his lips, kissing her palm. "I don't want you to leave—ever." He crushed her in his embrace, covering her face with kisses.

"You must decide, Willie. What happens if he sends me away?"

He sat on the dry sand, lying back, pulling her on top of him. Her skirt rose to her thighs as she straddled him. To his delight, she tugged at his pant buttons, while he explored.

21

Enthralled, Willie said, "We'll get mar—damn, are those riders coming here? Oh, shit! It's your father. Get back across the stream. Button your riding vest. Shake down your skirt."

While grabbing his boots in one hand and gun belt in the other, Willie slithered from sight within the tall grass. If Buxton and his riders crossed the stream, they'd trample him in the sheltering grass, or worse, shoot him if he dared to stand.

"Papa, what are you doing here?" she called when the riders reached her. "Can I have no peaceful time to myself?" She all but stamped her foot to complete a lip-pouting, faux tantrum.

"Where is he? Ya are too flushed to have been asleep. Why're yer clothes all wet?" Buxton twisted in the saddle, waving his men forward. "Search the woods over there. Trample the grass. That little coward is hiding over there." Standing in his stirrups, he pointed across the stream.

The Buxton's B-Bar-B riders plunged across Encina Creek to thrash their horses through the tall grass while they pushed farther into the cottonwoods growing in the basin near the pool's edge. Large puffs of cottonwood seeds, light as down feathers, sailed through the spring air.

Buxton's crew hadn't ridden twenty feet onto Muleshoe land when Theo Tuttle and four Muleshoe punchers trotted among the cottonwoods from the opposite direction.

"Howdy do, Mr. Buxton." The butt of Theo's lever-action Winchester rifle rested on his right hip. "We've always treated this pool as neutral ground, where any of our punchers could find a cool drink while resting in the shade. I sure hope ya ain't about to bullocks that notion?"

"Where's your boss? Is he hiding in the high grass behind you?" Buxton waved his arm.

"The *jefe* told me he'd be checking the grass up in the Encina's meadows today."

"Ya don't out gun us like ya did at yer place months ago," Buxton's voice rumbled in a low growl. "It'll go different today, Theo."

Theo spat tobacco. "Do ya reckon this ol' Reb will miss ya at this range? Oh sure, I'll be dead, but you'll be dead beside me. Young Willie'll be free to court your daughter in a fine style. Hell, them two might even combine their ranches if'n they marry—once't you're dead and buried. Won't that be sump'n? Muleshoe-Bar-B" Theo's smile revealed tobacco-stained teeth.

Buxton shot his daughter a scowl sour enough to have curdled milk. "Get on your horse. Go home. I know you can hear me, Little. I catch you with my daughter again, I'll shoot you."

The B-Bar-B crew re-crossed the stream, nodding "howdy" while exchanging grins with the Muleshoe punchers before they followed Buxton east from the cottonwoods onto his land.

Theo shouted into the trees, "Dang near got caught with yer britches down, ol' son."

The punchers joined Theo in laughing and teasing Willie when he rose from the lush grass.

"This is plumb embarrassing," Willie said. "It's bad enough being caught by her father, but witnessed by my crew. The B-Bar-B riders snickered aloud about catching us." He slapped his hat on his thigh as he reshaped the edge roll before he glanced at the man. "Thanks, Theo."

"Thank Curly. He seen ya ease into the cottonwoods, an' sent for me." Theo rode close to rap a knuckle on top of Willie's head before he mounted. "Trouble is, ol' son, he can shoot ya the next time. Ain't no jury in Uvalde County gonna convict a father after he done warned the boy."

The next day, Theo and Rattles, the cook, appeared at suppertime. "'Before we sit, Cookie has a sump'n to report from his trip to Uvalde for to get supplies. You tell 'em." Theo nodded.

"Didn't intend it to happen. They just busted in whilst I collected from a box from the floor, so I stayed down low 'til they rushed up front to the clerk," Rattles said in a rush of words.

"Slow down. Who came in? Why does this involve the Muleshoe?" Willie asked the cook.

"Buxton and the purty gal. Ever time I lay eyes on that man, he's angry 'bout something."

"What's he angry about now?" Willie bunched his brows.

"Buxton waggled his finger in her face, saying, 'I'll give ya one more chance. Ya mess up again, it's back to the Convent. No more playing the innocent novitiate for the high brows. Ya will serve the regular trade, day and night.'"

"What'd she say?" Willie asked.

"She grabbed his arm, crying, 'You promised I'd not go back to the Convent.' Then he snarled like a mad dog, 'Ya ain't done the set up ya promised. If ya don't do yer job in a week, it's on your back in the Convent.' I listened to his words, but it made no sense. We ain't got no Convent hereabouts. I figured best tell Theo when I gots back here," Rattles said, glancing between the other men to tell if he'd landed himself in trouble.

Theo patted his arm. "Ya done the right thang, Rattles. Thanks for bringing our supper."

After Theo escorted the cook across the threshold, he faced Willie. "Ya think her job is to distract ya while Buxton's rustling puts us out'a business?" he asked.

"That's the least of it. Greed does strange things to people. He's so intent on getting the Muleshoe, he's willing to ruin his daughter's life. Thanks for bringing Rattles in here."

"What do we do?" Theo stood hipshot with his thumb hooked on his Colt.

"We got no proof he's done anything wrong. We need to be cautious, not letting him sucker us into anything."

"What about the girl?" Theo asked.

"I sympathize with her living with a man like Buxton, but there isn't anything we can do unless she asks for help or reports him to the law." Willie heaved a deep sigh.

"Tread soft, ol' son."

Six days passed before Willie ventured off his land to conduct business in Uvalde. Theo and he argued about sending a puncher along with him. Willie settled it. "I don't need a wet nurse."

The Nueces valley lay flat near the river, but on the north side, rocky shoulders extended out from the highlands, bordering the deep watercourses draining the plateau. The mail road from Uvalde forded the Nueces five miles west of town before the road ran due west toward Del Rio on its way to El Paso del Norte. The Nueces formed the B-Bar-B and Muleshoe's southern border. The mail road, while straight west in general, veered away from the taller shoulders undulating in and out to provide an easier route for the stage's horses. Texans, however, tended to ride in straight lines, so Willie rode up one rocky shoulder to cut a few miles from his ride.

Before he reached the crest, two shots split the air, followed by a scream. Spurring his horse, he topped the shoulder in time to catch sight of two rough-dressed riders leading a third horse before disappearing into the tree-lined mouth of a rocky canyon.

The third horse looked like MarieClare's pinto. It seemed as though they'd tied her hands to the saddle horn, judging by how awkward she sat in the saddle, but hard to tell at this distance.

Damn and double damn. He should've listened to Theo. No way he'd let those men capture her. His only hope lay in meeting a B-Bar-B puncher. If Buxton's man didn't shoot at him, he'd send the man riding for help, while he tracked those men. They dressed like Mexican *banditos*, which meant they'd fight to keep their prize. He needed to be cautious when he overtook them.

He urged Chico down the rocky shoulder to follow their tracks as he rode deeper into B-Bar-B land. Small trees and heavy brush lined the bottomland along the edges of the trickling creek forming the canyon. Mesquite and post-oak trees gave him enough cover to hide. The *banditos* appeared to follow an old game trail or Indian trail into the highlands above.

MarieClare's lack of riding skills worried him, particularly with her hands tied—a fall in this rocky canyon might be fatal.

When the canyon narrowed, the tree cover thinned as the rocky walls grew steeper. The lack of cover forced Willie to wait under the few remaining trees. He observed the riders negotiate a series of switchbacks leading upward along the canyon's steep scree. He dared not follow until they completed their last turn before riding from sight, some four-hundred feet above him.

Willie had never ridden this area before, since it lay on B-Bar-B land. The highlands, by their nature, became too rocky and steep for cattle. However, many goat and sheep herds, such as his, grazed throughout the highlands. He urged Chico through the trail's switchbacks. After easing from the saddle to reduce his exposure, he ventured onto the next shelf in the rocky scree.

The canyon walls grew steeper for another four-hundred feet. Willie assumed it topped on the highlands of the Edward's plateau. He monitored the three horses, which followed in single file around a jutting rock outcrop. The goat trail around the rock didn't appear stable. Loose scree broke away, sliding down when each horse passed. When he brought MarieClare down the trail again, it might be tricky around the pointed outcrop.

The trail widened after the outcrop. The riders trotted abreast up onto the highland's plateau. Willie waited dismounted behind a large boulder, because one sombrero-topped hombre sat on his horse, surveying the trail behind for several minutes. Once satisfied no one followed, *el sombrero* rode from sight. Willie waited an additional few minutes to make sure the clanking of his horse's iron shoes on the rocky trail failed to attract the attention of *el sombrero*.

The narrow trail tested Willie's sorrel when Chico eased around the rocky outcrop, with one eye on the steep drop-off. Here, the rocky scree dropped eight hundred feet to the trickling stream. Again, Willie dismounted, removing his hat, before he peered over the rim to the plateau beyond. He spotted no one. More worrisome, he found few tracks on the rocky plateau.

The highlands lay at the plateau's broken edge. This early in spring, various shades of green grass and fresh-budded shrubs covered the area, but underneath lurked large rocks and stones, which made treacherous footing for horses and cows. However, the small feet of sheep and goats allowed them to forage with ease while growing fat in the rocky highlands.

After searching with care, he discovered they'd ridden west through an area of heavy brush and stunted trees along the plateau's overlook. He followed their scant signs of fresh broken limbs and crushed grass for a few miles before spotting the low roofline of a rundown shack. He expected to find an abandoned shepherd's hut.

Chico chomped the spring grass after he tied him to a stunted oak tree. Willie eased close to the hut. A small corral stood at the hut's rear, sheltered on one end by an extension from the roof.

An hombre, *el sombrero*, Willie guessed, unsaddled a horse. The slim man tossed the saddle on the corral's top rung. His actions alarmed Willie; it signaled the *banditos* intended to stay the night. Worse yet, they might expect MarieClare to provide their evening's entertainment.

Willie flushed with anger when her short scream ripped the plateau's quiet reverie.

"*Avanzar rapido.* Get a move on, Carlos," yelled an unshaven, stocky man as he stood in the doorway. "You won't believe her body." He cupped his hands over his chest, jiggling them.

"*Oye tú, estúpido. ¿Qué crees que haces?* (What are you doing?) *El patron* told us to bring her to him unharmed. He'll kill us if you've marked her," Carlos called from the small corral.

The man in the doorway cackled before he muttered a curse, while pushing the door closed.

Carlos's attention must've wandered inside the hut when he slowed in his tasks.

Willie slipped close to vent his anger, striking Carlos's head several times. The last blow from the butt of Willie's Colt cracked Carlos's skull.

MarieClare's loud yelp of pain sent Willie rushing through the hut's door.

Inside, the surprised hombre, his pants around his ankles, glanced at his gun belt on the floor.

Willie killed the man almost by reflex—like you'd shoot a snake. To make his point, he shot him again and then added a head shot as the unshaven hombre lay on the hut's dirt floor.

"Willie." MarieClare exhaled a gust of air, as if relieved to see him. She held a small fist to her mouth, sobbing with little jerks, while gulping deep breaths. She covered herself with the tattered remains of her blouse, but not before Willie glimpsed a vicious bite mark on her breast.

He stooped to grab the dead hombre's discarded wool poncho, wrapping the warm cloth around MarieClare's shoulders. Still in hot blood from the short-lived fight, he kicked the door open wide, while its bottom edge resisted, dragging in the dirt. He dragged the hombre's body outside by his collar, leaving twin lines of spurred boot heels into the brush.

Horses tend to get skittish and hard to handle when too close to the dead's scent, so he dragged *el sombrero* from the corral before he laid the two banditos together.

He'd become jittery once the action ended. Using his canteen, Willie splashed water over his head in an effort to settle his shaking nerves. Without being aware of how much time he'd spent following those hombres, the setting sun surprised him. He feared taking MarieClare down the rocky trail after dark. After retrieving Chico, he hobbled all the horses in nearby grass so they could feed overnight. He used *el sombrero's* water skin to fill a water bucket for the horses.

Willie knocked before he reentered the cabin. MarieClare hadn't moved from the far corner, where a wood-slatted cot had been nailed to the rough-hewn plank wall. She sat on a Spanish-moss filled mattress ticking, stiff with age. He offered her his canteen, but she shook her head.

"You ought to drink. This has been an awful shock. Try to rest, eat, and get some sleep. I'll carry you to your father in the morning." He pulled a three-legged stool close to sit near the bed.

MarieClare inhaled a ragged breath, but glanced at him once before dropping her gaze. "He bit ... he hurt me. I couldn't stop him." She snuffled, holding back a sob. "He waited to ... to have his way with me until ... his friend watched. He taunted me with the thought of ..."

"Hush ... hush, darling. You're safe now. You are all that matters to me," Willie whispered.

"He didn't ... take me ... I—"

"I know, MarieClare. You fought until I got here. I'm proud of you. You remained innocent."

"I'm not innocent. Those men, terrible as they are ... they died. I've never seen anyone die."

"It's what those men deserved—a swift and certain death."

"I've never seen death so close. You said this isn't Mobile; men would die because of me. I didn't understand. I never expected one to fall bloody at my feet. All this blood frightens me."

Willie reached to give her his canteen, but she shrunk away. It took him a few seconds to understand he must give her more time—she'd been shaken by this event. He mustn't crowd her until she recovered from their attack. He scooted his stool farther away.

"I have some venison jerky and Indian pemmican I carry in my saddle bag. You might want to eat a little food. I want you to drink more water before you sleep tonight. It'll give you more energy for your ride home tomorrow."

While opening a rawhide drawstring bag, Willie said, "Pemmican has a nutty base. Bite off a chunk to chew before swallowing with some water. Don't chew the jerky. Hold it in your mouth until it gets soft, sucking its juices. Chew after it softens, swallowing with lots of water, it's real salty." He set the bag on her cot in a slow, easy motion to avoid startling her.

While talking to her, from a well-established habit, he ejected the spent brass from his re-chambered 1861 Colt Navy before reloading ready-made .38-calibre rim-fire brass cartridges.

MarieClare studied his movements with wide-eyed alarm. "What are you doing? Are you going to shoot again?" She leaned away, quaking, while placing a closed fist to her lips.

"I hope not, but it's a good habit to reload after shooting." He slid the pistol into its holster.

"*S'il vous plaît*. It frightens me to see you handle a gun so carefree. Guns bring death." She pointed to a peg on the wall above her cot. "Hang it on the wall until we leave. Please."

"Tell you what; I'll go outside to settle the horses for the night. It'll give you a few minutes of privacy to … do your necessaries before you settle to sleep. There's a bucket in the corner for your use. I know it's crude, but it's all we have. The fireplace will give us a bit of light in place of a lantern or candles. I'll hang my gun on the peg when I come inside again. Will that do?"

She nodded before he turned to the door. He returned twenty minutes later, knocking to alert her. As promised, he hung his gun belt on the peg above her cot.

Stretched out on the cot, MarieClare closed her eyes as he draped a bedroll blanket over her.

Willie sat on the floor to block the door from opening, but soon fell asleep. He awoke with a start to find MarieClare sitting on the bedside watching him. He asked, "Are you okay?"

~~~~~~

31

MarieClare shuddered, the shooting with the blood disturbed her more than she expected. There had been death outside "the Convent" in New Orleans, but she'd never seen the bodies or the blood. She understood what Buxton planned, but seeing Manny killed shoved her nose in it. No man had ever treated her with concern or kindness unless he expected to get her into bed. Willie treated her as a friend who cared for her. His kindness confused her. Buxton had never been anything but cruel after he'd taken her in the plantation's *garçonnière*. She didn't know who to trust. Could she depend on Willie?

"I'm cold," she said. "I've been a silly goose. Please sit by me, hold me. I'm so frightened."

Willie sat on the bed, placing his arm around her. They shifted as she suggested. After a little squiggling, they became comfortable. She leaned her head on his shoulder.

After a few minutes, she said, "I'm frightened. I don't know what to do. Buxton is not who you think he is—he's dangerous. I didn't want to do this … he forced me to … to trick you."

"What are you saying? Is he coming here?" Willie asked as he sat up.

"Do you really love me? I don't want to go back to—"

"It's time for the truth about the Convent. I have my suspicions," he said, his lips a flat line.

"You can't imagine how evil Buxton is. He reveled in belittling my mother; he'd only bring her medicine if I submitted. I thought she'd die soon, letting me escape. When she passed, Mama's family placed me in a real convent in Mobile. I found peace and forgiveness there."

"How did you land in New Orleans? Surely, that wasn't a real convent?" Willie asked.

"Buxton convinced the Ursuline Sisters in New Orleans to send for me. He showed proof I was his child; it's true. Once the Church delivered me to New Orleans, I couldn't escape again."

"Such abomination can't occur in a convent." He squeezed his hands against his head

"His sister bought an old building in the French Quarter that once served as the Convent until the Sisters built the new one on Rue Ursulines. The Sisters never told me he would be there. What a surprise when they delivered me to him in a nearby hotel."

"How ... How ...?" he whispered.

"We must say the word that terrifies you, if we are to have our peace and forgiveness." She stroked his hair while he leaned forward burying his face in his hands. "I'm not a common whore. Few could afford my price, often only once a week. I performed skits that drew crowds."

"Dear God. Stop. Please, no more," he gasped.

"Yes, I must stop. You are out of time. Buxton—you notice I never call him my father. He's coming here to kill you," she touched his head with hers. "He ordered me to unload your gun."

Willie gagged like he wanted to vomit before burying his face in his hands again.

"He promised to set me free, if I seduced you. Can you imagine—freed from him at last?"

His head still in his hands, Willie rocked to and fro.

"I thought he intended to blackmail you. When I became suspicious, he said he wanted you on trial, so you'd have to sell your ranch to get the charges dismissed. After the incident at the creek, I knew he intended to kill. I've been forced into this life, but I'm not evil like him."

She lifted his head, sliding his hands away. She touched her nose to his. "I couldn't let him kill you. You're the only man who treated me like a real person, not a play toy. Even if you send me away, I'll cherish the time we spent together. Don't let him kill you, please. Set me free."

Willie sat on the stool in a wide-eyed stupor.

She rapped his head with a knuckle. "Reload your gun. Fight him. Put an end to this."

Willie rose as if sleepwalking, reaching for the pistol on the wall. He reloaded in the mechanical haze he used in reloading the first time. He cocked the Colt, pointing it at her.

She smiled in serene bliss. "It's okay. I'd rather die than live another moment with him."

Tears flooded Willie's eyes. Even with all her baggage, he loved her for being true to him.

The door exploded from its hinges as Buxton plunged into the room, his pistol firing twice. "You rapist," he screamed, but Willie didn't lie where Buxton expected—he missed both times.

Willie didn't miss; he centered his first shot in Buxton's broad chest from two feet away.

Buxton recoiled backwards into Sheriff Lancaster before staggering forward, his eyes focused on MarieClare. "Ya little whore. Ya betrayed me."

In the instant before Willie fired his second shot, Buxton shot MarieClare in the chest.

Sheriff Lancaster hollered, "Drop that gun, Little. Drop it I tell ya."

Willie dropped his Colt after he shot Buxton, turning away as the Sheriff spoke.

Lifting MarieClare into his arms, Willie wiped a cold sweat from her pale face.

The Sheriff, wide-eyed, asked in a loud whisper, "Did Buxton shoot his own daughter? It sure looked like it to me. What'd he mean, 'betrayed'?"

MarieClare coughed blood, struggling for breath. She grabbed the Sheriff's shirt. "Buxton set me up. Those two Mexicans raped me. He intended this scene to give him an excuse to kill Willie. Willie stopped the rape. Buxton would have got away with this if Willie and I died in this shoot out. He tricked us all. You most of all, Sheriff. You'll find the missing cows on his land in Frio canyon. You …" she coughed blood again, shuddering to rattle her last sigh.

Sheriff Lancaster's mouth hung almost to his chest. "He … he used his own daughter for … bait. Let the Mexicans use her just … just to get your ranch?" The Sheriff wagged his head, failing to accept the words he said. Shaken by the events, he shuddered after he straightened to stand.

After shuffling around in a circle, Lancaster removed his hat to wipe his face with a bandanna. Clearing his throat, he said, "I'll give you a bit of time with the poor little thing. It's awful to say, but I'll be three days getting a wagon up here and two days back. It's best we carry her to town over a saddle, getting there a bit after noon today, or wait for a wagon?"

"No one's ever treated her with the respect she deserved in life; no reason to treat her any different now," Willie said in a soft voice.

"Buxton carried a thick bedroll. I'll toss it inside before I haul them Mex's over their saddle. You bundle her like you see fit." Lancaster trudged outside, still wagging his head in disbelief.

By the time the Sheriff saddled the horses and loaded the Mexicans's bodies, the sky brightened with dawn. Willie and he strained to lift Buxton's bulk across his saddle. Lancaster tied the bodies in place while Willie tied the blanket-wrapped

MarieClare on her pinto. The two men never spoke a word aloud in all this time.

Willie mounted first, as if anxious to escape this place.

Glancing across his saddle at Willie before he mounted, the Sheriff said, "I don't know what I expected to happen when I rode here with Buxton. I gotta tell you, this ended a whole lot different for you than I expected."

After mounting, Lancaster shot Willie a glance with a twist of his head. "Now that this is over, what're you gonna do? You gonna buy Buxton's place, making this into one big spread?"

Willie released a long sigh. "I'm riding to the ranch to let Theo know what's happened, telling him where to find those missing cattle. After that, I'll gather a few mementos before I ride as far away from here as I can get."

The End

From the Author:

I appreciate you taking your precious quiet-time to read "One Way or Another." I hope the bittersweet ending met with your approval. My editor convinced me to let Willie ride away with a broken heart to thwart Buxton's schemes. Would abused and mistreated MarieClare overcome her tawdry past sheltered in Willie's kind-hearted guidance, or would she return to her wicked ways? Wait, that's the story the editor cut—oh, well.

As mentioned in the story, one puncher going along the trail talks to another, spreading the word by the moccasin telegraph. If you liked "One Way or Another," please tell your friends—the old moccasin telegraph—word-of-mouth is the best advertisement. Amazon (and other readers) rates a book by the number of reviews; I'd appreciate a review.

A critique group member, John O. Woods and I are co-writing a western adventure series. "California Bound" follows Josh and Zach, two confederate survivors of a Yankee POW Camp. They promised if they survived, they'd go west to find their fortune in the California gold fields. The road to California isn't always a straight line. Look for it Fall of 2017.

Please check my WEB http://frankkelsoauthor.com for my other novels and short stories. Click over to my WEB page to sign-up with your e-mail. While you are clicking, give a "like" to www.facebook.com/AuthorFrankKelso/ If you'd like to browse my books and short stories, or read samples pages, stop by my Amazon Authors page:
https://www.amazon.com/Frank-Kelso/e/B00N990V3A/
Thanks Again.

If you have questions or comments, please contact me: frank@frankkelsoauthor.com

Biography

Frank Kelso grew up around Kansas City, Missouri, the origin of the Santa Fe Trail. Historic sites, monuments, and statues abound highlighting the journey west, including the Wagons West, Pioneer Women, and the Indian Scout located on the bluffs overlooking the wide Missouri. Writing western themed books fit with his upbringing. His parents considered storytelling a family tradition, and the taller the tale, the better, when sharing around the supper table. A biomedical research scientist in his day job, Frank writes short stories and novels to keep the family traditions alive.

Frank has several of his award winning short stories available on Amazon, which he uses to promote a following for his coming novels, "The Apprenticeship of Nigel Blackthorn" to be released in Fall of 2017 and "A Message to Santa Fe," to be released in Spring of 2018.

Links to my books:

https://www.amazon.com/True-Union-Frank-Kelso-ebook/dp/B00LYJOL3I

https://www.amazon.com/Flop-eared-Mule-Frank-Kelso-ebook/dp/B00M3IQXCG

https://www.amazon.com/Windmill-Frank-Kelso-ebook/dp/B00LWIU540

THE SCHOOLMARM'S HERO
Lyn Horner

Lentzburg, Colorado; Autumn 1880

"Move aside," Marshal Trace Balfour ordered, pushing through the noisy throng gathered in the street outside the Golden Slipper Saloon. Their shouts and laughter had drawn him from his office farther along the street. Among the crowd, he identified the local Methodist preacher, the undertaker, and the owner of the mercantile across the dusty street. A half-dozen ranch hands, in town on Saturday, made most of the racket.

Trace also noticed the schoolmarm, Matilda Schoenbrun. With her brown hair wound into a tight bun at her nape, she wore a matching drab brown calico gown; she brought to mind a brown jay like those who pestered him when a boy in south Texas. After she spotted him, she drew her shoulders back, pressing her lips into a tight line to gaze down her bespectacled little nose, setting his teeth on edge.

"Marshal, please put a stop to this." she demanded in a haughty voice.

"Ma'am, that's what I aim to do." Touching his hat to her,

39

he shouldered aside bystanders whose laughter and catcalls almost overwhelmed the shrieks coming from a pair of females rolling in the dirt. Trace recognized them as saloon girls from the Golden Slipper. With red and purple skirts bunched around their knees, they fought like animals, scratching, biting, and pulling one another's hair.

He'd rather face a gang of bank robbers than deal with these snarling wildcats. Almost tripping over their tangled petticoats, he grabbed the flailing arm of one saloon girl while he snagged the back of the other's laced black bodice.

"That's enough." he growled, hauling them to their feet. One, a red-haired gal named Nellie, screeched a high note while raking his restraining hand with her sharp nails. The other, a blonde whose name he forgot, slapped his face. Cursing under his breath, he gave both snarling females a hard shake. "I said that's enough, *ladies*. Either stop this or spend the night in jail."

"I'll behave if she will." Nellie sneered, jabbing a finger toward the other woman.

"Let go, lawman. I won't touch her," said the blonde, glaring at her antagonist.

Trace glanced from one to the other. "I don't know what started this, and I don't care. Just remember what I said. Any more trouble from you two, I'll throw both of you in jail. Got it?"

After receiving a grumbled, "Yeah," from each, he released them. He watched them shake the dust from their tawdry clothes before flouncing into the saloon. Along the way, each gave the other dirty looks while pushing through the batwing doors. With them gone, he faced the crowd.

"It's over, folks. Go on about your business." While the onlookers dispersed, he examined his left hand. The scratches Nellie inflicted stung like the devil; blood dripped from two of them. A woman clearing her throat drew his attention.

Glancing around, he found Matilda Schoenbrun standing nearby, her brow wrinkled with worry. A thought popped into his head unbidden; she might be kind of pretty if she removed her specs, let her hair down, and smiled for a change.

"Those need cleaning," she said, pointing a slender gloved finger at his hand. "It could turn into blood poisoning."

He frowned at the oozing scratches. "Yeah, I reckon I'd better pay Doc Aikens a call."

"He's not in. I spoke with Mrs. Aikens at the mercantile a short while ago. She mentioned her husband is tending a patient who lives ten miles from town."

Trace shrugged. "In that case, I'll take care of it myself. Thanks for saving me a trip to the doc's place, ma'am." He shifted to stroll away, but her irritated voice halted him.

"I have a name, you know. It's Miss Schoenbrun or, or Matilda, if you prefer." Her cheeks grew red while her gaze skittered away. Her nervous hands twisted the drawstrings of her black reticule.

"Yes, ma'am, err, I mean Miz Schoenbrun. I know your name." He rubbed his mouth to hide a grin at her embarrassment. Behind her prim and proper lady act, he realized she was as bashful as a young girl just out of the schoolroom..

She cleared her throat, again, darting a swift glance at him. "I can clean and bandage your hand, if you like."

"That's right kind of you, Miz … Matilda," he said, uncertain how to proceed.

"It's the least I can do after goading you into ending the fight. I'm sorry that vile woman scratched you."

"Yeah, well, when you mess with a wildcat, you're bound to get scratched." He allowed himself a wide grin this time. "Besides, you didn't goad me into anything. It's my job to keep the peace."

Her shoulders stiffened before she lifted her chin. "Be that as it may, I believe it my duty to tend your hand. I keep bandages and carbolic at the schoolhouse for scraped knees and elbows. Come with me." She whirled, marching away. She expected him to obey like one of her students.

"Blasted female," Trace muttered, following in her wake. He always thought of her as the skinny old maid, but from this view, she wasn't all that thin. He canted his head, finding himself admiring the sway of her rounded hips while her skirt swished back and forth.

A short while later, after suffering the cold sting of carbolic acid on the raw scratches, he sat on a student's chair beside the schoolmarm's desk, watching her wrap a white bandage around his hand. She stood leaning forward next to him, filling his nostrils with the sweet scent of honeysuckle and woman. Her bosom rose and fell mere inches from his face, making him even more aware of the curves hidden beneath her ugly dress. He never expected to become attracted to this straight-laced spinster, but he couldn't deny the hot blood rushing to his groin. It caused him to shift, unsettled in the small chair.

"Good thing it's my left hand," he said in an effort to distract his wayward thoughts. "I'd have a hard time drawing a .45 with my gun hand in a cocoon."

She glared at him, her fine dark brows tilting downward above her wire rims. "If you don't like the way I'm doing this, you can do it yourself."

He raised his free hand. "Whoa, I ain't complaining. Don't get your feathers ruffled, Miz Mattie."

Her breath caught in her throat. Then her breasts rose and fell like she'd finished running a race. "Don't call me that. N-no one calls me that anymore." She shifted her attention to his hand.

"Anymore?"

"My mother called me Mattie," she said, following a tense silence. "So did my grandmother when I lived with her."

"Why'd you live with your granny? Did your folks pass on?"

She nodded. "Papa died fighting the Rebs in the second battle of Manassas. Mama died of cholera a few years later."

"Sorry to learn of their passing." Trace hesitated, wondering how she might react if he told her his family fought for the South. Deciding he needed to test the waters, he said, "My brothers both died in the war, too ... fighting Yankees."

Her head jerked up. She stared with hooded eyes for a moment before she lowered her gaze. "Where did they fall?" she asked, tying the end of his bandage.

"Grant, the oldest, fell at Shiloh. Frank, the next oldest, got struck by a cannon ball at Gettysburg. A friend who served with him reported he lost both his legs, bleeding to death before anyone could get to him."

"Oh, how terrible. I'm sorry for your loss." She heaved a deep sigh and shook her head. Biting her lip, she paused in gathering the extra bandages and bottle of carbolic. "Did you fight for the Confederates, too?"

"No. The war started before my eleventh birthday. Even so, I'd have gone with my brothers if they'd let me." He shrugged. "I reckon I'm grateful they didn't."

"I am too." A blush rose from her neckline to her hair. "I mean your folks must have been devastated after losing two sons. I'm glad they didn't lose you, too." She gave a bashful smile, making him notice what a tempting shade of rose colored her plump lips when she didn't flatten them into a frown.

Letting the subject drop, he watched her stash the

doctoring supplies in a desk drawer. A wild hare got the best of him, causing him to blurt, "Say, are you going to the church picnic tomorrow?"

"No." She busied herself straightening a pile of books on her desk that didn't need straightening.

"Why not?"

She cut him a sharp glance. "Because I don't like going by myself."

He stood, hat in hand, clearing his throat. "I'd be honored if you'd go with me, Miz Mattie."

She went ramrod straight, glaring at him. "You joshing? I don't appreciate that kind of joke. Why would you want to attend with a drab old maid like me?"

Trace rounded the desk to stand in front of her. "You're not drab, Mattie. If you let your hair loose and didn't wear glasses, I bet you'd be downright pretty."

In a bold act, he removed her spectacles, drawing a gasp from those alluring lips he found himself longing to kiss.

"Marshal Balfour." she whimpered, lovely green-gold eyes wide with alarm.

"Easy, honey, I just want to see what you really look like." Stepping so close their bodies all but touched, he reached around her, removing pins from her hair. He held her wary gaze the whole time.

She caught her breath when he dropped the pins on her desk, blinking fast as he spread her long, wavy dark hair over her shoulders. Shot with red from sunlight streaming in the nearby window, the fiery strands glided through his fingers like silk. He transferred his hands to her face, caressing her flushed cheeks.

"I guessed wrong, you're not just pretty, Mattie. You're beautiful." Drawing her into his arms, seconds ticked by as he lowered his head.

"Marshal Balfour," she repeated, gasping for breath.

"Call me Trace, honey." He kissed her closed eyes before brushing her lips with his.

"Oh, Trace." Her breasts plumped against his chest, heart beating as fast as a captured bird's while he set about convincing her to attend the picnic with him.

~~~~~~

Arriving at Sunday's church picnic on Trace Balfour's arm, Mattie imagined she floated over the ground. Could this be real? Did she dream strolling beside the most handsome man in town, the man she adored in secret ever since he arrived to serve as the town marshal a year ago? Her emotions reeled as if she lived one of the fairytales her grandmother once enthralled her with as a child.

To please Trace, she wore her hair down, held back by a blue ribbon that matched her blue calico dress, the prettiest one she owned. She'd also left her spectacles in her room at the boarding house where she lived. She needed them only for reading, but wore them every day since accepting her teaching position in Lentzburg four years ago. They made her look more studious, a desirable quality when facing a roomful of fractious students, or their parents. The eyeglasses also served as a barrier between her and the world, a blessing for a shy spinster.

"Where do you want me to spread the blanket?" her tall, raven-haired escort asked.

"Maybe under the trees along the creek?" Away from the people who stared at them, at *her,* to be more precise.

"Un-uh, we're not gonna hide. I want to show off my pretty gal. How 'bout over there in that sunny patch?" He pointed to a spot surrounded by picnickers, then led her through the crowd, nodding and greeting townspeople, thereby forcing Mattie to do likewise. She didn't want to appear unhappy beside him.

Once they settled on the blanket, she opened her picnic basket. She lifted out a tin pan of fried chicken before gathering a clay bowl of potato salad she'd prepared, along with smaller side dishes.

"Mattie, this is a feast," Trace said, his eyes bright.

"I hope you like it." Smiling, she loaded a plate, handing it to him.

He bit into a drumstick, closed his eyes, and chewed blissfully. "Delicious," he declared after swallowing. "Woman, not only are you beautiful, but you can cook. You'd do a man proud as his wife."

Dumbstruck, she choked on a mouthful of potato salad, dropping her fork on her plate with a clatter. Coughing, she dabbed at her watering eyes with the cuff of her sleeve.

Trace chuckled, patting her back. "Didn't mean to make you choke, honey."

"I'm sorry," she wheezed, unable to look at him. "Y-you took me aback. I've never thought of myself that way."

"You mean as becoming a man's wife?"

Nodding, she retrieved her fork, pushing food around on her plate.

"I don't know why not." He used two fingers to lift her chin, urging her to meet his caressing gaze. "You best start thinking about it, Matilda Schoenbrun, because—"

Gunshots rang across the churchyard.

~~~~~~

Cussing under his breath, Trace leapt to his feet while the townsfolk around him gasped or cried aloud. "Stay here, Mattie," he ordered. Dodging picnickers, he ran toward town, where the shots broke the noonday peace.

When he entered Main Street, he spotted three cowboys with pistols drawn on the boardwalk outside Big Jake's Saloon. Two took cover on either side of the batwing doors while they fired an occasional shot into the saloon. The third man fired from a squatted position beside the shattered front window. At least two men returned gunfire from inside.

Another man lay in the street clutching his bloody thigh. A twinge of guilt jerked at Trace when he recognized his deputy, Walt O'Brien. The older man had offered to remain at their office, keeping the peace on what should have been a quiet Sunday afternoon. He'd volunteered for the duty, allowing his boss to escort the pretty schoolmarm to the church picnic. Walt sure as hell hadn't bargained on, and didn't deserve, getting shot by a trigger-happy cowpoke.

"Toss away your guns." Trace shouted, drawing his Colt. He strode toward the troublemakers, huffing and puffing like a steam engine.

Three cowboys pivoted to face him. Two were young bucks sowing their wild oats, but the third, an older cowhand with curly, rusty orange hair, oughtta know better. From the bleary-eyed look of them, they'd spent their payday money getting liquored in Big Jake's.

The older one, whose Stetson hung from its chinstraps down his back, glared from beneath bushy brows the same rusty orange as his curly hair.

"Who says so?" he challenged.

"I do. The name's Balfour. I'm the law in this town. I'm ordering you to drop your guns. Now."

"Like hell we will," yelled the wild-eyed waddy. He fired a shot at Trace, striking the ground a foot in front of him.

Trace dodged behind a nearby horse trough, returning fire. He missed, but his bullet convinced the curly-haired loudmouth, the time to git had come. Hollering for his cronies to run, he bounded into the street, dashing to his horse, tied to a hitch post a few feet away. The two youngsters followed his lead.

Determined to prevent their escape, Trace sprang to his feet, taking aim at the leader. Before he squeezed the trigger, Jake Driscoll, the saloonkeeper, charged from his establishment waving a shotgun. He stomped down the boardwalk steps into the street while the three cowboys spurred their mounts toward the south end. Big and burly as the name of his place implied, Jake blocked Trace's clear shot.

"You bastards killed my piano player. You ain't gettin' away scot-free." he bellowed. Aiming his shotgun, he fired both barrels. The blast exploded with a deafening roar, knocking one of the young riders from his horse. The lad hit the ground face down in the dirt, never to move again.

"Shep." yelled the other youngster, a dark-haired kid on a paint horse. Gazing at his fallen friend, he reined in for a moment.

"He's done for. Ride." shouted the curly-haired galoot.

The two tried to make a run for it, but by this time, four shopkeepers and another man blocked the street's south end, pointing guns at the cowboys—now outlaws—racing toward them. Finding their way blocked, the pair swung about, galloping back the way they'd come.

Trace had run south after them, intending to grab his horse at the jail. When they turned to ride toward him, he halted, firing a shot as they raced past him in the opposite direction. He winged the dark-haired lad. The kid screamed, rocking from side to side, but he managed to stay on his horse. When he and his gun-happy companion neared the north end of the street, Trace witnessed more citizens gathering. Fresh from the picnic, the crowd included several families. Eight of the men who carried firearms formed a line, blocking the street.

Trapped, the fleeing pair jerked their horses to a dusty, skidding halt. Trace's stomach knotted. Fearing what the fugitives might do, he ran, spurs jingling, toward the threatening conflict. Before he could get there, the carrot-topped *cabrón* prodded his horse into a group of shrieking women and children, sweeping low to grab one of the women. She screamed when he hauled her in front of him. Spotting her blue dress and flying dark hair, Trace recognized Mattie. He shouted her name, running faster, his heart hammering in his chest.

"Let us pass or I'll kill her," her rusty-haired captor hollered at the crowd. He pressed the barrel of his six-shooter to her head.

"No!" Trace roared. He didn't know if he shouted at the bastard not to shoot or at the crowd not to let him get away with Mattie in his clutches. It didn't matter—the townsfolk parted, allowing the outlaws through. Watching them thunder away, Trace froze, overcome by fear for the woman he respected and desired.

Shedding his shock, he ignored the cries of people around him, spun on his heel, and sprinted for his horse at the far end of Main Street. Breathing hard, he gathered the reins, vaulted into the saddle, and spurred his chestnut gelding in pursuit of Mattie's kidnappers.

Why hadn't the little idiot stayed at the picnic grounds like he'd told her? He'd shake some sense into her when, not if, he freed her from the snake who snatched her.

He took heart knowing he'd wounded one outlaw while the other's horse carried double with Mattie. That ought to slow their escape. Minutes later, his guess proved correct when he spied riders on the horizon. Sure he'd catch them, he spurred his gelding into an all-out run.

The horse stumbled, shrieking in pain. Trace hollered, throwing himself clear as the gelding toppled tail over head. The marshal landed on his back, knocking the wind from him. Unable to move or breathe, he lay there, listening to his horse thrash and scream. At last, he managed to drag air into his lungs. Rolling to his feet, he swayed unsteady. Once he gained control, he crouched beside the injured horse. The fall broke its right front leg.

"Ah, hell." he muttered. The chestnut must have stepped in a prairie dog hole. "It's my own damn fault." He should have been more careful instead of driving the animal so hard. Squinting into the distance, he saw the two outlaws disappear in a cloud of dust with Mattie. Cussing a blue streak, he pulled his gun.

"Sorry, Red." He ended the gelding's suffering. He removed his saddle and bridle, swinging them on his shoulder before he trudged to town. A distance that took minutes to cover on horseback, took him well over an hour on foot, sick with worry for Mattie the whole time.

Concerned citizens greeted him, stepping from stores and houses along the street. Several asked about the schoolmarm.

Trace explained what happened. "After I check on Walt O'Brien at Doc Seaver's, I'll fetch another horse and head after Mattie's—Miz Schoenbrun's kidnappers. I'd be obliged if a few men ride with me."

Five men raised a hand, volunteering to go. They included Mayor Ben Lambert, Charlie Putnam, a miner turned storekeeper, Saul Davis, the town blacksmith, and two former Indian fighters. He thanked them before they hurried home to collect their gear. Of course, they needed to tell their families they joined his posse. Meanwhile, Trace stopped by the doc's office.

"Walt is asleep," the balding, stoop-shouldered sawbones announced as soon as Trace stepped across his threshold. He dried his hands with a towel as if he'd just washed up. "I removed the bullet from his leg and I stitched him closed."

"He'll be okay?"

The older man shrugged. "He lost a fair amount of blood, but if the wound doesn't fester, he'll do fine. I'll keep him here a few days to make sure he takes things easy."

"Thanks, Doc," Trace said, breathing a sigh—one less worry. "When he wakes up, would you tell him I'm going after the coyotes who shot him? They carried away Mattie Schoenbrun."

"I'll be glad to tell him." Seavers pushed his wire rimmed specs up his nose. "Good luck, Marshal. I hope you bring our schoolmarm home safe."

"So do I." Trace strode to the livery where he saddled a new mount. Minutes later, he rode from town at the head of the posse, resolved to catch the fleeing outlaws while hoping to God they wouldn't be too late to save Maddie.

~~~~~

"Please let me go. You don't need me anymore," Mattie begged the man whose arm clamped around her, locking her against him on his galloping horse.

Her captor snorted. "You're wrong, little gal. You'll make a good hostage if that two-bit marshal comes after us. 'Sides, I wouldn't be much of a gentleman if I set you loose in the middle of nowhere." He laughed at his inane remark before he slid his hand up to cup the underside of her breast.

"Don't you dare," she said, grabbing at his wrist to jerk his hand away.

"Ah now, don't be like that, darlin'. You and me can be good friends if you act nice."

Terrified, and sickened by his rank odor, she tried to twist free, wanting to throw herself to the ground. If she broke a bone or two in the fall, it would be worth it to get away from him. But her struggle proved useless. In response, he tightened his grip, bruising her ribs while wringing a cry of pain from her lips.

"I gotta stop, Finn," his friend called. "My shoulder hurts something fierce. It's bleeding bad."

"Hell, Billy, you're already slowing us down," Mattie's tormentor grumbled.

"I can't help it. I gotta rest for a spell, gotta stop the bleeding, If I don't I'm gonna fall off my horse."

"Alright, alright. We'll stop by that knob ahead." Fin waved his arm, pointing to a rocky hillock a hundred yards away. He said, "It'll give us cover if that marshal is close on our trail."

Mattie said a silent prayer, urging Trace to come after her, wanting him to catch them before it grew dark.

They halted behind a rocky outcrop of the hill. Billy slid from his saddle to stumble to a flat-topped boulder surrounded by scrub grass. He collapsed on the rock in a heap, clutching his wounded shoulder. Pale beneath his tan, he closed his eyes while sagging with a weary groan. She guessed him sixteen or seventeen years old. A stab of pity for him squeezed her heart.

"I'm gonna set you down, girl, so's you can tend to Billy," Finn growled in her ear. "If you try to run, I'll make you wish you didn't."

She nodded, shaking inside at his threat. When her feet touched ground, she gulped a breath of fresh air, lurching to where Billy sat. "Let me look at your wound," she said, crouching beside him.

He opened his eyes. Pain filled the bright blue orbs, yet he gave her a crooked smile. "Yes ma'am." He slid his hand away, allowing her to peel away his shirt. He sucked in his breath when she removed the blood-soaked bandana he'd stuffed against the hole in his shoulder.

She hoped the bullet had penetrated clear through. To check, she rose, leaning over him, searching for an exit wound but didn't find one. Frowning, she said, "The bullet is still inside. I don't have any way to get it out."

"That's okay. We'll find a doc somewhere. Just plug it with somethin'."

She thought for a moment before she spun around. The vision of Finn standing by his horse, arms crossed, watching her every move stayed in her mind. Doing her best to ignore him, she ripped a strip from the bottom of her petticoat. Far from clean after today's rough wear, the linen would make do. She folded it several times before pressing the pad atop Billy's wound.

"Hold that in place for a minute." He did as directed while she ripped off another strip of linen to use as a binding. "I need to wrap this around you to hold the bandage in place. We'll have to slip your arm out of the sleeve first."

He swallowed hard. "Yes ma'am, I kind of figured that."

With a struggle, they managed to free his arm. Billy gritted his teeth while she worked. His so-called friend didn't lift a finger to help. When she leaned close to wind the linen strip around him, he raised his good arm to stroke her hair. The surprise move made her jump, almost dropping the binding. Her lips trembled.

He dropped his hand. "Don't be afraid. I won't hurt you. I just wanted to see if your hair is as soft as it looks." He smiled. "It is and it's real purtty, too, Miss."

"Th-thank you. You can call me Mattie if you want." Returning a quivering smile, she concentrated on her task. After tying the strip tight across his chest, they maneuvered his arm into the shirtsleeve. Billy reeled, ready to keel over. Calling up courage from deep inside, Mattie stiffened her spine, facing Finn.

"Billy is too exhausted to ride," she said. "He'll never stay on his horse."

"He'll ride or I'll leave him behind." The lout scowled,

causing his broad pockmarked face to grow even uglier.

She balled her fists, glaring at him. He showed no concern for the youth he'd led into this calamity. Forgetting her own danger, she opened her mouth to tell him what she thought of him, but Billy spoke first, saving her a beating, at the least.

"Let her ride behind me, Finn," he said. "She can hang onto me. It'll keep me in the saddle."

Finn frowned while running his gaze over Mattie, her breasts in particular. His glance made her skin crawl.

"I had my mind set on her riding with me again, but you've got the right of it, for now." He gave a toothy sneer. "I reckon you won't have no trouble staying awake with her rubbing those boobies against your back."

Mattie gasped at his crude remark.

"Don't talk like that," Billy protested. "Can't you see she's a lady?"

"Watch your mouth, boy," Finn snarled, jabbing his finger at Billy. "I don't need you telling me how to talk. Now you and your *lady* get mounted. We can't waste anymore time." Turning away, the nasty devil climbed on his horse.

Billy rose slowly, weaving on his feet. Mattie grabbed his good arm, helping him to his paint mare. He dragged himself into the saddle, finding the strength to lend her a hand up behind him. She hurried to adjust her skirts to cover her legs.

"You'd best hang onto me, Miss Mattie," he said over his shoulder.

She rested her hands at his waist and clutched him tight when he spurred the mare into a gallop after Finn, who had already charged away. They caught up with him, but he maintained the blistering pace for the next several hours. Weak from loss of blood, Billy sagged against Mattie. She soon had to wrap her arms around his slim torso to steady him. He had a musky odor, but not near as bad as Finn's disgusting stink.

~~~~~~

Trace learned to track as a boy from his half-Cherokee father in Texas. Later, he'd served as an Army scout for a spell. The outlaws left an easy to follow trail west across the grassy plains of eastern Colorado.

Around mid-afternoon, he raised his hand, calling a halt at the base of a low hill. "Stay here," he ordered, dismounting.

"What do you see, Marshal?" asked Ben Lambert, a graying, middle-aged man who could still handle himself in a fight.

"They stopped here. I want to see why. Stay clear, all of you, so you don't mess up any footprints."

Inching across the site, studying the ground, Trace glimpsed two sets of boot prints, one larger than the other, and Mattie's dainty shoe prints. The smaller man's and her prints led to a large rock, where the man appeared to have sat while Mattie moved around him.

He spotted something dark red in the grass nearby. Squatting, he lifted a wadded, bloody bandana from the grass. It told him what had happened here. Mattie had bandaged the kid he wounded in town. With what, he wondered.

He tossed away the rag, rose, and followed their tracks away from the rock to where a horse had waited. Both sets of footprints stopped there. Mattie had mounted to ride away from here with the young outlaw, not with the carrot-topped bastard who grabbed her in town. Trace tipped his hat back to gaze into the distance, hoping the change boded well for Mattie.

"What did you find, Marshal?" Ben Lambert called out.

"They stopped to let Mattie—Ms. Schoenbrun—doctor the kid I wounded." Returning to his horse, Trace stepped into the saddle.

"Huh. Now why'd she want to do that? She ought to have let him bleed to death," Charlie Putnam said.

"Maybe they didn't give her a choice," Trace said.

"Yeah, I reckon you're right. Too bad, though. She'd have been better off with only one of them owlhoots to fight off," Ben said.

Not liking the implications of that remark, Trace scowled at the man before he kneed his horse, leading the posse west toward the mountains.

~~~~~~~

Occupied with holding Billy upright, Mattie struggled to ignore her own misery but found it impossible. She wasn't used to spending hours bouncing up and down on a horse's rump. Her bottom ached to the point of pain while the saddle blanket scraped the insides of her bare thighs raw.

Finn called a halt near dusk in a small clearing surrounded by trees along a narrow stream. Mattie stifled a groan as she slid to the ground. She hung on to Billy's leg for a moment to prevent her own legs from collapsing. Then, gathering her strength, she caught him around the middle when he all but fell from the saddle, managing to keep both on their feet.

"I need to take care of Polly," he muttered. "My horse."

"I'll see to her after we get you settled," she said, supporting him with his good arm across her shoulders while she wrapped her arm around him to grab his belt.

"But she has to be unsaddled."

"Don't worry about it. I grew up on a farm. I know how to saddle and unsaddle a horse."

He didn't argue further. Together, they staggered to a spreading box elder tree, where he more or less slid down the trunk to sit, leaning against it. Glancing around, Mattie saw Finn squatted by the sluggish stream, drinking his fill without a thought for his injured partner.

What a poor excuse for a man.

"You rest," she told Billy. "I'll take care of Polly."

He caught her hand, whispering, "Watch out for Finn. I think he's got some no-good ideas about you."

"I know he does," she said, suppressing a shiver.

Mattie ignored Finn while unsaddling the paint. Hearing him snicker when she attempted to lift off the heavy saddle, she locked her jaw in anger, yanking the darn thing off. It landed with a thud at her feet. Intending to drag it to Billy's resting place, she bent over to take hold of the saddle horn. She yelped when a hand grabbed her bottom.

Shooting straight up, she whirled to find Finn standing there with a lewd grin on his pockmarked face.

"Mmm, mmm, mmm, you sure are a handful, honey girl. How 'bout you take off that dress? Let me get a good feel."

"No. Stay away." she cried, sidestepping past the saddle, tasting fear.

His grin turned mean. He started to come after her. She shifted to turn and run when Billy's voice rang out.

"Leave her be, Finn"

Darting a glance at him, Mattie's jaw dropped open, astonished to see him on his feet. He leaned on the tree trunk for support. His right hand hovered over his holstered gun.

Finn pivoted to face him. "You fixin' to draw on me, boy?" he snarled.

"If I have to."

Holding her breath, Mattie slid aside, afraid of flying bullets. While grateful for Billy's intercession, she prayed he didn't get himself killed. If he did, she would be at Finn's nonexistent mercy.

To her surprise, the nasty villain gave Billy an ingratiating smile, rubbing the back of his neck. "Ah hell, she ain't worth slappin' leather over. Let's dig out some grub. We daresn't start a fire, but we can still eat."

Not believing his change of tune, Mattie remained wary

while she finished caring for Polly, leading her to the creek for water, then staking her in a patch of grass for the night. Exhausted by then, she collapsed next to Billy, who had resumed his seat beneath the box elder, with his pistol by his side, she noticed.

"Thanks for tending Polly," he said, handing her a tin plate holding a strip of jerky and a small pile of canned beans.

"You're welcome." The grub didn't suit her taste, but she forced it down, knowing she must keep her strength for whatever the following days might bring. Even though she now trusted Billy, she feared his condition would worsen if they didn't find a doctor to remove the bullet in his shoulder. If that happened, he'd be unable to protect her from Finn. Once again, she prayed Trace would come to save her.

~~~~~~

Three days passed without sighting the outlaws. Their trail led into the foothills of the Rocky Mountains, climbing over stony ridges, winding through creeks, and following low, rugged canyons. The rougher the route grew, the longer it took Trace to find their tracks. The process slowed the posse, causing his men to grow restless. They'd brought enough grub to last a week or more, but they hadn't really expected the hunt for the fugitives to last that long. Worse yet, the excitement of the chase had worn off.

Ben Lambert fought for the Yanks in the Civil War. Strong as an ox, Saul Davis could flatten a man with his fist alone. Charlie Putnam wasn't a big man, but he learned how to fight in his silver mining days. The other two men, Jim Curtis and Joe Wilkes were veterans of the frontier army. All five knew how to handle a gun and defend themselves, but not so their wives and children back in town. This was still a wild country. Trace knew the men wanted to get back home soon to protect their families and property.

The posse members' discontent boiled over when he lost the outlaws' trail. He'd followed their tracks down into a steep-sided, dry arroyo that split into a tangle of smaller outlets, barely wide enough in some places for a single man and horse to negotiate. After picking his way through three of these winding defiles without finding a sign of the fugitives' trail, he backtracked to where the arroyo split. The grumble of muttered curses from the men grew loud.

"Marshal Balfour, this is pointless," Ben Lambert said. "You'll never find their trail in this maze. It's time to face facts and turn back.

"Yeah, we might as well go home," Charlie Putnam said. "It's too late, anyhow. The schoolmarm is likely dead or wishing she was by now."

Fury flared inside Trace. Charging his horse at Putnam, he caused the man's mount dance sideways. Charlie's eyes widened in fear just before Trace landed a hard right on his jaw. The storekeeper cried out and nearly tumbled from his saddle.

"I won't abide talk like that," Trace growled.

He backed his horse to face the group, drawing a deep breath to calm down. "Whoever wants to turn around can leave now, but I'm going on. I'll find Mattie or die trying." He realized he'd revealed his feelings for her but didn't care. The other men needed to know where he stood.

He surveyed the group, gazing into each man's eyes. No one challenged his statement and none made a move to turn back. Putnam hung his head, rubbing his jaw. "I'm right sorry, Marshal. I oughtn't to have said what I did. It was cold of me."

Trace acknowledged his apology with a nod. Ordering them to wait where they sat, he set his hat and rode into another of the narrow offshoots of the arroyo. Lucky for Mattie, this one proved to be the right one. He spotted the outlaws' tracks ascending a rock ledge from the depression. Backtracking once again, he was pleased to see every man sat where he'd left them.

"I picked up their trail," he announced. "Let's go." Getting no argument, he led them out of the troublesome web of false trails onto a dry, rolling plateau, where the wind blew bunch grass nearly flat, threatening to whip off their hats.

The trail they followed angled northwest. He pondered if Mattie's kidnappers had a destination in mind, or were they wandering where the wind took them.

Late that afternoon, dark clouds billowed in the west, with distant flares of lightning. As a stripling, Trace had punched cattle down along the Rio Grande, where he grew up. He carried vivid memories of another rider who got hit by lightning. It had killed both man and horse. He didn't want to witness such a thing again.

"We need to find shelter fast," he said, to which the others readily agreed. Rain pelted them by the time they found an abandoned sod house in the side of a low hill. A pole corral stood nearby which offered no protection for their horses, but at least, they would be there when the storm passed. The men hurried to unsaddle the animals before closing them in the coral. Trace and his men crowded into the dank, pitch-black soddy.

Saul Davis struck a match. It briefly illuminated a small patch of dirt walls and floor. A plank shelf hung crooked on the wall. A broken slat bunk without a mattress stood beneath the shelf. "Hell of a place to call home," Saul commented in his deep, barrel-chested voice. He blew out his match as the flame neared his fingers and lit another.

"I lived in a hole in the ground like this one when a kid in Kansas," Charlie Putnam said. "My Dad had set his mind to growing wheat and corn there. He promised to build us a fine big house one day."

"Did he succeed?" Trace asked.

"Naw, the border troubles started and pretty soon he went off to fight for the Union. He never came back." Changing the subject, Charlie said, "You know, there might be a lantern in here somewhere." He lit his own match, poking around in the dark corners. Sure enough, he recovered a dented lantern. Although low on kerosene, it provided steady light until the storm blew away two hours later.

By then, night was upon them. Although Trace begrudged the time lost to the storm, he knew they must wait for daylight. Standing at the corral where the horses stood drowsing after being drenched, he leaned his arms on the top rail, staring into the starlit night, thinking of Mattie. Had her captors sought shelter or had they ridden into the teeth of the storm with her? The thought made him sick with rage and frustration.

Footstep squished through the mud behind him. Turning, he made out Saul Davis's bulky form approaching. The big man halted and leaned on the corral next to him.

"Nice night. The rain cooled things off a might," he observed.

"A might."

After a moment's silence, Saul said, "Reckon you're worryin' about our pretty schoolmarm, eh?"

"Yeah." Trace shifted his stance, uncomfortable with putting it into words.

"You think you can find a scrap of those buzzards' trail after all the rain?"

"I don't know." Saul had put his finger on Trace's worst worry. If the rain washed away the outlaws' trail, he'd have no choice, but to send his men home. As for himself, he would search every acre of Colorado, and beyond if necessary, until he found Mattie.

~~~~~~~~~

Maggie's tense shoulders relaxed when Finn called a halt in a sheltered hollow beneath a towering slab-sided ridge. Below them spread a night-shaded meadow with ghost-like trees silhouetted against the moonlit sky. The cold air carried the clean scent of rain and wet vegetation.

Mattie shivered so hard her whole body shook as she slid off Billy's mare. She didn't hurt as bad as the first night, having learned to pad her tender parts with folds of her skirts. The driving rain chilled her legs and feet to the bone while encasing them in yards of rain-soaked material. At least her upper-half stayed dry; thanks to the slicker Billy shared with her. Nevertheless, her wet skirts clung to her legs, promising to make the night long and miserable.

Billy wanted to find shelter before the storm rolled in, but Finn insisted they continue to ride, smearing their trail. He feared pursuit, a fact that caused her bitter amusement. Her hope of Trace, or anyone else, rescuing her hung by a thin thread.

She braced Billy as he stepped from his saddle. He clung to her shoulder a moment before he managed to stand alone. He'd long since stopped bleeding, but he still carried the bullet in his shoulder, and judging by the heat he exuded, the wound festered with blood poisoning. How he kept going, she didn't know. If he didn't get medical help soon, she feared he wouldn't make it.

"Those wet duds are gonna give you the ague," he said, his blue eyes fever-bright in the moonlight. "You'd best get out of them."

She shot an alarmed glance at Finn, who stood a few feet away, making a noisy racket while shaking raindrops from his slicker. He glanced around at Billy's comment to grin at Mattie. In the moonlight's shadows, Finn took the shape of a demented ghoul.

"That there's a mighty good idea, Billy."

"No. I'm n-not taking off a-anything." She hugged herself, teeth chattering.

"You oughtn't to scare her like that," her young protector told his lecherous partner. Untying his bedroll, he shook out the blanket as well as he could one-handed, giving it to Mattie. It was a little damp but not soaked through. "Wrap that around you. I'll hold it closed while you shuck your dress and all."

She sent a wary glance at Finn again, wanting to refuse.

"I won't peak, I promise," Billy said, one corner of his mouth curving up.

It wasn't him she distrusted, but he had the right idea. She needed to shed her wet clothes. "Okay. Th-thanks."

Wrapping the blanket around herself up to her neck, she welcomed the blessed warmth, not even minding the strong odor of horse. Once Billy took a good hold of the overlapped ends, she worked fast behind the woolen shield. Unbuttoning her bodice, she slipped her arms out of the sleeves and let the dress fall. Her petticoats followed.

"I've got it," she said, gripping the blanket. When Billy backed away, she stepped clear of her soggy garments.

Watching the whole procedure, Finn sneered. He sent Billy a mocking laugh. "Kid, you're treatin' her like she's your woman instead of our hostage."

"I'm only showing her the respect due a lady, Finn." Billy bared his teeth. "That's more than you can say." His right hand came to rest on his pistol butt.

Finn's sneer turned into a scowl. Eyes narrowing, he stuck his thumbs under his gun belt, adopting a hipshot stance. "You might be a fast draw with that iron, boy, but you ain't lookin' so good. I figure before long you'll be too sickly to stand up or pull a gun. Then we'll see who holds the reins to yonder filly, and I don't mean your paint mare." He jerked his head at Mattie.

She shivered again, but not from the cold this time. If the day came when Billy couldn't protect her from Finn, she had no reason to live. What man would want her after this vicious animal violated her?

"I ain't that bad yet," Billy said with a smile. "You'd best keep your distance from her." Turning to her, he said, "Miss Mattie, you might should hang your wet things over a branch so they're dry by mornin'." He gestured toward the skeletal outline of a nearby tree.

Swallowing the lump of fear in her throat, she nodded and snatched her wet clothes from the ground. While she hung them to dry, he had managed to unsaddle Polly He attempted to rub her dry with a handful of grass. She noticed him stumble, before leaning his shoulder against the mare, Mattie hurried to his side, touching his arm.

"I'll do that. You need to rest."

He hesitated, then nodded. "Alright. I'll spread my ground cloth. It's waterproof. You come to lay beside me when you're done. I'll keep my hands to myself, I swear."

Noting Finn had already sprawled in his blankets with his hat covering his eyes, she smiled. "I believe you, Billy. Thank you for being a gentleman."

~~~~~~

Trace slept little, rising in the gray light of pre-dawn. He'd ridden several circles, widening each, searching for sign of the outlaws, before the rest of the posse rolled from their blankets. He rode back into camp in time for coffee and a plate of greasy potatoes and bacon.

"I cut their trail," he told the others, squatting to eat next to the soddy.

"Humph. I'm surprised to hear that," Ben Lambert said,

sitting cross-legged nearby. He spoke around a mouthful of potatoes.

"Yeah, me too," Jim Curtis chimed in. "I figured the rain woulda washed out their tracks."

"It mostly did, but one of their horses chipped off the corner of a sandstone rock about a mile that way." He waved in the general direction.

"How far ahead of us do you reckon they are?" Ben asked.

Trace shrugged, thinking. "Depends if they holed up during the storm."

"Even if they didn't, they'd have to stop for a few hours to sleep and rest their horses," Saul commented.

"Right. It might be they figure the storm threw us off their trail for good. In which case, they might take their time moving on this morning."

"I think we oughta surprise 'em," Saul said with a deep rumbling laugh.

No one argued. Five minutes later they rode toward the mountains again.

~~~~~~

Mattie's clothes had dried overnight. While Billy kept a weather eye on Finn, who lay rolled in his blanket, she sought privacy behind a patch of red-leafed sumac. She rushed to don her petticoats and dress. She rejoined the young man in time to see him poke the snoring oaf in the ribs with the toe of his boot.

"Quit it," Finn mumbled.

"Get up, cowboy. It's getting late. Sun's broke clear of the horizon. You're the one who's always wanting to light a shuck."

Grumbling, Finn sat up. "Ain't no need to be in a hurry today, kid," he said, scraping a hand through his filthy hair. "That storm we rode through wiped out our tracks sure as hell." He waggled a finger at Mattie. "Get your gal there to gather dead limbs to help you build a fire. I want me some coffee after I tend to business."

Expecting them to do his bidding, he shoved his feet into his boots before he tromped into the bushes. When he returned minutes later, he carted his saddle to a pinion tree to sit with his back propped against it. Crossing his arms, he watched Mattie boil water for coffee. She needed to bite her tongue to keep from calling him a lazy good-for-nothing.

However, the aroma of Arbuckles' coffee soothed her anger. The rich, dark brew boosted her flagging spirits, if only for a short time. It also warmed her and filled her empty stomach with more than the last small piece of jerky Billy gave her, saying he couldn't stomach even a bite.

"We're out of food and I need a doctor," Billy said, cupping his left elbow. Over the past days, he'd done his best not to show how much pain he suffered, but it became obvious, he'd grown worse. His face also appeared more flushed than yesterday.

"Yeah, I've been thinkin' the same thing. There's a burg maybe a day south of here. Castle Rock it's called. I reckon we'll head that way."

Finn didn't care a bit about Billy's suffering, Maggie thought. His kind only cared for themselves. He didn't like going hungry.

Leaving Finn to kick dirt on the fire, she helped Billy with Polly. He managed to bridle her before tossing the saddle blanket on her. That effort left him weak; he could no longer heft the heavy saddle by himself. They struggled together to lift it onto the mare.

"Stay where you are. Drop your guns," a man shouted from beyond a projection in the rocky wall behind them.

"Trace." Mattie gasped the instant she recognized his

voice. Her heart leapt in her chest. She lost her grip on the saddle, failing to realize Billy let it drop at their feet.

"What the hell? It can't be." bellowed Finn from beside his as yet unsaddled horse.

Billy grabbed Mattie's arm. "Come on," he ordered, trying to drag her into the trees.

"No. Let me go." She dug in her heels, twisting from his grasp, yelling, "Trace, I'm here."

"Mattie, take cover," Trace shouted to her.

She glanced around, frantic for a place to hide. She noticed Billy made it to a clump of aspens, where he sheltered. Twisting around to follow, Mattie hadn't taken two steps before a thick arm clamped around her middle from behind. A sickening odor attacked her nostrils.

"Finn, let go." she shrieked, tearing at his arm with her nails.

"Not a chance. Stop scratchin', you little hellcat." He tightened his arm around her, forcing a whoosh of air from her lungs. Drawing his gun, he held the barrel to her head like he had done when he abducted her.

At that moment, several men burst from cover behind the rock outcropping. Trace was in the lead, but Mattie recognized Lentzburg's leading citizens among the others.

"Release her." Trace roared at her captor.

"You must think I'm stupid, lawman," Finn scoffed. "The minute I turn her loose, you and your boys will plug me full of lead."

"I think you're a killer and a mangy dog, but if you let her go and throw down your gun, I promise you'll get a fair trial."

Finn laughed. "Followed by a hanging? No thanks. I've got a better idea. One of you boys saddle my horse. I'll climb aboard with the little lady. If you want to see her alive again, you'll give me two hours head start. When I'm a few miles up the trail, I'll set her free. Deal?"

"No deal," Trace barked. "You're not going anywhere except back with us. So you might as well release her right now."

"Un-uh. I'll put a bullet in her head before I let you take me in." Finn cocked the hammer of his gun, making Mattie catch her breath.

"No, you won't, Finn," Billy called from behind them.

Finn swung her around to face the young man who approached from out of the trees. He wove a bit on his feet, but the gun he pointed at Finn's head proved he meant business.

His vicious partner must have read death in Billy's feverish gaze. Without saying a word, he shot the young man.

Struck in the chest, Billy jerked, coughing a choked cry. His gun blazed, the bullet whizzing far wide. His body folded like a rag doll, dropping to the ground. It happened in the space of seconds.

"Billy!" Mattie screamed. Enraged, she scratched Finn's restraining hand, kicking him in the shins. Happy to hear his cry of pain, she didn't care if he killed her. She refused to let him use her as a shield any longer. Elbowing him hard in the ribs, she twisted, breaking his grip on her before staggering backward. In wide-eyed terror, she watched his pistol come up. She expected to die.

Then shots rang out. Finn's body bucked several times. The gun fell from his hand while he dropped like a stone, dead before he hit the ground. For a moment, Mattie stared at his body, unable to move or think.

Movement to her left caught her eye. Trace appeared beside her, drawing her into his arms.

"Thank God you're alive," he said in a raspy voice. "I was afraid I'd lost you."

"So was I," she choked out, clinging to him. Tears of

gladness spilled down her cheeks. Then she thought of the young cowboy who'd taken a bullet for her sake. Pushing at Trace's chest, she said, "I need to go to Billy. He protected me from Finn. He just saved my life."

Although frowning, Trace nodded, releasing her. She ran with her skirts lifted to where Billy lay. Dropping to her knees beside him, she gaped at his blood-soaked shirt and his barely moving chest. He didn't have long, she realized.

"Billy," she whispered, brushing back a lock of dark hair from his forehead. His skin was clammy and cold.

He winced before opening his eyes. A weak smile flitted across his lips. "Miss Mattie, you . . . you alright?" he struggled to ask.

"I'm fine, thanks to you." Biting her lip, she wrapped his cold hand in hers.

"I didn't . . . do much."

"Yes, you did. I'll never forget how you saved me from Finn. You're my hero, Billy." Tears she'd been suppressing overflowed.

"Me, a hero?" His words were hardly audible.

"You truly are." Bending down, she lightly kissed him.

A smile curved his lips. This time it lingered as he breathed his last. Mattie laid his hand at his side while she knelt there, weeping until Trace crouched beside her.

"He's gone, honey." Curving his arm around her, he raised her to her feet. He shifted her into his embrace, pressing her face to his chest, absorbing her sobs.

A while later, after they buried the dead men, Trace helped Mattie onto Polly's back. Billy would want her to have the paint mare, she was certain. She would make sure someone always cared for the horse.

The ride back to Lentzburg passed without incident. The members of the posse accepted Mattie's word that her captors had not molested her—thanks to Billy. She made sure they knew. The men treated her with tender concern, Trace in particular. Yet he always seemed somehow distant. She wondered why but didn't ask, fearing the answer.

After they arrived in town, the citizenry came out to congratulate the victorious posse. The women made a fuss over Mattie, seeking reassurance she hadn't experienced what they feared. Knowing what they meant, she assured them she'd survived intact, relating how Billy, the young cowboy, had protected her.

It astounded her to see skeptical looks from a few women. Since she had no way to convince them she spoke the truth, she ignored them. She wanted to put the tragedy behind her and think about normal events, such as resuming her teaching position. Uppermost in her mind, she wondered if Trace Balfour had decided he was no longer interested in her.

~~~~~~

A week later, Trace stopped by the schoolhouse in the afternoon, once he checked that Mattie's students had gone home. She sat at her desk in the front of the room, head bent over school papers she was reading. When he stepped across the threshold, her head popped up at the sound of his jingling spurs.

"Trace." she blurted, eyes huge behind her specs. "I-I mean Marshal Balfour. What are you doing here?"

He cocked his eyebrows at her flustered expression. Strolling toward her between rows of child-size desks, he halted in front of her, hands riding on his hips. "Why so formal, Mattie? I thought we moved to a first name basis."

Her cheeks turned a pretty shade of pink. "I'm sorry. Of course we are." She fiddled with papers on her desk, avoiding his eyes. "You didn't answer my question. What are you doing here?"

"I've been thinking about our ruined picnic." He crossed his arms, waiting until she glanced at him.

"How about you and I try it again?" Trace said.

Her eyes widened again. "You mean another picnic?"

"Yup. Just you and me this time. What do you say?"

She hemmed and hawed but settled on yes. The next day was Saturday. He rented a buckboard to drive them to a secluded meadow near the creek. Spreading a blanket, he relaxed beside her while she set out an assortment of delicious looking foods. His stomach rumbled at the sight and scents.

He complimented her on her cooking, and they made small talk while they ate. Nervous over what he planned to say, he noticed she also acted jittery.

Once she packed away the leftovers, he caught her hands. "Mattie, I have to ask you something."

"Alright." She nodded, smiling with a nervous tick at the corner of her mouth.

"When that kid, Billy, lay dying, you acted broken up. I listened when you told him he was your hero, and then you kissed him. Were you in love with him?"

Shock swept over her face. "Good heavens, no. He protected me from Finn. You saw that for yourself, and he treated me with respect. I'd come to care for him but I wasn't in love with him." She dipped her chin. "I'm sorry if I gave that impression, Trace."

He sighed in relief, a weight lifted from his chest. "Okay then." He cleared his throat. "Uh, at the church picnic, I said you'd do a man proud as his wife. You said you didn't think of yourself that way. Remember?"

"Y-yes." She bit her bottom lip, blinking fast.

"I wanted to say more but the gunshots erupted." Stroking his thumbs across the top of her hands, he gazed into her eyes. "I wanted to say you'd best start thinking about being a wife because I aimed to marry you. And I still do, if you'll have me?"

She stared at him in wide-eye disbelief as her mouth formed an "O."

He feared he'd just opened himself up to a bucket-load of hurt until, she shouted, "Oh, Trace." She leapt into his arms, kissing him with fierce ardor. A joyful sound rose from his chest. He crushed her to him, happier than any man had a right to be.

Tearing her lips from his a moment later, she murmured, "Trace Balfour, I'll have you now and forever. You're the hero of my dreams." Then she kissed him again, proving for good that she was no shy spinster.

The End

From the Author:

Thank you for taking your valuable time to read The Schoolmarm's Hero. I hope you enjoyed Mattie and Trace's ride through 1880 Colorado. If you did, please tell your friends. Word of mouth is an author's best friend. Posting a review on Amazon will also be a great help.

I'm a longtime Texan and a lover of stories about the Old West, from the iconic works of Zane Grey and Louis L'Amour to the western historical romances I adore reading and writing. If you would like to browse my books and maybe sample a few, stop by my Amazon author page http://amzn.to/Y3aotC or website Lyn Horner's Corner. A word to the wise: My full-length romances are for folks 18 and over.

Happy trails!

Biography

Lyn Horner, California-born and Minnesota-bred, has lived in Texas for over thirty years. She resides in Fort Worth – "Where the West Begins" – with her husband and several very spoiled cats. Trained in the visual arts, Lyn worked as a fashion illustrator and art instructor before she took up writing. She loves crafting passionate,  highly emotional love stories, both historical and contemporary. Lyn also enjoys reading, gardening, visiting with family and friends, and cuddling her furry, four-footed children.

Celtic myth and folklore, as well as unusual powers of the mind fascinate Lyn, influencing most of her writing. Recently, she has also become interested in Native American mythology.

The author's **Texas Devlins** series blends authentic Old West settings, steamy adult romance and psychic mysteries. This series has earned multiple awards and nominations, including Crowned Heart reviews and a Rone Award nomination from **InD'Tale Magazine**.

Readers can also find short works by Lyn Horner in collaborative western anthologies such as **Rawhide 'n Roses**. From that book, she has expanded a flash fiction piece into the short story now included in **The Posse** anthology. A spinoff from her Texas Devlins series is part of the popular Christmas collection **Silver Belles and Stetsons**, which features more than a dozen novellas by best-selling and award-winning authors.

Branching out into modern times, Lyn is now hard at work on her paranormal-romantic suspense series, **Romancing the Gaurdians.** These books combine her trademark flashes of psychic phenomena with Irish folklore and a chilling apocalyptic sub-theme. Along the way, readers are treated to thunderous action, terrifying suspense and sizzling romance.

Horner is a member of Romance Writers of America (RWA) and Pen & Pixels, a local Dallas-Fort Worth writers group. All of her books are available on Amazon, most in Kindle and print format. They may also be read for FREE by members of Kindle Unlimited.

Thank you

Profiling Nathan

Book Description:

Nathan Maguire just wants to make a living inking tattoos, but trouble dogs him. A serial killer is murdering young women in Tampa, near Nate's shop. Latino gangbangers are threatening him. Worst of all, he's a Guardian of Danu charged with protecting an ancient scroll handed down through his family, a dangerous job.

When sexy FBI profiler Talia Werner delivers a message from one of the other Guardians, she turns Nate's life upside down. First, he doesn't trust her, suspecting she wants to steal the scroll. Then, to save her pretty neck, he must help catch the murderer. His deadly psychic gift may come in handy.

Five Star Review
By Craig A. Hart on December 2, 2016
Format: Kindle Edition

Lyn Horner doesn't waste any time getting into the meat of the story with this book. One thing that bothers me about a lot of writers is they take forever to get to the actual story—not an issue here!

I also enjoyed the characters. Nathan Maguire, a psychic tattoo artist, and Talia Werner, a sexy FBI profiler are both larger than life and help move the story along.

The story itself is a good mix of romance and murder mystery, so there's something for everyone! Horner also does a good job of creating some great Florida atmosphere, although early on in the book, I got hungry for a Cuban sandwich and had to stop reading to eat something!

A great read!

Profiling Nathan (Romancing the Guardians, Book Five)
https://www.amazon.com/dp/B01MG3S4ZY

If you have questions or comments, contact me at:
Website: http://lynhorner.com
Facebook:
https://www.facebook.com/lyn.horner.author
Twitter: https://twitter.com/LynHornerauthor
Amazon Author Page:
http://www.amazon.com/author/lyn.horner.award-
winning.books

BAD DAY AT ROUND ROCK
cj petterson

A boyish man with a broken shovel in his hands kneels in the sand, his dark mustache dripping sweat. He digs hard and fast ... and listens for the sounds of footfalls. No one must find what he needs to hide. -----

CHAPTER ONE

Talley Munroe dismounted his skewbald Pinto under the sparse canopy of stubby mesquite trees at Prairie Dell. He looped the reins around a branch then tugged a Sharps rifle out of a hand-tooled leather scabbard, two prizes he'd recently claimed off an ex-Union cavalryman in a game of stud poker. He unsaddled and wiped the sweat off the animal's back with the coarse saddle blanket, all the while checking for the telltale dust clouds of company he wouldn't welcome. Waves of heat writhed skyward and dust devils whirled in the distance. Talley pulled off his blue Stetson, ashy with caliche dust, and swept a shirtsleeve across his wet brow before resettling the rumpled hat over the few strands of gray hair still clinging to his head. He scanned the horizon again then unfolded a thin sheet of yellowed newsprint he dug out of his hip pocket. No one ever taught him to read, but he knew his numbers and had heard the story about the Union Pacific train robbery. It wasn't hard to put two and two together when his eyes fixated on the $30,000 in the headline: *$30,000 Still Missing From Train Robbery.* He'd heard the rumors that Sam Bass had taken to burying parts of his share in different places. He'd also heard that some of those golden double eagles might be buried in a cave near Round Rock. He was counting on his lucky streak at the poker table holding long enough to lead him to it.

He tenderly re-pocketed the paper, then draped the sling of the Sharps over his shoulder and tied a canteen of water and his new prospector's shovel to his belt. Patting the horse's rump, he took a last look around before he skidded on his boot heels down the craggy knoll. A small cascade of dirt and stones followed him down.

At the bottom of the hillock, Talley spat out his chaw, wiped a tobacco drool off his chin, and walked into the shade of a cave. He halted in front of a column still bright with reflected sunlight and blotted by dark smudges where Texas's Confederate soldiers had once mixed gunpowder for their muzzle-loading carbines.

He pondered the passageway in front of him, the only one in the eleven-mile cavern he hadn't yet explored. Talley held to his gut feeling that the cave would give up its secrets before another day passed.

His fringe of dirty hair flopped stiffly against his collar as he checked the depth of kerosene in the miner's lantern he'd stashed in the cavern days before, scratched a match against the wall, and touched the flame to the strip of gauze wick. The lamp held high in front of him, Talley moved deeper into the cave—a labyrinth of underground dry riverbeds and golden limestone columns that resembled pulled taffy, carved by receding waters of a prehistoric sea. The temperature dropped with each step, until his sweaty shirt felt like a cool, wet towel. With the weak lantern light illuminating only a few feet ahead, he ran his palm over the coarse sandstone walls, feeling for hidden niches or loose stones. He studied the floor a step at a time as he headed deeper into the musty darkness.

He groaned softly as his legs threatened to give out when the passageway sloped and forced him into a deepening crouch. Finally, the opening compressed into a space too small and too debris filled to pass through.

"Damn, damn, and double damn."

Then the lantern's light swept over a footprint-shaped, dark blotch on the limestone wall.

"This is it. This is it," he hissed. "A lamp's done sit here a spell."

He knelt awkwardly and dug into the sand with his hands. When the sand gave way to gravel, he switched to the short-handled spade. Before he could break a sweat, the shovel hit something solid. He brushed aside the last of the pebbles and sand and rocked back on his heels. He exhaled a soft whistle and lifted the lid of a green strongbox. Except for $10,000, he didn't know and didn't much care what was printed on the three canvas bags bound with thick twine. He rocked back on his heels, looked around, and then untied one. The gold lit up under the dull flicker of the kerosene lamp.

"Good Gawd-amighty," Talley breathed and started laughing. "Much obliged to ya, Mr. Sam Bass. Them that said you buried it in this here cave spoke true, all right." Talley grabbed fistfuls of shiny twenty-dollar gold pieces with both hands and let them drain through his fingers, relishing the feel and sound of his new-found riches.

Suddenly, the cave magnified the sound of a rock tumbling somewhere.

He turned the lamp wick as low as it could go without flickering out and hid the dimmed lantern behind him. After several minutes of darkened silence, Talley cranked up the lamp, re-buried the box, and retraced his steps. He set the shovel and lantern down just inside the entrance then scrambled back up the rise to the Pinto.

"Shhh," Talley whispered, gently moving his palm over Apache's velvety brown muzzle. The only sounds were the whisper of prairie winds blowing through the mesquite, the crunch of his boots on the ground, and the intermittent stomp of the nervous horse. Talley's head swiveled, looking and listening while he re-saddled the horse. With a final tug on the belly cinch, he led the Pinto down the far side of the knoll, carrying his lucky rifle in one hand.

"Stand easy, boy. Gotta wait til nightfall to get that gold."

Talley eased down to the ground with a groan—the ache in his back a constant reminder of years of busting broncos and driving cattle. He twisted his whiskered chin in a slow side-to-side, working out the audible cricks in his neck. He expected it'd be a long while before the stiffness abandoned his shoulders and the hollow in his lower back, if it ever did. He didn't much miss the cowboy life, though he reckoned he'd still be cowboying if a wild mustang hadn't taken a particular dislike to him and stomped him nearly to death.

He opened a saddlebag and pulled out a wadded-up red neckerchief that held the remnants of his breakfast at the café in Round Rock. He used his pocketknife to slit the hardened baking-soda biscuit in half and set a spicy pork sausage patty in the middle. He took small bites and chewed slowly, savoring the flavors. "Cook makes a mighty fine biscuit." He washed down the dry crumbs with a long pull of tinny-tasting, almost-hot water from the canteen. Talley settled in to keep watch over his treasure as the sun dropped below the horizon, painting mauve and blue edges on the mare's tail clouds sweeping the darkening sky.

When a full moon added its pale glow to unstinted starlight and the fat shadows of the mesquite smeared blackness across the cave entrance, Talley rose on all fours like an arthritic spider, leveraged his body upright, and returned to the labyrinth.

The cavern that was as bright as churned butter in daylight had turned into a black hole. His stride overtook the meager light of the lantern, and he stumbled, fell, and cursed his way back to his fortune. He reopened the strong box and stuffed handfuls of gold double eagles into his pockets. Then he cradled the three sacks in his arms. Feeling their weight, he decided to drag out the strongbox with its cargo intact.

The trip out was harder and longer than he thought it would be, and he sat down hard on the strong box to catch his breath. "Wisht I could-a found this a few years back." He wheezed and coughed for several minutes before he hurriedly hefted the box high enough to get one knee under its weight. The horse's withers rippled, and his eyes rolled.

"Whoa now, 'Pache. Ain't nothing to be feered of. They been a-calling me a fool fer looking for this, but lookie here. We got us our pot o' gold."

The skewbald sidled away when the box brushed against him.

"Hold still, hoss," Talley growled and pushed on the box until it sat balanced on the horse's rump behind the saddle. "We get this done, and it'll be a soft bed and fine whiskey for me, green pastures and sweet water for you."

Apache's nose flared, he snorted, danced, trying to get out from under the weight of the box.

"Settle down, hammer head."

Talley heard the click of a gun cocking and twisted around just as a muzzle spat fire. He spun into the horse's side, grasping at the saddle horn to stay upright. Apache reared, pitched wildly against the reins and bucked the strongbox to the ground. The gun flared again, and Talley Munroe was dead before the echoes of the shot resounded from the cave.

CHAPTER TWO

Seventeen-year-old Lilly Malmstrom thought morning calm was the best time of any day—before the sun burned away the cool of the night, before hot winds drove the fine West Texas sand under the windowsills, before the town of Round Rock fully awakened. By seven a.m., when she stood on tiptoe to twist the key in the wall clock to wind it, she had the doctor's instruments scalded and air-drying on the table and fresh-washed huck towels hanging on the line behind the building. To mark the end of the work week, she drew an "X" through the date on the calendar with the stub of a lead pencil and sighed.

"July 19, 1878," she said, pronouncing the month as "yulie". "One year. One whole year."

It'd been exactly a year since she'd left Sweden, but her new life hadn't turned out exactly as she'd planned. Now she had a new plan: Once she'd worked off the debt, she'd be free to start anew. She blinked back the tears that filled her blue eyes, grabbed the corn-straw broom, and attacked yesterday's dirty floor with a flourish.

Out on the boardwalk, Lilly twisted a strand of black hair around her finger and poked it into the bun at the back of her neck then draped her palms over the top of the broom handle and rested her chin on her hands. She watched the town begin to stir. A wire-haired dog, nose to the ground, made his way to the back door of the café. An old woman, her white hair mostly hidden by a black bonnet, flicked a whip at the rumps of two mules as her buckboard rattled up the dusty road. Two Texas Rangers walked down the hotel steps and crossed over toward the New Town Café.

Startled by a horse's snort, she turned to see Shorty vanDyne slide off his roan. He wrapped the reins around the hitching rail and strutted toward her, chaps flapping and the silver rowels on his Mexican spurs jangling.

Lilly felt her eyebrows knit together. "I say the same thing as before, Mr. vanDyne. Go away."

"Whoa, now, Miz Lilly. You ain't heard what I come all the way from Dallas to say."

"If you come to say 'goodbye,' I hear you. Goodbye and good riddance to you. Now go." She made no attempt to keep the contempt out of her voice.

Shorty chuckled. "Don't go gettin' all uppity on me, pretty lady. I told you I'd leave the Chisholm Trail and come for you when I got my fortune. Didn't I tell you that? Well, I done it. I got my fortune, and I'm here to make you my wife."

"You got no fortune." Lilly swept the broom roughly across the toes of Shorty's boots.

Shorty pulled a twenty-dollar gold piece out of his pocket. "See this here? This ain't but a tiny bit of it. I'm telling you, I'm rich."

She stared at the coin. "Maybe you're rich. Maybe not. Don't matter to me. I don't need no husband to tell me what to do and when to do it."

Shorty's smile stretched into a thin line. "A woman alone ain't seemly. Folks in these parts might think unkindly things about her."

"The folks I care about in these parts know me better. The others don't matter to me much."

"Better think on that a bit more," he said. "Mean gossip can bring a person down. Sure would hate for someone to start some ugly rumors about a pretty lady like you." He took hold of her wrist. "I can put a stop to that when you're my missus."

"Let. Me Go!"

A moment later she was sitting on the boardwalk, looking at Shorty sprawled face down in the street. A moment after that, two strong arms quickly lifted her to her feet, and she heard Anders Olsson's smooth-as-warm-whisky voice as he steadied her.

"I'm sorry, Miz Lilly. I'm sorry to knock you down." He pointed at Shorty. "You got no business bothering the lady. Get on outta here while you're still able."

Shorty got to his feet, sputtering dirt. He slapped both palms against his empty holsters then grabbed his hat off the ground. "You just bought yourself a ticket to hell," the wrangler yelled as he swung a leg over the saddle.

Lilly straightened to her full five-foot height, brushed dirt off her skirt, then looked up into eyes as dark blue as midnight as Anders handed her the broom. She saw the flash of uneven white teeth under the nut-brown mustache he kept waxed into fine curls on the ends. Because she knew he rarely smiled, she was pleased that he smiled for her. "*Tack*," she said.

"You're welcome. I don't think he'll bother you again."

"It is good the law says he cannot wear his pistols in town, but I think he will come for you some time. You must be careful."

He shrugged. "Is Doc in?"

"Pretty soon. Why do you—?"

Anders unwrapped a blue bandana from his right hand and held it out for her to see. A deep gouge marked the beginning of a long, angry tear across his palm. "Bob wire."

"Cutting fences gets a man killed in Texas," she murmured, concern in her voice.

"Needed new graze." His eyes held hers for a long moment. "The fence and the land are mine."

She believed that was more than likely true, but the uncharacteristic show of pride in his property made her smile. Not wanting to seem like a flirt, she dropped her eyes to his hand. "When'd this happen?"

"Two days."

"Morning, folks," Doc Green called as he crossed the street from the livery stable where he'd left his hack. "From what I saw, Swede, you just made an enemy."

Anders nodded. "Wouldn't be the first one. Won't be the last."

"I'd be a mite careful from here on if I was you. Shorty vanDyne is a coward all right, but he's vengeful, sneaky, and mean as a snake." Doc bent over Anders's outstretched hand and shook his head. "That's a nasty gash. Pretty close to infected, I'd say. Come on in, and let's get it cleaned out."

~~~~~~

After Anders had paid his bill and left the office, Doc grabbed a bar of the lye soap Lilly made for him and dropped his hands into water in a white enamel basin. Lilly began to clean up. When she sensed that he was watching her as she put away the suturing thread and washed down the table top with water and a splash of carbolic acid, she stopped working and returned his gaze.

"I am doing something wrong?"

85

"You're doing fine. Shorty pestering you again about getting hitched?"

"He is a fool. Maybe this time Anders makes him stop for good."

"You've had a hard year, Lilly."

"Not so bad," she murmured with a shrug. "You were kind to help me when my money was stole. Except for you, I would still be in New York City. Maybe I might be dead."

"Your sister, Selma, stood good for the money, and you'll have it worked off soon. What are you going to do then?"

Her breath caught for a moment in her throat. She was desperate to have the term "indentured servant" removed from her records, but the thought that she might not have a job terrified her. "I cannot keep working for you?"

"I can't pay you enough wages to live on. I barely make enough to live on myself."

"I can make do. Already I have spent a year with no money. Selma will be happy if I can give her only a little bit."

"Anders is sweet on you, Lilly. I see the way he smiles and how his eyes light up every time he looks at you."

"He is not interested in me that way. He was being nice to help me."

"You couldn't do much better than young Anders for a husband. He's a good man, and he's no hardscrabble dirt farmer neither. Got himself 160 acres and a nice herd of longhorn. I hear tell he's also got three or four of those new, hump-backed cattle that come all the way from a country on the other side of the world. India, I think. From what I've heard about what it cost to buy one of them cows, I'd say Anders is pretty well off."

"And he speaks Swedish," she said with a laugh. "You say this every time he comes to town. Ya, Anders is a good man, a nice and handsome gentleman, but I feel the same as I say to Shorty. I don't want a husband. Not even Anders."

She knew that wasn't quite true. She wanted a man who would make her heart jump into her throat. She wanted her pulse to race until she felt her fair complexion flush warm with a rosy glow. She didn't think Anders was exciting. Anders was comfortable.

Doc smiled and headed for his desk. "A good man needs a good woman," he said over his shoulder. "And you are that. A lot of the ladies in this town has got their caps set on him."

"They will be very lucky to have him," she said and picked up a months-old copy of *The Round Rock Sentinel.* Every day, she would read aloud every word in every column to practice her English.

Lilly had just turned to page three of the newspaper when a towheaded boy threw open the door.

"There's going to be a killing!" he yelled. "There's going to be a killing at the stables. I come to fetch the doc."

"Who?" she gasped.

"That waddie, Shorty, and Mr. Olsson. Gotta find the deputy." the boy said then disappeared out of the doorframe.

Doc stepped out of his office, his round face and halo of silver hair giving him a monkish look. "That sounded like Jonah from over to the livery. What'd he want?"

"*Ett skjut,*" she managed, her words more breath than sound.

"English, please."

"A shooting." She waved a trembling hand toward the street. "Anders, Shorty, the livery."

Doc left the building in his shirtsleeves, sprinting across the street. Lilly followed, skirt lifted high, and passed him at a dead run.

She jumped up on the fence rail, saw Shorty holding a rifle belt-high, and heard him order Swede to beg for his life.

"I'm counting to three," Shorty said.

"You aim to kill me whether I beg or not. Get on with it. How about I make it easy for you and turn my back?"

Before he could move, Shorty shot off a round that threw up a divot between Anders's boots. "I ain't no back-shooting coward!"

"*Nej!*" Lilly screamed. "No!" She dug her fingers into Doc's arm. "Make him stop. Make him stop. Anders has no gun."

"I'd stop right now if I was you, vanDyne," Doc hollered. "There's Texas Rangers in town. You kill an unarmed man, and they'll hunt you down, and they won't quit 'til you end up in jail or dead."

Shorty hesitated then cradled his rifle. "There'll be another time," he said.

Lilly was standing in Anders's shadow before Shorty had backed out of the corral. The towheaded boy and the deputy arrived just in time to watch a dust cloud follow Shorty out of town.

"Everything's okay, Caige," Doc hollered. "Shorty vanDyne had got his dander up, but it's over now."

Anders shook his head. "Didn't expect him to come this soon. I'm indebted, Doc."

"Didn't want to see all my good work on your hand go to waste. Go home, Swede. You got a ways to travel, so best be watchful."

Lilly stroked her fingers over the wet trails on her cheeks. The thought that a friend, that Anders might have died had terrified her to tears. "Ya. You best watch."

Anders mounted his buckskin, tipped his hat to Lilly and headed out of town. She watched until he disappeared into the glare of the sun then switched her gaze to the three men in trail-dusty, tenderfoot clothes riding slowly up the street. She'd seen the strangers earlier in the week, and this time, the one that looked about her age nodded and smiled at her as they headed for Kopperal's Store. She smiled then ducked her head and silently admonished herself for being so blatantly flirtatious with someone she'd never been introduced to.

The deputy also noticed the men and swore softly under his breath. "They got guns," he murmured and turned to follow them.

Lilly and Doc had just made it back to the office when the gunfire started. Startled, she yelped and twirled to see what was happening. "Get down!" Doc yelled as he shoved her inside and slammed the door. She crept to the window in time to see a man wearing shaving cream and a barber's cape burst out of the barbershop at a dead run, firearm blazing. Two of the strangers galloped past, one firing a gun; the other hunched over, gripping the saddle horn, doing all he could to stay on the horse. Round Rock lay silent for a few moments, then the town erupted in shouts and screams. Doc grabbed his black bag and ran out the door with Lilly close behind.

CHAPTER THREE

On Monday morning, the July 22, 1878, issue of the newspaper quaked like a leaf in Lilly's hands. In the second column, next to Kopperal's full-length column of advertising for trimmed and untrimmed hats, for silks and dry goods, for all manner of great bargains, the headline for the first item under the masthead screamed at her from the front page:

3 DEAD IN BLAZING GUN FIGHT

—Williamson County Deputy Sheriff Alijah Caige Grimes was killed Friday in a shootout with outlaws Sam Bass, Seaborn Barnes, and Frank Jackson.

The conscientious Deputy Grimes happened to see the Bass gang ride into town wearing pistols, which is against the law in Round Rock. He followed the outlaws to Kopperal's Store whereupon Bass fired six shots, killing the lawman instantly.

The outlaws were already on their horses when Texas Ranger Dick Ware ran out of the barbershop, still wearing shaving foam and a barber's cape, and shot Bass and Barnes out of their saddles. Barnes was dead when he hit the ground. The resourceful Jackson laid down covering gunfire while he helped the injured Bass climb back onto his horse after which they rode out of town. Jackson was heard to yell at a negligent parent to move a small child to safety.

Texas Rangers tracked down the mortally wounded Bass on Saturday and brought him back to Round Rock where he died on Sunday, July 21, his 27th birthday. The sheriff said he believed the gang came to town intending to rob the Williamson County Bank, unaware that the Texas Rangers had been tipped off and were waiting for them.

The Rangers warned residents to be on the lookout for gang member Frank Jackson, who is still at large.

Lilly had recognized the outlaw firing his gun as the two men rode past the window as the handsome, young man who'd smiled at her. "His name is Frank Jackson," she said, pronouncing the "J" like a "Y," and was shocked and ashamed she'd smiled at a bank robber. "I will pray for no more days like that in Round Rock," she whispered. "That was a bad day." She started to turn the page when her eye caught sight of two familiar names under another column headline.

Two men found dead.

—A posse of Texas Rangers hunting down the outlaw Sam Bass on Saturday found Shorty vanDyne, a Chisholm Trail cowboy, shot dead on the Georgetown Road. Sheriff Barry arrested local rancher Anders Olsson for the crime. Several people saw Olsson and vanDyne shouting threats at each other at the Round Rock livery on Friday. The victim was known to carry two pearl-handled pistols and a Winchester repeating rifle. His guns and his roan horse are missing.

—Talley Munroe, a buffalo hunter and prospector, was found shot dead near the Prairie Dell cave on Saturday. Mr. Munroe was known to carry a Sharps rifle and ride a Pinto horse. Both are missing.

—Anyone having information about these two killings should contact the sheriff's office in Round Rock.

"I go to the jail!" Lilly yelled on her way out the door. "Anders is there."

By the time Doc got to the jail, Lilly was leaning across Sheriff Barry's desk with both hands planted in front of him, yelling.

"Anders did not kill Shorty!"

"I think otherwise, Miz Lilly. Seems Swede had a motive."

"What's a motive?"

"Means witnesses seen them fighting."

"Like banty roosters," she spat out. "They fight because of me. I am no reason to kill for. *Gud i himlen.*" Exasperated at not being able to convince him of Anders's innocence, Lilly turned to Doc. "This man listens to you. Tell him."

"Swede had a bad gun hand Friday," Doc said. "I know because I stitched it up that morning. Besides which he didn't have a gun with him neither."

"Don't mean nothing. Didn't nobody say vanDyne got killed on Friday. Even if he did, Swede could-a used his other hand and Shorty's own gun to kill him," the sheriff said. "And Swede had a couple of twenty-dollar gold pieces in his pocket. Shorty'd been flashing a few of them gold eagles around town and bragging about making his fortune. I figure Swede killed him for it. You feeling all right, Doc?"

"I reckon maybe Sarai's biscuits ain't sitting too good right now."

"I fix you a tonic when we get back to the office," Lilly said, momentarily reverting to her job of tending to the doctor's needs. "Tell him, Doc. You tell him Anders is no killer. You know he is a rich man. To have two pieces of gold is no problem for him."

"One, maybe, two, but we're talking about a fortune in shiny, new gold pieces," the sheriff said. "Gold's a mighty big temptation, Miz Lilly. Doc'll tell you the same thing. It can make the best good man go bad. There's no question in my mind but Swede done the killing. Rangers figured they was gonna take Sam Bass back to Austin. I guess they'll take Anders instead, and they'll see he gets a fair trial before he hangs."

"*Nej*! He did not kill no one. Doc, you tell him again."

"Ain't no use wasting any more breath on someone as stubborn as my mule. Sheriff's got his mind made up. Come on, let's get out of here."

"Wait. When will the Rangers take Anders to Austin?"

"Friday, I suppose," the sheriff said, "but don't go thinking you're going to get him out of jail before then."

Out on the street, Lilly peeled Doc's fingers off of her arm. "I thought Anders was your friend. Why didn't you tell the sheriff some more that Anders did not do this?"

"It's exactly because Anders is my friend that I couldn't say anything more back there." Doc leaned closed to her ear. "When the sheriff said Anders had two twenty-dollar gold pieces in his pocket, it brought to mind that Anders paid me with a twenty-dollar gold piece. That means he had at least three."

"You think he ...?"

"No, I don't think he shot Shorty. Not for a blamed minute. But if the sheriff found out Anders had three gold pieces ...."

She suddenly felt cold and shivered. "A wealthy man can have three gold pieces. He can have more than three, can't he? Anders did not kill Shorty. We must help him."

"How do you propose we do that? I'm a doctor, not a lawman, and you're just a girl."

Lilly stopped walking and buried her face in her hands. Doc was opening the door to the office before he noticed that he'd left Lilly standing in the middle of the street, crying.

"Aw, come on, Lilly. Get on in here out of the heat. We're gonna figure something out."

The New Town Café droned with excited voices as people speculated about the wild shoot-out, something that had never happened before in Round Rock. Between bites of chicken-fried steak, boiled potatoes and baking-soda biscuits, all of it smothered in sawmill gravy, the lunch crowd opined on the death of Shorty vanDyne, the guilt or innocence of Swede, and the whereabouts of Shorty's alleged fortune. Two men sitting at a table near a wall conversed softly. Not coincidentally, they became silent while the waitress refilled their mugs with chicory coffee and then leaned in close to restart their whispers.

"Swede needs to say where he hid that gold. He won't have no use for it after he's hung. It'd be a crying shame for it to be lost forever."

"You think you can just go ask him, and he'll tell you? He's got no reason to tell you nothing."

"Maybe if we threaten to set fire to his spread and rustle his cattle, he'll have a reason."

"Yeah, you go ahead and make all the threats you want. He'll just yap to the sheriff and the Rangers, and then what?"

"I heard tell Swede about knocked Shorty ta hell and back because he bothered that girl that works for Doc."

"You thinking he's sweet on her?"

"That's what I'm thinking, and I'm also thinking maybe she can find out where the gold is hid."

"What if she ain't willing to help us?"

"Don't expect her to be. Probably take some persuading. I expect Swede'll be real happy to say where the gold is hid when he hears how persuasive we are."

"How about the sheriff and them Rangers? She'll go running to them, and they'll be all over us like ticks on a hound."

"That's the thing. She ain't gonna say nothing to nobody unless she wants to get killed—her, Anders, and Doc, too. The whole lot of 'em."

CHAPTER FOUR

On Tuesday morning, Lilly marched into the jail with a covered plate of food. "I bring breakfast to the innocent man."

"The sheriff says he ain't innocent, and I'll have to take a look-see under that towel," the sheriff's new deputy said. "Make sure that's all you brought."

She set the plate on the desk with a clunk and whipped off the towel. "Take your look-see."

The deputy snatched a thick slice of crisp-fried salt pork before she could pull the plate away.

"Now you open the door, and I give him his food."

"I'll give it to him. You stay here 'til I say come on."

She watched him palm a bakingsoda biscuit as he opened the cell door and handed the plate to Anders.

"You can come on now," the deputy said as he set a chair a couple of feet away from the cell door. "This is where you hafta sit."

When the deputy was back at his desk, she scooted the chair closer to the bars. "The eggs are picked fresh this morning."

"I thank you for your trouble. It looks real good," Anders said. He bit into a buttered biscuit slathered in homemade peach preserves. "Tastes even better. You need to hear this from me, Lilly. I didn't kill Shorty vanDyne."

"I just know you didn't. The sheriff says you killed him because of that fight you had, and he found gold pieces in your pocket. That's not good reasons."

"A while back, I sold one of my bulls," he said in answer to the unspoken question. "One of them humpbacked cow mixes they call Brahmans. There ain't many of them in Texas, so I got a good price. The man paid in gold."

"Who bought it? He must come tell the sheriff right now."

Anders shook his head. "The man's named Steve Luce, and he can't come right now. He's got the Lazy L spread over near Lake Travis."

"But he must come back and tell the sheriff."

"My vaquero, Luis, rode out Sunday to get him. It's a day's ride there and a day back, so I expect they'll be here sometime Tuesday. Plenty of time before the Rangers plan on taking me to Austin."

Lilly nodded, then silently fingered the lock on the cell door and studied the window bars while Anders sat on the end of his cot and ate. "The bars on the window are old," she whispered.

"*Nej*," he said. "They are only rusty. I looked at them."

When a smile gentled his stoic face, she cocked her head and smiled back.

"Can't break me out, if that's what you're thinking," he said. "This jail, everything in it, is new and strong."

She wrapped her hand around a steel bar, sighed, and leaned her forehead against it. "I come to America," she said in Swedish, "for adventure because everything in Sweden is always the same, boring, but aye, yi, yi …."

96

"None of that Swede jibber-jabber in there," the deputy yelled. "Talk so I can understand."

"I don't think you understand English so good either, because when I tell you Anders is not guilty, you do nothing."

When Anders used the last lump of biscuit to wipe a final smear of drying, yellow, egg yolk off the plate, she stood.

"I will bring more at lunchtime."

He came close to the bars with the empty plate and brushed her hand with fingertips as coarse as sandpaper. She was surprised when her heart seemed to skip a beat.

"'Preciate that," he said, "but no need. The deputy can bring me some grub from the café."

"Won't taste as good as mine."

He nodded. "That's true. You're a fine cook. I'm much obliged."

She hesitantly reached through the bars to touch his hand, and as he curled his fingers gently around hers, she felt her heart begin to race and her face flush warm.

~~~~~~~

Lilly was crossing the narrow alleyway between the café and the house of the demimondes when a dirty hand, smelling of horse sweat, sour beer, and the stench of someone who pees against a wall, smothered her scream. With one hand over her mouth and an arm around her waist, the man half-dragged and half-carried her down the alley and threw her face-down behind a pile of building debris and a trash barrel. When she lifted up, the man waiting there knelt and jabbed a gun barrel against her forehead.

"Scream and you're dead," he said.

"I won't scream," she whispered, then rubbed the palm of her hand across the blood that tickled down her face after the bearded man holstered his gun. She looked at her hand then wiped off the blood on her skirt and swept her fingertips across the tears welling in her eyes.

He yanked her up and slapped her hard, knocking her back down. He knelt again and waited while she caught her breath.

"You're going to ask Swede where he hid Shorty's gold. Then you're going to come back here this same time tomorrow and tell me. And iff'n you talk to anyone but Swede or tell anyone else about this, I will kill you and Swede . . . and Doc, too, for good measure. Do you understand?"

She nodded.

He grabbed a fistful of her hair and yanked. "Let me hear you say it."

"Ya, I understand."

Lilly lay in the dirt, crying until the men disappeared around the corner of the building. "Enough," she said. She got to her feet, wiped her face with the bottom of her skirt, and ran back to Doc's office, ignoring the stares of passersby.

She was out of breath when she slammed the office door behind her.

"What happened to you?" Doc asked. "Who—?"

"Orton and Wesley Schmidt. They want me to ask Anders where he hid the gold and then come tell them. But Anders doesn't have the gold. How can he tell what he doesn't know?"

"We're going over to the sheriff's office. You tell him what happened."

"Orton said if I tell anyone, they will kill us. Me, you, *and* Anders. They'll be watching me, and if they see us go there right now, they'll know I told."

Doc filled a white-enamel pan with water from the kettle on the Franklin stove and began to clean the cut on Lilly's forehead. Her eyes watered in pain, but she sat impassively while he daubed on an antiseptic carbolic solution. When he'd finished, he reached into a desk drawer and pulled out a gun belt.

"That's against the law, and you're no gunfighter."

"I ain't about to let them yahoos get away with this. I got to do something."

"It's two against one, and all you'll do is die. I have thought about this. I think we can set a trap. After I get back from bringing Anders his lunch, I'll take your buggy and drive toward the place where they found Shorty. When I drive out of town, they will follow. Then you tell the Rangers."

"You mean the sheriff."

"*Nej*. I mean the Texas Rangers. I heard one of them say something to the sheriff about a 'Bass War' and how they had come to Round Rock on purpose to find Sam Bass and his gold. Now, they believe Anders knows where the gold is. I think they will be very happy to keep Orton from having it."

~~~~~~

Lilly set a towel-covered plate of food on the deputy's desk. "I say again, Anders did not shoot Shorty."

"Nothing I can do about it. Tell it to the sheriff. What happened to your face that it's all bruised like that?"

"I tripped and fell."

"Guess you need to watch better where you're walking," he said as he pulled off the towel and snatched a chicken leg from the mound of fried chicken and potatoes boiled with their jackets on. She waited at his desk while he handed the plate to Anders then placed the chair where she was supposed to stay.

"You can come on back, now."

When the deputy reached his desk, she pulled the chair close to the bars, and sat quietly with hands folded in her lap.

Anders's eyes narrowed and he set the plate on the floor. "I heard you tell the deputy you tripped and fell. That might account for the knot on your forehead, but who put that handprint on your face?"

"I cannot say."

"Can't or don't want to?"

"They are the same thing."

"Then it's because of me and the gold people think I've got. Whoever left those marks on you meant to send me the message that he means business. That kind of man ain't about to back down, Lilly. You have to bring me a gun."

"Orton Schmidt," she burst out. "Wesley, too. They want me to ask you where the gold is. They gave me until tomorrow. Orton said he will kill me if I don't do what he says, and that he'd kill us all if I told anyone but you. I'd rather tell the sheriff what happened than have you die trying to get out of jail."

"The law ain't about to do nothing. It'd be your word against theirs."

"But you could die."

"Luis got back a while ago. Empty-handed. The man who bought my bull is on the trail somewhere, driving a herd up to Wichita. So, if you don't bring me a gun, the Rangers are going to take me to Austin, and Orton and Wesley will get away with what they done to you. Bring me a gun."

She glared at him. "Ya, and now you make me think I have fallen in love with a dead man," she snapped. "I forget the tea," she told the deputy as she stomped out the door. "I'll be right back."

Fifteen minutes later, Lilly handed the sheriff's new deputy two Mason jars filled with sweet tea then stood back with balled fists jammed into her apron pockets.

"I say again that Anders didn't kill Shorty."

He grimaced, shook his head, and hefted one of the tea jars. "Mine?"

She nodded, and he walked the other Mason jar back to Anders then sent her a come-along wave with his fingers. When the deputy sat down at his desk, Lilly set her back to him and pulled Doc's double-action revolver out of one apron pocket, a handful of cartridges out of the other, then passed them through the cell bars to Anders. He slid the cartridges into a pocket and pushed the gun under his waistband at the hollow of his back. He searched her eyes then reached through the bars for her hand.

"*Tack.*"

"You're welcome, I suppose," she said and twisted around when the sun's glare came through the open jail door and the vaquero, Luis, walked in, asking to see Anders.

"Not 'til Miz Lilly leaves. Can't be two people back there at the same time."

"I can come back for the plate later," she said and ran out the door.

"Go on back, Mex," the deputy said. "Like I told you before, don't get close to them bars."

Luis lowered his eyes as he passed the lawman, paused for a minute in front of the cell, then returned to the desk.

The deputy raised his head and stared into the barrel of a Smith and Wesson revolver. He rose without a word and unlocked the cell door.

"This ain't gonna go well for you, Anders. Your Mex, neither."

"Why don't you go have a seat on the bunk there, rest a spell?" Anders said.

The deputy eased down on a corner of the bunk. "You won't outrun a posse of Texas Rangers."

"The consequences of getting caught don't mean much when the alternative is hanging." Anders locked the cell door and nodded at Luis who left the jail.

Ten minutes later, Anders had the deputy's gun belt strapped onto his right hip with Doc's Smith and Wesson snugged down in the holster before he stepped through the door and mounted the horse that Luis left tied to the hitching post. He rode the buckskin at a walk behind the buildings, headed for the café.

CHAPTER FIVE

Anders did not intend to kill the brothers. There had been too much killing in Round Rock. What he knew for sure was that Orton and Wesley could not, would not remain unpunished for the assault on Lilly. He would leave the option to live or die with them. He also did not intend to run from the law once his mission was accomplished. He knew he would never outrun or outlast a posse of Rangers. Luis was already on the road to Austin to employ the legal services of Anders's good friend, Elisha Pease, the former governor of Texas. The sheriff's accusation notwithstanding, Anders knew that all the evidence against him was circumstantial, and the ex-governor still had considerable clout in a courtroom. He figured if he could stay alive, he had a good chance of being acquitted.

Anders dropped the reins on the ground in the alleyway next to the café, walked around the back and in through the kitchen door. The cook frowned then stepped back from the stove with his hands spread wide and empty when he spotted the gun in Anders's hand. Anders acknowledged him with a nod and stopped next to the counter long enough to spot where the Schmidt boys were sitting. When he stepped into the main restaurant, every sound in the place slowly died as patrons recognized who he was and what he was carrying.

"Sorry to disturb your lunch, folks," he said, "but I got some business with Orton and Wesley there."

Murmurs, chairs scraping, and boots clumping on the wood plank floor took the place of silence as some customers hurried to leave. Others, those who wanted to get a first-hand look at the excitement that was about to happen, stayed in their seats.

"We ain't got no guns," Wesley said, his nasal voice made tinny with fear.

"Never did have much use for them myself. Today seemed an exception. I wanted to be sure to get your undivided attention. Miz Lilly tells me you have a question for me."

Orton's voice was braver. "I reckon that's right. We kind'a figured since you was going to hang anyways, you won't have no use for that gold and wouldn't mind telling us where you got it hid."

"I mind a lot, Orton. I mind because I didn't kill vanDyne and have no idea where that gold, if there is any gold, is hid. And second, I mind because I'm particularly unhappy with how you went about asking the question." Anders waved his arm toward the customers still in the restaurant. "Why don't you tell our friends here how you two cowards roughed up Miz Lilly then threatened to kill her?"

"She's lying. We never—"

This was the response Anders hoped for. He wanted a public reason to exact the punishment the brothers had earned. His face turned to cold stone. He drew back his arm and raked the gun barrel hard across Orton's face, sending him crashing to the floor with a gash that angled from his temple to his chin. Orton screamed like a girl, grabbed his bloody face, and rolled side to side, moaning and cursing.

"Where's your manners, Orton? You never call a lady a liar. How about you, Wesley?" Anders said in an even voice with no trace of anger. "You man enough to own up to what you did?"

Bug-eyed, Wesley stared at him, then at his brother, and then inhaled a shuddering breath. His mouth gaped like a fish out of water, but no words escaped. It took several seconds of hard swallowing before he found his voice.

"We didn't mean to hurt her much. Just wanted to scare her some."

"You should'a asked me yourself." Anders switched the gun to his left hand then threw a short right jab straight from the shoulder that caught Wesley square on the chin. Wesley's head snapped back as the force of the blow knocked the cowhand out cold and tipped him and his chair backwards to the floor. Anders returned his attention to Orton who had gotten up as far as on his knees.

"It takes some kind'a yellow-bellied cowards to beat on a woman. Two grown men against one little woman. You hurt Miz Lilly bad enough that she needed Doc's attention to that cut on her forehead, and it'll be more'n a week before that handprint of yours leaves her face. I want you to confess in front of God and all these witnesses what you did to her. I see the postmaster there, and he'll be a fair, upstanding witness. Afternoon, Mr. Oatts. We won't take up too much more of your time." Anders jammed the barrel of the Smith and Wesson hard against the crease between Orton's eyebrows. "If you don't spit it out before the law gets here, it'll be too late, because I'll shoot you between the eyes the minute they come through the door."

Orton jerked his head back to get away from the gun and shifted his shoulders nervously. "It's like he says," he murmured. "Wesley and me might'a got a little too rough with Miz Lilly."

Anders jabbed the gun barrel into his chest. "Speak up, Orton, and tell it right. People can't hear you way back there in the corner."

"Awright!" he shouted. "I ain't got nothing personal against Miz Lilly, but I figured I had to work her over a bit so Anders could see we was serious about knowing where the gold was hid. All you folks want to know where it is, too. I know you do."

"How many times do I have to say it? I didn't kill vanDyne, and I don't know where his gold is." Anders punctuated his statement with a left hook to Orton's temple that sent him back to the floor.

"Anders Olsson! This is Sheriff Barry, and I got two Rangers with me. Better give it up."

"You got good timing, Sheriff. I've done what needed to be done, so come on in." Anders laid his weapon on the table in front of the postmaster and spread his arms wide. "Ask the people in here. They'll tell you. I'm unarmed."

The three lawmen stepped cautiously into the café with drawn guns. Lilly followed them in and was grabbed by one of the Rangers when she tried to run past him to Anders's side.

The sheriff studied the unconscious bodies of the Schmidt brothers then holstered his gun.

"What'd you have against these two boys, Anders?"

"You see Miz Lilly's face? That's what I have against them."

Lilly pulled away from the Ranger to stand next to Anders. "See," she said and pushed her hair back and cocked her head so the sheriff could see the knot on her forehead, then turned her cheek to him. "Orton hit me and said if I told anyone, he'd kill me."

"You don't have to take our word that he hurt her," Anders said. "Ask these people. Mr. Oatts will tell you true. Orton confessed in front of everybody that he beat Miz Lilly to get me to tell him where vanDyne's gold is."

"I did hear Orton admit to whupping on her, Sheriff," Mr. Oatts said. "Of course, it came at the point of a gun, but it sounded like a true confession to me."

"I didn't kill vanDyne," Anders said, "and I don't know where the gold is, but nobody wants to believe me. I figured if I didn't get these men to confess in public what they did to Miz Lilly, they'd get away with assaulting her."

"I will testify against them," Lilly said.

"I don't think you have to worry 'bout that, Miz Lilly," the sheriff said. "I can see the proof of what they did to you. I got a couple empty cells in the jail that they can fill for a spell. But you, Anders. I figured once you got out of jail you was going to make a run for it. Get as far away from Round Rock as you could. Why didn't you run?"

"I don't want to spend the rest of my life dodging the law," Anders said. "I want my day in court to clear my name. I got a cattle spread to take care of." He wrapped his arm around Lilly's shoulders and drew her close. "And this wonderful woman to love."

CHAPTER SIX

Shortly after noon on Thursday, Jessiemae Hartley halted her buckboard in front of Kopperal's Store. The dour-looking woman dressed in widow's weeds wrapped the reins around the hitching rail and tromped across the boardwalk into the store.

"Need supplies," she said to the storekeeper and then spent a few minutes pointing to bags of flour, cornmeal, beans, sugar, and chicory coffee. It took her nearly an hour to decide on a measure of blue cloth, a packet of oyster shell buttons, and threads for a new dress.

"You want me to add this to your bill?" the clerk asked as he summed up the purchase.

"Jez' tell me what I owe. I'll pay it all."

He pulled a ledger book from the shelf under the counter. Adjusting his wire frames, he found her name, added up a column then spun the book around to show her.

"Don't know sums. Will this pay it?" She pulled two shiny gold pieces out of her tiny, black clutch.

He turned the coins over in his hand. "And then some. I'll have to go over to the bank to make you change. Don't keep that much money in the store. You wait right here. My hired man will load your purchase for you."

Jessiemae, her mouth curled down and a crease between her eyebrows, sat atop the loaded buckboard when the storekeeper returned with Sheriff Barry at his side and Lilly trailing behind them. The storekeeper counted out Jessiemae's change, but before the widow could slap the reins against the horses's rumps, the sheriff grabbed the bit of one of them.

"Hold on a minute, Miz Hartley. Seems you got some evidence here concerning a murder." He patted the horse's neck and smoothed his palm down its muzzle.

"Don't know nothing about no murder. What evidence you talking about?"

"Them shiny new gold pieces you gave the storekeep for one thing, and these horses for another. Got a right pretty Pinto here, and this here roan looks familiar. Where'd you get them?"

"They're mine, and I ain't murdered nobody to get 'em."

"Mind telling me where you did get them?"

Her narrow face pinched tighter. She rubbed both hands against her skirt as she talked. "Got my homestead out by the cemetery."

"Yes, ma'am. I know where you live."

"Well, the day that Sam Bass fella got buried, a rider come by towards evening, threw a clod on the grave, and stood a spell. I reckon he seen me working in the cotton field 'cause pretty soon he come over and give me some gold pieces."

Mild disbelief raised the sheriff's eyebrows. "A stranger just up and gives you twenty-dollar gold pieces, out of the goodness of his heart?"

"Not exactly. He said he'd be obliged if I tended to the grave ever' now and again. Keep the weeds down and chase away the grave robbers. Said there'd most likely be a mess of grave robbers, so I was supposed to keep a vigil. Told me where to catch these here horses, too."

"I told you!" Lilly shouted. "That proves Anders didn't kill Shorty."

The sheriff held up a hand to shush Lilly, "Doesn't prove anything," then turned again to the widow. "Tell me why I should believe you, Miz Hartley."

"'Cause I ain't no liar."

"That so? Then why didn't you speak up sooner?"

"Speak up for what?"

"Didn't you know a man is in jail and about to hang because of these horses and them gold pieces?"

"Don't recall."

"Everybody in this town knows about the story and nobody is keeping quiet. Think real hard, now. You sure someone didn't mention something in passing?"

"Maybe I might'a heard something about it. But I didn't know the name they said, so it weren't no skin off my nose. Anyways, I had chores to tend to."

Lilly pointed a finger. "You go to the church and ask for forgiveness, old woman. A man's life is more important than your chores."

"How many of them gold pieces did that good-hearted stranger give you, Miz Hartley?" the sheriff said.

"Ain't got no need to tell you that, Sheriff. I ain't done nothing wrong."

"Maybe you did, and maybe you didn't, but you got to come with me 'til we get all this sorted out."

Lilly grabbed hold of Sheriff Barry's arm. "You're going to let Anders out of jail now, aren't you?"

"Are you out of your mind? He's still accused of murder; he made a jail break; and he carried a gun in town. All of them things are against the law."

"This old woman just told you about the money and the horses, and Anders didn't really try to escape. He only wanted to make Orton and Wesley tell what they did to me. The deputy would've never let him out of jail to take care of that business if Anders didn't have a gun. That's why I brought it to him."

"You saying it wasn't the Mex that brought him the gun?"

"I brought it."

"You sure you're not messing with me to protect the Mex?"

"I said I brought Anders the gun."

Sheriff Barry shook his head. "Never can tell what a woman won't do. Now, I can't just up and let Anders out of jail. I guess I don't have to file charges for him breaking out of jail, but it's up to the Rangers to say if he's going to have to go to Austin to stand trial for a murder charge. If it's any comfort to you, I've changed my mind about Anders. After listening to what the widow Hartley said and seeing the horses and the gold, I can't say I flat-out believe that Anders killed vanDyne."

Lilly squealed, "Yes!" then stepped in close and wrapped her arms around the sheriff's ample girth. "Thank you. When the Rangers hear the old widow lady's story, they must say to let Anders out of jail."

~~~~~~

Doc Green rocked his chair back on two legs and leaned against the jail's whitewashed clapboard siding. "You see how Lilly and Anders look at each other? Ain't love grand?"

Sitting next to Doc, the sheriff rubbed the stubble on his chin. "Sometimes."

"You ask me, that gold's cursed," Doc said, puffing on a pipe of sweet-smelling tobacco. "When you think about it, everybody that's touched it's been killed or bedeviled. Starting with the man who stole it at the very beginning, Sam Bass. A person would have to be a damned fool to want any part of it."

"That's true." The sheriff flicked a match head with his thumbnail and set off a flame that he touched to one end of his misshapen, hand-rolled cigarette. He inhaled a deep drag to set the tobacco to smoldering then squinted at Doc through a wisp of smoke. "Wonder where that gold is now?"

"If we're lucky, it's in some hidey-hole where us two old fools can't ever get at it."

The End

From the Author:

I appreciate you reading Bad Day at Round Rock. I hope you enjoyed my tale. Please leave a review on Amazon; it helps other readers identify enjoyable stories.

The idea for "Bad Day" story came from a family legend about my great-grandfather who emigrated from Sweden to Georgetown, Texas, in 1877. The story goes that great-grandpa was in town on the day that Texas Rangers shot down the outlaw Sam Bass in the streets of Round Rock.

There are four protagonist sketches in "Bad Day at Round Rock," all are linked to a hidden cache of $30,000 in uncirculated twenty-dollar gold coins that Sam Bass stole from the Union Pacific railroad. The story surrounding Sam Bass and the gold is as true as newspaper reports and lore can make it.

Thanks again for reading it.

Biography

Author cj petterson is the pen name of Marilyn A. Johnston. An incorrigible wordsmith, Marilyn/cj is published in several genres, from haiku and free verse to non-fiction and fiction to short stories and novels.

As cj petterson, she has written two novels, *Deadly Star* and *Choosing Carter*, published by Crimson Romance. Her strong protagonists and supporting characters will take you on a fast journey through stories filled with suspense, action, and sassy dialogue. Her work in progress is about a female private detective. She plans to let sales and reviews decide whether Jake Konnor's story will be a stand-alone novel or the first in a series.

She has served as a judge for Romance Writers of America's Daphne du Maurer contest and is a member of several writing groups, including Mobile Writers Guild, Alabama Conclave, and the Alabama Writers Forum, as well as the international Sisters-in-Crime and their on-line Guppies group.

Born in Texas and retired from a career in the automotive industry in Michigan, Marilyn now lives with her family on Alabama's Gulf Coast.

If you have questions or comments, contact me at: cjpetterson@gmail.com

Links to other books by cj petterson:

Choosing Carter -- Kindle / Nook / Kobo / iTunes/iBook

Deadly Star -- Kindle / Nook / Kobo

Amazon Central Author Page: http://amzn.to/1NIDKC0

WEB:

Visit author cj petterson at her blog site at www.lyricalpens.com and on Facebook at http://on.fb.me/1xRVDej

THE POSSE

THE RECKONING
Charlene Raddon

Ohio, 1818

Gavin McAllistair watched his blood tumble and swirl around the rocks at the edge of the pond.

Crush the arnica leaves on a rock, make a paste, Grandson. Let the water carry the pain to your forefathers.

The twelve-year-old boy obeyed his dead grandmother, grinding the bitter leaves to paste. Her face faded in and out of his mind. The Shoshone medicine woman would guide him through whatever this hellish day brought.

At least, the girl was safe now. He'd seen to that. Buffalo Brother—his Shoshone self— had seen to that.

The day had turned hot. Even the butterflies panted as they fanned their wings atop the broad, white heads of yarrow blossoms. Not a leaf stirred. The sun sat on the earth, heavy and moist with sweat. Mayflies that the trout refused to leave the cool depths of the pond to leap for, hummed above the water. The kind of day Gavin used to enjoy growing up in his mother's Shoshone village.

A fierce pang of homesickness struck him. He buried his bruised face in his arms and fought off the urge to cry.

115

"Hey, Injun scum."

Gavin surged to his feet in the middle of the pond. Arch Willsey, Jason Dey, George and Jim Candor, and Timmy Lee stood on the bank. Gavin spat out the arnica, his fists clenched.

"You must want more," Jason said, "seeing as you're still here an' all."

"I ain't afraid of you." Blood trailed from his nose over his lip and into his mouth. He spat that out too.

"No? Well, come on then." Jason held up his fists. "But I warn ya, you'll get more'n a bloody nose this time."

"Yeah, Gavin," Timmy put in. "You don't mess with Jason, or you pay."

"We was just havin' a bit o' fun with that little gal. We weren't hurtin' her none."

Gavin snorted at that. "You had no right to hold her down like that and try to get under her skirts."

"Hell, half-breed, she's only a tart. Lots'a fellas been under her skirts." Jason laughed and danced along the bank like a prize fighter.

"She told you no. I heard her." Gavin took his time leaving the water and climbing onto the bank to give him more time to prepare. His wet canvas trousers clung to his legs and weighted him down, but he didn't care. If Jason wanted to go another round with him, fine. He could only hope the other boys stayed out of it. "A man doesn't keep after a girl after she's told him no, no matter who she is."

The boy laughed. Not only was he three years older than Gavin, but he also weighed more. A lot more. He threw a mock punch. Gavin didn't blink.

"Oooh, gonna play the stoic Injun, eh?" Jason danced around him. "Okay by me. I'm looking forward to beating the crap outta you. Grab 'im, boys."

Before Gavin could ready himself for battle, the other four

kids jumped him. Snarling and grunting, he fought hard, kicking and trying to strike out. They had hold of his arms. Jason kicked his feet out from under him, and he went down, taking the other boys with him.

The next thing he knew, stakes were pounded into the ground, and his wrists and ankles bound to them. He lay in the dirt, face down and spread eagle, unable to move. He clenched his fists, bucked, and tried to kick. Didn't help.

"Now comes the fun part, Injun. We're gonna see how tough you are." Jason cut down a sapling and whipped it through the air several times. Gavin flinched inside with each snap, though the lash never touched him. The rest of his body he kept still as death. They wanted him to cry, beg, and wail. He refused to give them that.

The first strike of the rod on his back forced a whoosh out of him and set his skin on fire. He made no sound. Let them do their worst. Let them kill him. He would go to the Other Side with his pride intact and the image of their disappointed faces in his mind.

Whap! Whap! Whap!

"Shit, Jason," Arch whined. "He is tough. Whip him harder."

"Hell, his back's already bleeding," George said.

WHAP!

Gavin caught himself praying to the white God Uncle James and Aunt Melissa tried to insist he worship, and bit his tongue to stop. He did not believe in this white God who was supposed to be so merciful, yet let His red skinned people suffer. Jason and the other kids were wrong, the Shoshone—all the tribes—were as good as the whites. No, better.

WHAP!

His entire body burned. Blood filled his mouth from his bitten tongue. He did not cry out. He did not beg.

117

"This is a waste of time," Jimmy muttered.

"Gavin?" Uncle James's voice called from a distance. Gavn wanted to cry out for help but stayed quiet.

"Gavin McAllistair! Where are ye, lad?"

The boys grew nervous. Jason stopped the whipping. "Who is that?"

"I think it's his uncle," Arch said. "They live near here."

Their feet moved nervously around him. Scuffed boots, mostly. Some bare feet. No moccasins like Gavin wore.

"Let's get outta here before the old man catches us," Jimmy said, panic in his voice.

"Ah, shit!" Jason muttered. "I hate having my fun ruined. We'll finish this another day."

The battered and bloodied sapling landed next to Gavin. A boot with the sole nearly wore off slammed into his ribs. The boys ran. He coughed at the dust they raised with their clumsy white man's shoes.

A movement at his side told him not everyone had gone. Uncle James could not have reached him yet.

"One more little thing to make sure you remember what happened today," Jason said.

Gavin heard the rustle of clothing, then a stinging wetness on his back that nearly had him screaming in pain as Jason pissed on his torn flesh.

Finished, the boy chuckled. "That should help you heal."

He bolted through the trees.

"Gavin?" Uncle James's voice came again, closer now.

"Here," he answered around his swollen tongue.

The bushes rustled. "Gavin!" His uncle's work boots hurried up beside him. "Good Lord, lad, who did this to ye?" James knelt beside him and worked at the ties. "What happened?"

One hand came free. The second one, then James moved to

Gavin's feet.

"Dear Christ, whoever it was even raised welts on yer soles." He helped Gavin sit up. "You tell me who did this. I swear I'll—"

"Do nothing, Uncle. I am a half-breed. The people here hate me. Punishing them will only make it worse."

James rubbed a hand over his bearded face and hummed in his throat. "Reckon yer right, lad. But, damn it!" He got on one knee, slipped his arms under Gavin and lifted him to his chest to carry home.

"I can walk, Uncle."

"Like hell. Not on those feet. Lay still and shut up."

Aunt Melissa stood up from the garden where she was picking peas when they arrived. "What's happened, James?"

"Someone whipped the bejesus out of our boy." He hurried through the house into the back room where Gavin slept. Gently, James laid him on the bed, facedown.

Aunt Melissa rushed in with her medical supplies, poured water into a basin and set to work cleaning him up. "Ye poor, poor lad. Why would someone do this to ye?"

Gavin said nothing. His aunt was such a good soul, she found it difficult to believe people could be so cruel to others. Even without seeing her, he knew there would be tears in her pale blue eyes.

"Was it the boys from town, Gavin?" Uncle James asked.

He gave no answer. He didn't want James going after the kids. He'd likely only end up hurt as well, old as he was at age thirty-five. Gavin did not want to see anyone else harmed. He should not have interfered when he came upon the boys trying to have their way with Eloise, but she was screaming, bawling, and begging them to stop. He had been raised by the Shoshone to revere the women of his family, of his village. To force a woman was wrong and he could not allow it and still think of himself as honorable.

To a Shoshone, honor was everything.

"Ye left that field half-tilled, Gavin." James chuckled as he paced the floor, but the sound held anger. "The furrows look like the meanderings of a blind mole. I'd best go finish it." Instead, he knelt at the side of the bed and brushed the hair from Gavin's eyes. "Ye've been a good lad, Gavin, me boy. Your da has a right to be proud o' ye. 'Tis been nigh onto five years since he brought ye here for some learnin' and ye've done well." He rose and shuffled about for a minute as if seeking something more to say or do, then, with a weary sigh, he left.

"Your uncle is right, Gavin," Aunt Melissa said as she gently bathed his back. "Ye're a good lad. We love ye, we do, as if ye were our own."

Gavin kept his face buried in his arms, eyes closed, and fought for control of his emotions. The faint aroma of violets came to him through the window, reminding him of the tea Rain Woman used to brew for him before he came to Ohio. As a medicine woman, his grandmother had taught him much of the healing powers of herbs. They had spent many pleasant hours searching for arnica, bee balm, wild licorice, and other medicinal plants.

The memories only heightened the need to bawl. His throat and chest ached with it. Even his jaw hurt from his efforts to hold back the tears.

~~~~~

Three weeks passed, and Gavin healed strong and healthy. He wiped the sweat from his brow with his forearm and adjusted his hat. Another hot day. He'd finished weeding the vegetables. Maybe he could steal off for a quick swim before starting on his next chore.

Going to the pond did not give the same pleasure it once

had. Always there were the memories of Jason Dey whipping the flesh from his back. Gavin approached with caution, making certain he was alone before removing his clothes and going into the water. In winter, the pond nearly froze his balls off, but now, in July, the water felt warm and good. The skin on his back had healed tough and thick in spite of all the fat and lotions Melissa had doctored him with. He could feel the scarred flesh pull as he swam and worked his muscles. Melissa hated that he bore scars. He hated that the sight of his bare back upset her.

He hated anything that upset Aunt Melissa.

Life here was not so bad, he told himself, not for the first time, all the while wishing his pa would come for him and take him back to the mountains. He ate fat meat here in Ohio, even in winter, and his aunt and uncle treated him with kindness. He wore good clothes, though less comfortable than his old breechclout, leggings, and tunic made by Rain Woman from softened buffalo hides. He had grown used to the bed in his room and enjoyed the books Aunt Melissa taught him to read.

But another boy lived inside his skin. That boy, Buffalo Brother, had been on a vision quest, received a spirit helper, and learned he would become a brave warrior some day. Every hour of the long years in Ohio, Gavin McAllistair and Buffalo Brother had battled for dominance.

Gavin McAllistair—a white man.

Buffalo Brother—Shoshone.

He washed quickly, redressed and hurried back to finish his chores. As he rounded the barn, he nearly ran over his aunt.

"Gavin, dear, I'm glad you're here." Melissa tucked a strand of blond hair under her bonnet and re-tied its blue ribbons beneath her chin. "I must go to town for salt and thread. I want you to drive me, and I've already told James. Any chores you didn't finish can either wait, or he'll take care of them." She smiled. "We'll stop at Clara's on the way."

The happy anticipation in her eyes that softened the haggard look of her gentle face banished the groan forming in Gavin's throat. She enjoyed few pleasures at the lonely farm. He could not deny her the joy of visiting with another woman for a while.

But, oh, how he detested going to town. He did not want to see the boys or for them to see him, did not want to hear the taunts, the name-calling.

Still, he said nothing, went into the house and put on clean clothes. Then he hitched the old nag to the buckboard, helped Melissa onto the seat, joined her and took up the reins. The wheels creaked as he drove the rutted road toward town. Melissa smoothed her skirts, straightened her bonnet, and smoothed her skirts again.

He smiled. Only when excited did his aunt fuss as she did now.

At least no wind had risen yet to coat them in the dust raised by the wagon wheels. Gavin clucked at the swaybacked mare in the traces and thought about the book he suspected Melissa had ordered for his thirteenth birthday next week. Byron or Wordsworth? Perhaps he should take advantage of today's visit to the store to show his aunt the rifle he yearned for. Not a new rifle—James and Melissa could not afford that—but an old Kentucky flintlock with an octagonal barrel and a carved stock worth drooling over.

Yes, life was good here, he told himself for the thousandth time as a breeze brought welcome coolness to his heated body.

"Melissa! Melissa, hello." Clara Dibbs waved from the porch of her cabin as they turned into her lane. "I'm so glad to see you. I've a new tin of English tea. Come, come."

Gavin brought the wagon to a halt and secured the reins before jumping down to help his aunt alight. Clara danced around them like an overeager pup. All she needed was a tail to wag. He smiled at the image that popped into his head.

"The boy can wait by the porch," Clara said, taking Melissa's arm to lead the way up the steps to the shaded porch.

"Heavens, Clara. Slow down. You'll make me trip on my skirts." Melissa's laughter softened her complaint.

Their voices faded as they entered the cabin. Alone in the sweltering sunlight, Gavin unhitched the horse and hobbled him where he could find grass to eat. He kicked a few pebbles down the lane, then went over to lie in the cabin's shade. Overhead, in the eaves of the sod roof, a pair of swallows took turns feeding their young. Their black wings changed to blue as they emerged from the shadowy nest into the white light of day. The urgent cries of the infants faded.

From a nearby window came Melissa and Clara's voices, along with the clatter of cups and saucers.

"Why do you waste your time on that little heathen, Melissa? He still refuses to cut his hair, I see. Seems proof enough to me you'll never tame him. A savage he was born and a savage he'll remain. I only hope he doesn't take too many lives when he's full-grown and returns to his wild ways."

"You're wrong, Clara. Gavin's a good boy. Why, he can read and write as well as anyone, and he loves poetry. Does that sound like a savage?"

"Humph. He's got you fooled." Utensils clinked, and the scent of pastry wafted under Gavin's nose.

"I heard he was caught accosting one of the town girls," Clara said.

Gavin grimaced and tossed a rock at the outhouse. It struck with a thud and bounced into the grass. No wonder Clara's husband ran off. No man wanted a cantankerous shrew for a wife.

"Nonsense," Melissa replied. "Gavin would never do such

a thing. The truth is that he stopped several town boys from raping Eloise Benson."

"Humph. That girl, she's no virgin, more shame to her parents. Didn't raise her right."

Silently, in his heart, Gavin thanked his aunt for her faith in him, and vowed never to disappoint her. But the pleasant mood he'd managed to work up vanished. He moved away, out of hearing range. By the time Melissa came out and called for him to hitch up the wagon again, he felt surly and angry. She did not seem to notice. For that, he was grateful.

The town of Wildwood was oddly quiet for a Saturday afternoon as they drove down the town's main street. A few horses stood at hitching rails, swatting flies with their tails. A man came out of the bank and disappeared into Macpherson's saloon. The high-pitched voices of children came from the alley in between.

Two women approached on the boardwalk. Melissa raised her hand to wave at them. Disgust entered their eyes at the sight of Gavin, and they turned into the mercantile pretending not to see Melissa.

The click-clickety-click of typesetting came from The Daily Dispatcher as Gavin halted the wagon beside the boardwalk. The delicious smell of Mrs. Cross's fresh bread drifted from the bakery. Gavin's keen senses, on full alert now, took in the sights, sounds, and smells. Nerves tautened his muscles. He frowned, seeing a bay mare at the hitching rail, head down, hide damp with sweat. He sensed her thirst and fatigue. A roar of laughter came from the saloon--from men too eager for liquor to care for their animals.

This is not how The People behave, my son. The words of his Shoshone grandfather came to him. Gavin had been gobbling boiled meat while his pony stood lathered and thirsty. *Do you want to see your old grandfather taunted by those who believe a mixture of red and white blood produces a weak, useless being like the old ones who can no longer chew their own food?*

Gavin squirmed, remembering.

You are Shoshone, my son. The blood of your white father can make you no weaker than you choose to allow. It is for you to decide.

Two Hearts—as he had been called before his vision quest—had wondered, in the white-coned village of his youth, what Grandfather meant by that. He was a half-breed; what was there to choose? He made up his mind that day that he would be the best warrior the Shoshone ever knew and the wisest of chiefs. Grandfather's cronies would smile on him then.

A few weeks later, his father had come and fetched him here to the white man's world.

"'Tis time ye learn to read and write, Gavin. Ye'll live with me brother, James, and his woman. They be good people and will treat ye right. Learn well, son. To learn the white man's ways will stand ye in good stead when ye're older. Promise me, ye'll no' let me down."

Gavin had done his best. It hadn't been easy. His eyes yearned to see the towering white reaches of the mountains that witnessed his birth. His heart ached for the freedom he had known then. To race his pony with his friends, practice with his bow, and join a buffalo hunt. The smothering white men's clothes made him sweat. He longed for his breechclout Aunt Melissa had burned.

"Goodness, Gavin." Aunt Melissa startled him from his memories. "You nearly walked over the top of me. Are you daydreaming again?"

He jumped back and bent down to brush the dusty imprint of his toe from her hem. While she deliberated over the mercantile's selection of ribbons, he sniffed at the pickle barrel and eyed the peppermint sticks in glass jars on the counter. In the small area set aside as the post office, he looked over the paper-wrapped parcels stacked on shelves, seeking one bearing his aunt or uncle's name, and found none. Disappointed, he assured himself his birthday gift would arrive tomorrow.

At thirteen, he would be considered a man in the Shoshone village. He could go on pony raids, not as a helper to the warriors, but as a warrior himself. He could compete in games and contests. None of the other boys in Wildwood could shoot as well as he, or ride as well either. He yearned to show them he was as good as any of them. Nay, better.

Carrying his aunt's purchases, he followed her outside. They crossed the street and walked past the marshal's office. Gavin paused to admire a handsome blue dun stallion being ridden past by a hard mountain of a man when something stung his cheek. Glass shattered behind him. Beside him, Melissa gave a startled yelp. The dressmaker ran from her shop to see who had broken her window.

Instinctively, Gavin swung about in a low crouch, his dark eyes darting left and right. He gnashed his teeth and cursed himself for allowing Uncle James to take the rabbit-skin quiver and the bow Grandfather had made him. How did Uncle expect him to protect Melissa? At least he had the knife hidden in the stiff, uncomfortable boots they made him wear.

"My gracious." Melissa stepped delicately over the shattered glass littering the walkway. "Look at this damage."

"Someone call for the marshal," the dressmaker called out. "This heathen boy broke my window."

"No, he did not." Melissa, hands on her hips, faced the woman down. "Did you see who did do it, Gavin?"

"No, Aunt. Stay behind me. I will protect you."

She smiled. "I appreciate that you want to shield me,

Gavin, but I won't have you fighting. Remember now." Using her handkerchief, she wiped a fleck of blood from his cheek.

Muttering, the dressmaker went inside for a broom.

Melissa took Gavin's hand and dragged him past the Red Lady Saloon. "Come, I've another errand to run before we head home."

Across the street, furtive figures dashed from the alley to duck behind a watering trough. A red head rose above the side of a buckboard. An arm reached up and let go with a large horse dropping.

Gavin gave Melissa a gentle shove. "Run, Aunt."

"What? Stop that."

The messy clod missed him and splattered her blue-striped skirts.

"Oh! Oh." She tried to shake the offal from her dress. Across the street, redheaded Timmy Lee prepared to throw another such missile, but she spotted him. "Timmy, you put that down this instant. What would your mother say if she saw you throwing horse manure at innocent people?"

Timmy laughed. "No disrespect to you, ma'am. But my ma would thank me for runnin' off scum like you have standing next to you. He's who I was aiming at."

Three other heads popped up from behind the wagon and watering trough, mouths open in laughter. Gavin reached inside his boot and brought out the worn skinning knife Uncle James had thought lost.

"Gavin McAllistair!" Melessa's hand flew to her cheek. "Where did you get that? Never mind. Hand it over."

"Go on, little squawman," Arch Willsey yelled. "Be a good boy and give your auntie the knife."

"Squawman!" the boys chanted. "Squawman!"

Gavin stared at his aunt's impatient, outstretched hand. Did she truly expect him to do nothing to protect them? Did she want to see him shamed?

"Injun scum! Hey, Injun scum."

Along the street, heads emerged from windows and doorways. Men laughed and pointed. Women shook their heads and ignored their bullying offspring. Through narrowed eyes, Gavin watched. His innards drew up into his chest, and his fingers tightened on the bone handle of the knife. At that moment, it came to him what his grandfather's words had meant.

The blood of your white father can make you no weaker than you choose to allow. It is for you to decide.

"Ignore them, Gavin," Aunt Melissa said. "They're hooligans. Show them what you're made of by walking away as a man would do."

He looked at her. "You mean as a white man would do, Aunt?"

His voice did not sound his own, nor that of an almost-thirteen-year-old. The tone held a hard bitterness that tasted like bile.

I am not a white man, he screamed silently. I am Shoshone. I have gone on a vision quest and won a spirit helper. I have carried moccasins for great warriors during horse raids and stole my own pony. I am no longer a boy—except in the eyes of the white men.

Regret filled him. He could not make it through this one day without breaking his vow not to disappoint Melissa. It was done now. Taking off his hat, he let the black braids she had made him hide underneath fall to his chest. Chest puffed out, chin held high, he wished for the powdered paints in the medicine bag James had taken from him, along with all other vestiges of his Indian heritage. He would paint his face and show these worthless white eyes the Shoshone warrior inside.

He would set Buffalo Brother free.

A rock whizzed past his ear.

"Hey, breed. You gonna hide behind women's skirts?" Timmy Lee swung back his arm and heaved a rock with all his might. It slammed into the clapboard wall behind Gavin and clattered onto the boardwalk.

"Now, you stop that, you hear me?" Melissa yelled.

At that point, Jason Dey stepped out to stand in the open, a grin on his face, his hand over the placket in his trousers—a reminder of the day he'd whipped Gavin and pissed on the wounds.

Something inside Gavin snapped.

"Stay out of the way, Aunt." A sudden calm came over him. "For five winters I have been a white boy for you and for my father who stays where I wish to be, in the Shining Mountains. My blood is mixed. Red like my skin and the skin of my mother's people, and white like the face of a coward. This is why these people hate me, and that will never change."

He turned from her and glowered at the faces peeking out at them up and down the street. "Now," he said quietly, "let them see why they should fear me."

With Melissa's shouted commands echoing in his ears, Gavin bolted across the street, a flesh-freezing Shoshone war cry issuing from his throat.

Timmy's throwing arm froze in mid-swing. Billy Thornton gulped and stumbled over Arch Willsey, in an attempt to escape the knife-wielding savage thundering toward them.

Nancy Lee and her older sister, Ruth, stopped laughing in the doorway of their mother's boarding house.

More boys came out of shock, wheeled about, and ran. Jason stayed put, waiting and laughing.

"Someone fetch Marshal Spence," a man yelled.

Gavin came to an abrupt halt before Jason and stared him in the eyes. When the boy's gaze flickered, Gavin anticipated the coming blow, ducked, fisted his hands, and brought them up in a vicious strike between Jason's legs.

Howling with pain, Jason fell to the ground and rolled in the dirt, cupping his privates.

Gavin's gaze zeroed in on Timmy Lee's red hair; a fine scalplock to present to a loving Shoshone grandfather.

Inside, his stomach tightened like a fist. His heart pounded. He gave another chilling war cry. Then, softer, he sang the nearly forgotten medicine song given him during his vision quest.

> I am the eagle.
> I come.
> See me.
> My enemies flee before me.
> I am the eagle.
> Victorious I come.

As the last word died on his lips, he flung himself on a wide-eyed, wet-panted Timmy. An instant later, he held up a handful of fine red hair, severed close to the scalp without shedding a drop of blood or harming the boy. Howling with pride, he leaped over the water trough, slit the suspenders on Billy Thornton's britches, and vanished up the alley between the boarding house and livery stable.

All Marshal Spence found of Gavin McAllistair was a red linsey shirt, canvas trousers, and a pair of boots, size nine. Clutching them to her bosom, Melissa sobbed.

Gavin McAllistair no longer existed. The boy fleeing through the woods west of town was headed for his true home in the Shining Mountains. His name was Buffalo Brother, a warrior of the Shoshone Nation.

The End

From the Author:

I hope you enjoyed *The Reckoning*. Gavin McAllistair was the first "hero" I ever wrote for my first book, a time travel called *Time Weaver*. The book hasn't been published yet, even though it was written long ago. *The Reckoning* is a sort of prequel to *Time Weaver*. Gavin returns to the mountains he loves and eventually becomes a fur trapper. I hope to have his story released later in 2017. Thank you for reading my short story. I hope you will post a review on Amazon and/or Goodreads.

It would be very helpful and much appreciated.

Biography

Charlene Raddon began her fiction career in the third grade by telling her class she had a (nonexistent) little sister killed by a black widow spider. Her first serious attempt at writing came in 1980 when she woke from a vivid dream and decided it had to be in a novel. She dug out a portable typewriter, and she's been

writing ever since. Her first book was a Golden Heart Finalist published by Kensington in 1994.

All of her full-length books have won or placed in contests and received high reviews. In 2016, she received a "Pioneer" award from *Romantic Times Book Club.* Even as a child, Charlene believed she'd been born in the wrong time period and truly belonged in the Old West. When not writing, Charlene likes to travel, crochet, read and spoil her grandchildren. She also designs book covers at Silver Sage Book Covers, specializing in historical and western covers.

Links:

http://charleneraddon.com

https://www.amazon.com/Charlene-Raddon/e/B000APG1P8/

https://silversagebookcovers.com

HEADED FOR TEXAS WITHOUT LOOKIN' BACK
Chimp Robertson

Colorado and Oklahoma Territory 1868

The sun, glaring bright and hot, scorched the back of Rowdy Hawkins' neck. He splashed across the Pigeon River into a meadow, its grass reaching almost to his stirrups. His horse limped into the sleepy little village of Silverplume in the northern Colorado Mountains.

He only stopped in this place after his horse pulled up lame. Upon leaving Montana, he rode hard, anxious to return to Texas. The rugged mountain trails took their toll; the horse needed rest before hitting the trail again.

Not yet twenty, Rowdy stood tall and slim with broad shoulders and a narrow waist. His curly hair, black as night, fell below a weather-beaten hat. A seasoned cowhand, proved by his deep suntan, he wore dusty, brush-scarred chaps and the silver rowels of his spurs scraped the aged heart pine floor with every step. He moved with the athletic grace of a swift-moving puma. A gun belt let a holster hang on his right hip.

Nothing in the mountain village held a special attraction for him. When he asked Ed Wilson, the man who managed the livery stable, about Silverplume, the old fellow sat on a keg before he leaned back against the rough-hewn wall.

"The people in Silverplume are either drifters, miners, trappers, or poor Mexicans," Wilson said. "There's a few scratch-gravel farmers livin' nearby, and most times, visitors find it a quiet place. Now and then, a miner or a couple of freight-wagon teamsters go loco. The rough-and-rowdy-type drift into town to disrupt life at the cantina for a few days of drinking, fighting, and being loud and obnoxious, before they move on."

"Not much different than other western towns, I guess," Rowdy said.

"The village leaders appointed an eighty-year old man as sheriff," Wilson added. "He only has vision in one eye and when he speaks, his missing front teeth show a wide gap. While a good shot with a revolver or a rifle, he hasn't lived this long by taking unnecessary risks so when a rough bunch come to town whooping and hollering, he just stays in his office."

After Rowdy stabled his horse in the tumbledown livery, he ambled across the dusty street to the town's only cantina. When the dealer invited him to join a poker game, he slid a chair close, sitting at the table with three men.

"Been here long?" asked a broad-shouldered man with thick black hair and a greasy handlebar mustache. He wore a heavy wool, hip-length, plaid Mackinaw that gapped open in front showing the mother-of-pearl handle of a Colt forty-five.

"Just got here," Rowdy said, glancing about the room. "Trailed a herd to Montana, but now I'm headed home."

The chunky Mackinaw man's lips twitched.

"Didn't ask where you was headed. I asked if you been here long?"

Rowdy's hands shook once with a slight tremble, but he didn't answer. Instead, he focused on the card game while he lowered his head, watching Mackinaw from the corner of his eye.

"You're sittin' in my chair." Mackinaw's voice grew cold as death, goading him for a fight.

The threat echoed when the ten other men in the cantina fell silent.

The bartender, Herb, banged the glass he just finished cleaning on the bar before he leaned forward, jutting his chin at Mackinaw. "Alright, that's enough of that talk." Herb's job involved keeping the cantina's drunken customers from shooting its paying customers.

"You want it that bad, you can have it," Rowdy said, as he rose from the chair to step across to the bar.

"Careful," Mackinaw snarled. "Everything you say offends me."

In the looming silence, Mackinaw stepped into the cantina's center and nodded, signaling for Rowdy to open his coat, exposing his gun, while Mackinaw did the same. Before Rowdy could react, Mackinaw drew his Colt, firing first.

The bullet pierced Rowdy's left side; the lead nicked the bottom edge of his floating rib when it passed through. Pain filled his eyes as he reeled backward, crashing against the bar before sliding to the dusty pine floor. Blood pooled beneath him. Mackinaw's attack came as a complete surprise.

In a drunken stagger, Mackinaw moved in for the kill, his gun wavering from side to side with each step.

Rowdy didn't wait. When his Colt cleared the holster, he fired point blank, not once, but two times. His lead kicked the heavyset man backward, tumbling him into the card table. Mackinaw's lead-riddled heart quit beating before he hit the floor. From habit, Rowdy reloaded while he leaned his left elbow on the brass foot rail.

Anger stirred in him, but the gunplay confused him. Why had Mackinaw picked a fight? Rowdy didn't know anyone in Colorado, let alone any who wanted him dead. Only one thing he knew for sure—he had a bad wound. He lay still, waiting.

The men in the cantina paused at first, glancing at one another, but no one stood to complain. Mackinaw's friends glared at him, growing angrier by the minute.

"Let's get him," a brawny man shouted. His soggy, lace-up calf-high boots squeaked with each step. A rough, burly brute with ham-hock hands, he coughed the wet, hacking cough that plagued deep-rock miners.

"Hell of it is," Rowdy said, as he grabbed the bar's edge to pull up while staggering to his feet. "You do, I'll kill you, too." He hoped his bravado might hold off a charge, at least long enough for him to get out the door.

A short silence followed before another drunken man with a twitchy eye pushed through the crowd. Dressed in bib overalls, he wore the mud-caked, lace-up brogans typical of a farmer. While the twitchy eye winked, his head wobbled around and he laughed aloud, crazy as a loon.

"You gonna kill us all?" he yelled, drawing an old cap-and-ball pistol.

"Not all of you," Rowdy said. "Just you first, then him," nodding toward the heavyset miner. "After you two, I don't much care who dies next."

In blunt truth, the mob scared him. He reloaded six cartridges, but he knew he couldn't stop a mad rush. With his elbow on the bar to keep him upright and a hand on the hole in his left side, he shoved away from the bar. Shifting aside, he took slow steps toward the swinging doors of the smoke-filled cantina, his long-barreled Colt pointing at the drunken farmer's head. His bluff went in vain when the remaining customers surged forward.

"Get him," someone yelled. "Don't let him get away," another shouted. It became clear; their idea of justice consisted of a fair trial before they hanged him.

Rowdy pulled the trigger. The drunken farmer's arms flew wide with a jerk. He fell like a chopped tree while his rusty cap-and-ball pistol skittered across the dirty pine floor. In the next instant, Rowdy fired again, striking the burly miner in the forehead. His blood splattered across the faces of the men behind him.

The splatter granted him time, at least for the moment, when the crowd reeled away, scrambling over one another. Rushing outside, Rowdy mounted the first horse tied to the hitching rail, a wild-eyed, long-legged, blaze-faced sorrel.

He never considered fetching his horse from the livery; its sore tendon would fail in a hard run. The horse's wild-eye bothered him. He'd learned while picking horses from a remuda that a wild-eye spooked quicker, often getting the bit in its teeth to run wild—but he had no choice. The pain from his wound caused him to yelp when he swung onto the saddle of the spirited animal.

~~~~~

The cantina's gunfire alerted the old sheriff, who stepped from his office onto the boardwalk. He headed for the saloon just as a cowboy rode toward him. The lawman didn't know the commotion's cause, but he drew his Colt, firing from the hip, grazing the cowboy's left hand.

~~~~~

Answering with a quick shot, Rowdy knocked the new shooter over, who fell on his back. Only after Rowdy fired did he get a glimpse the sheriff's badge as he raced past. He regretted the hasty shot, but he had to keep riding to escape the lynch mob.

The men from the cantina stormed outside. They shouted and shot at Rowdy while he spurred the sorrel horse into a run along the short, dusty main street of Silverplume. He raced toward the snow-covered mountains to the east. If he could reach the timber, he figured he could lose them, at least long enough to get through the pass. Once over the pass, he knew this wild-eyed horse could outdistance the lynch mob on the front range.

Rowdy didn't slow down until he reached a grassy plateau about two miles above town. He slowed to a walk to let the horse blow while he reloaded his revolver. He carried a heavy-barreled, forty-four caliber Navy Colt he'd converted to brass cartridges. His grandfather, a former Texas Ranger, had given the Colt to him on his twelfth birthday.

A rifle bullet splintered his saddle horn. The jolt spooked the wild-eyed horse to lunge forward, bucking. It stampeded down the mountain, sprinting toward the oncoming lynch mob. Caught by surprise, they held their fire as the big sorrel charged them.

With his left hand injured, Rowdy yanked on the right rein, managing to pull the panicked horse into a sweeping right hand circle away from the charging gunmen. Bullets slapped nearby branches while others splattered on rocks at the racing sorrel's hooves, causing him to charge faster up the mountainside.

The lynch mob split into two groups, with half of them cutting across a meadow, trying to get in front of him.

Rowdy touched the blaze-faced sorrel with his spurs, on toward his only hope of escape—the pass. Forcing the tired horse to climb the steep, rocky slope, he slapped its shoulders with the long reins. The big-hearted sorrel responded as well as any great horse could, galloping toward the snow-covered pines edging the timberline.

A sharp pain smacked Rowdy's right shoulder when a slug tore through his heavy coat, driving him forward in the saddle. He rode hard with the mounted men only two hundred yards behind. Another lead slug struck his left boot heel, knocking his foot out of the stirrup, but he clung to the saddle, firing over his shoulder as fast as he could re-load.

The lynch mob charged up the mountain below him, climbing toward the timberline, hard and fast. Another bullet grazed Rowdy's right side. The pain twisted him sideways in the saddle, while his left foot almost dragged the ground.

He tied the reins in a knot, tossing them on the horse's neck. The big sorrel lunged on and on up the steep hill. He leaned to one side, sliding from the saddle. Landing in deep snow drifted behind an ancient, gnarled pine tree, Rowdy rolled under its low hanging, snow-ladened limbs.

The lynch mob raced past the gnarled pine in hot pursuit while the blaze-faced sorrel, without a rider, easily outdistanced them as it sped toward the mountain pass. When the sorrel reached the pass, it plunged ahead, racing down the trail on the other side. The lynch mob urged the spooked sorrel to continue running by splattering hot lead on the nearby rocks.

Rowdy shook his head to clear jumbled thoughts. Bruised and injured, inside and out, his mettle had been tested a mean-spirited enemy, but his boldness and strength had prevailed— he made his escape. Glancing above, he noticed the sun setting behind the mountains, telling him to expect a bitter cold night.

He shifted, settling his back against the pine, while peering through the low-hanging, snow-covered branches. Drawing his knees up under his chin, he placed his hand on the wound where a bullet had pierced his left side, pressing hard to stop the leaking blood.

Rowdy hated leaving his good horse and saddlebags at the livery stable, but he didn't have a choice. A nagging thought caused him to ponder; did Mackinaw know he carried a money belt? The belt contained one-thousand-seventy-five dollars in gold coin from a year's pay plus a bonus from the cattle sale. He rested the old Navy Colt on his lap while he leaned his head against the pine's trunk before sleep closed his eyes.

All through the night, he tossed and turned. He slept on a bed of dry pine needles under the pine tree, aching with pain, burning with fever. In fevered delusion, he thought he climbed into the saddle before riding to the top of a ridge. In his dream, he marveled at the breathtaking autumn view as golden aspen shimmered in the sun-drenched Colorado Mountains. A hard chill caused a shiver that forced him to shake his head to awaken.

"Damn, is it morning already?"

He drew an achy, raspy breath. Hesitating, he wondered if he still dreamed. His mouth watered, aroused by the scent of coffee and bacon. He gathered his coat tight around him after he struggled to stand, while one hand rested on the sheltering pine.

The steep, rocky trail caused him to stumble often while he staggered through the pass—the lure of food and hot coffee urged him forward. Time slipped away while he limped down the long grade toward a small flickering fire in the distance. The dark sky hid his surroundings while he continued tottering toward the campsite.

A grizzled old man wearing a fringe-trimmed deerskin jacket jumped as if he'd seen a ghost. His face paled when Rowdy stepped between two fir trees. A few feet from the fire, Rowdy staggered to tumble forward, falling face-first into the deep grass and snow. He lay unconscious from shock and loss of blood.

Amos Thomas, or Old Amos, as most people knew him, functioned as the wrangler and hood for a trail herd up from southern New Mexico on its way to the Bozeman gold strike. Besides working with the horse remuda on the trail, he helped the cook.

The herd boss had charged him with stocking supplies for the "hoodlum" wagon that followed the chuck wagon. He'd left from old Fort St. Vrain with food and supplies when darkness, and a sudden mountain snowstorm, overtook him, forcing him to stop for the night.

He dragged Rowdy to the supply wagon before propping him against a wheel. Holding a cup of hot coffee under his nose, Old Amos soon brought him around.

Old Amos patched cuts, scrapes, and horse bites on the cattle-drive's crew. He tended Rowdy's wounds as best he could before feeding him, but he hadn't said a word. While making ready to drive away, he hitched his team before he squatted in front of Rowdy and grinned.

"You're a tough one, ain't you?" he said, after he spat aside a string of tobacco.

"I don't feel so tough," Rowdy managed.

"Yeah, well, you got dinged with enough hot lead to put you down for good, but here you are tryin' to get up. You an outlaw?"

"I shot four men in Silverplume," Rowdy said. "So, if that's what it takes to be one, then I guess I am ... but it was self-defense."

Old Amos leaned his head back and laughed.

"That's what they all say. Is the Silverplume sheriff after you?"

"No, he ain't," Rowdy said. "He's one of 'em I shot."

"Wanna tell me about it?"

"Still a little dizzy," Rowdy shook his head no. "I just need a ride. Can I ride with you?"

"Sure," Old Amos said. "I'm about twelve miles behind the herd but only about eight miles over to Abbeville, so I best get you there, what with all the blood you lost."

After dark, the rickety old supply wagon's iron-rimmed wheels creaked as it rolled along. Old Amos drove down the main street of Abbeville, a noisy, rambunctious mining town. Saloons, dance halls, and gambling houses lined the main street, where drinks and money flowed.

Old Amos flipped the reins at his team of mules as they picked their way through wagons, pack mules, and saddle horses along the street. Beside him, wrapped in a canvas wagon cover, sat Rowdy Hawkins, sick with fever, hallucinating, and babbling to the world.

"Take it easy, kid," Old Amos said, as he wrapped an arm around Rowdy's shoulder.

A fat man exiting the saloon called to him. "Better get your wagon around back, old timer. Tom Dixon is on the rampage tonight. If he comes out of the Lost Cache Saloon to find you a sittin' there, he'll shoot you fer sure."

Amos swallowed his chaw of chewing tobacco, gulped for air, then nodded.

"Get up, Jack," he called to the tall white mule on the left. Next, he popped the reins against the smaller brown mule on the right. "Come on, Mable."

Ever since he could remember, little frontier towns harbored tough drunks who bullied people around. Tom Dixon had earned a bad reputation. Amos wanted to avoid crossing him. Carrying a sick man, he needed to find a doctor.

He drove Jack and Mable up the rutted street. The summer sun baked it hard, while winter rains turned it into axle deep mud. Amos halted beside a group of people standing in a circle, watching two men fight.

"Howdy," he called to a tall man standing on the circle's edge. "Can you tell me where to find a doctor?"

"Yeah, but not right now," the tall man said, as he resumed gawking at the fistfight in the middle of the street.

Old Amos drove farther along the street before stopping near two rough-dressed buffalo hunters arguing over a gambling debt one owed the other.

"I've a sick man here," Amos said. "I need a doctor."

One of the hunters ambled over, staring up at him. The man stunk so bad, Old Amos had to set the wagon's brake to keep his mules from pulling away.

"There's only one doctor in Abbeville," he said. "And he's over there in the saloon drunker'n old Cootie Brown. You'd do better takin' him up to Millie's place. Miz Curry lives in a big white house at the end of that side street." He pointed to a lane. "There's a 'Rooms for Rent' sign on the fence," he added.

Old Amos released the brake, popping the reins. His mules, their eyes wide, their nostrils flared, lunged against their collars as they strained to pull the wagon into the lane.

He spotted the house without a problem. Millie Curry lived in a large, three-story frame house with a wraparound porch and a white picket fence encircling it. His eyes fell upon several prominent ladies of the town while they idled on the porch in Mexican, woven reed chairs, enjoying the cool evening and sipping coffee.

"Good evening, ladies," he said, holding his greasy hat in his work hardened-hands. "I've a wounded man here and I'm lookin' for the owner."

"I'm the owner," Millie Curry said.

She towered above the other women, reminding him of a tall volcano with her shiny, short-cropped red hair fluffed on top. She smiled often, but a crooked front tooth caused her to cover her mouth with one hand.

"If you don't mind," Old Amos said, avoiding the risk of lingering glances. "I've a sick man what needs attention. He came down with the fever, and to tell you the truth, he's got a couple of bullet holes in him, too."

Millie rushed to the wagon to look at Rowdy. "Why, he's just a boy."

Old Amos shot her a glance. "Don't let that baby face fool you, ma'am. He can get plenty mean when he's riled."

"Is he an outlaw?" she asked.

He sent her a sly grin. "He said he ain't, and that's good enough fer me."

"What's his name?"

"All I know is he said it was Rowdy Hawkins and he'd been in a shootin' scrape over at Silverplume."

"Well, it don't matter anyway," she said. "I've seen fever … and I've seen bullet holes. Can you get him into the house?"

Casting a sideways glance at the other women, Old Amos ducked his head. "He's a strapping lad. I could use a little help."

Within the hour, Rowdy wore a long-tail nightshirt while he slept on a straw mattress bed. Old Amos handed Rowdy's gun belt to Millie. "He'll ask about that when he wakes up."

He thanked Millie Curry before he kicked the brake off and popped the reins.

"Get up, Jack. Come on, Mable," he yelled, rolling forward in his long journey to catch up with the herd and its chuck wagon.

~~~~~~

Three days passed after Old Amos drove his wagon away from Abbeville, but Rowdy's face remained haggard and pale.

For the first time, he managed to sit upright in the bed. He gazed at Millie for a moment in wide-eyed confusion.

"Where's my clothes?" Rowdy asked.

"Right over there," she said, nodding at a chair in the corner. "You hungry?"

"I guess I was born hungry," he mumbled.

Her dark brown eyes stared with excitement at the first words he'd spoken since he arrived. She awarded him a tired, happy smile before she left the room. Returning several minutes later, she brought him a bowl of hot potato soup.

In her absence, Rowdy managed to get dressed. He sat on the bed's edge. With a quiet, "Thank you," he accepted the bowl of soup she offered. After a glance outside, he remembered he liked sunny days like this, a good day for riding the trail.

Millie Curry studied his thin, drawn face, thinking of her own sons. They died in the damned war; Billy fought for the North, Bobby for the South. She swallowed hard, managing a smile.

"I'm glad you're stronger," she said, filling the long silence. "I wondered if you have plans. Think you might stay in Abbeville? I'm sure my husband can help you find work. That is, if the law isn't after you."

"They are." Rowdy ducked his head in shame. "But it was self-defense."

"I figured that much," she said. "Another tenant left a wanted poster about you in one of the rooms last night." She stepped across the room, lifting a paper from the dresser before handing him the wrinkled wanted poster. "You might want this for a souvenir."

"They don't waste much time, do they?" When he took the poster and glanced at, he folded it into quarters before stuffing it into his shirt pocket.

"Shooting a sheriff is pretty bad," she said.

"Even in self-defense?"

"Even in self-defense," she said. "But why would the law be after you if it was self defense?"

"They didn't even give me a chance to explain," he said. "They just started shootin'. I was dang lucky to get out alive."

"I don't blame you," she said. "Most men would probably do the same."

"Well, it don't make no difference anyway," he said. "If I can buy a horse and saddle, I'm pullin' out. Do you have my money belt? I hope Old Amos didn't help his-self to it." He glanced about the room. "Once I'm mounted, I'm headed for Texas without lookin' back."

She opened a drawer in the dresser before handing him the heavy money belt. "Headed for Texas without looking back, huh? What about all that talk of Oklahoma?"

"What talk?"

"If you said Oklahoma once while fevered, you said it a dozen times."

"Oh," he mumbled. "Well, I meant I'm headed for Texas without lookin' back after I stop in Oklahoma … to see someone."

"Your sweetheart?" She canted her head with a wide smile.

"No, ma'am," he answered. "I ain't even met her, official like anyway. I just saw her twice when we drove a herd up through there. She's a young Indian girl."

"Oh, my," Millie said. "You need to be careful. They have Indian problems in that part of the country, you know."

"Yes, ma'am, I know, but her grandfather is Black Kettle," he said. "He signed a peace treaty. They're supposed to settle on a reservation, so I ain't worried about him."

"If you don't mind me asking," Millie said. "How do you plan on making friends if you've never even met her?"

"I have a friend in the army who delivers provisions to her grandfather's camp," Rowdy said. "He told me he'd get me hired on as a supply teamster. That way I could visit her every time we delivered their monthly allotments."

Rowdy and Jake met when Rowdy helped trail a herd from Texas to Missouri where Jake worked in the loading pens. After the herd shipped out, Rowdy returned to Texas with the other cowboys. A few months later, Jake joined the army. The two men crossed trails again when Rowdy rode north with a herd that they drove to Kansas after Missouri banned Texas cows. The trail herd passed near the Indian camp where Jake hauled supplies for the army.

"Do you even know her name?"

"Yes, ma'am, I do," Rowdy said. "It's Pretty Girl Sleeps."

"Well, I wish you luck with it," Millie said. "When do you plan on leaving?"

"Today," he said. "And I sure do thank you for patching me together again." He touched the brim of his hat in the Texas way of taking your leave.

Rowdy bought a horse and saddle, and then a packhorse. Next, he stopped at the mercantile to buy a bedroll and a stash of food. He groused a little bit about paying the premium prices for supplies in a gold-rush town, then rode from Abbeville at five past noon.

Six days later, he struck the Canadian River in eastern New Mexico. He followed it across the Texas panhandle into western Oklahoma. He cut across an ox-bow bend in the river, and then rode due south fifteen-miles to pitch camp alongside Washita Creek.

The next day he rode downstream to an Army remount station. A platoon of soldiers bivouacked in a small grove of trees against a high bluff where they stored provisions in a cave at the base of the bluff. They located the camp about two miles upstream from Chief Black Kettle's village. From that camp, they rode out on regular patrol routes, hunting, capturing, or killing Indians who fled the reservation.

~~~~~~

The bad memories of 1854 troubled Black Kettle, the Southern Cheyenne Chief, as he stroked the coal black hair of his granddaughter, Pretty Girl Sleeps. He'd raised her since finding her in a deserted Cheyenne village ten years earlier. She alone had survived—all that remained of a band of over two hundred souls.

The white man spread cholera among the Southern Cheyenne with malice and forethought. Their vile plan succeeded when over two-thousand of his people, two-thirds of the Southern Cheyenne tribe, died from cholera that summer.

Black Kettle stood proud and erect, holding the reins of a bald-faced, blue-eyed palomino as the wild horse shuffled its hooves, restless to run.

"I will go once more to meet with the whites," Black Kettle told his people in 1864. "I will sign the treaty ... hoping we will have peace at last." He never wanted to leave this place, even though the nearest buffalo herd lay two hundred miles away. Over time, he had grown weary of running, and tired of the white man telling him where to live.

Black Kettle wiped his mouth with the back of his hand. "This little stream, Sand Creek," he said, his voice carrying an edge of indignation. "full of green grass along its edges with those tall trees, I think it is a good place to live if the whites will leave us alone."

Pretty Girl Sleeps moistened her lips. "Grandfather, are you afraid the whites will kill you?"

The question created an awkward silence, broken at last by Black Kettle.

"I am not afraid of whites for myself," he said. "I am only afraid of what they might do to our people if we cannot find a way to live together."

Black Kettle and his life-long friend, Lean Bear, mounted their horses. They agreed to meet Governor John Evans in Denver, over two hundred miles north of the Cheyenne camps near Ft. Wise along the western Arkansas River. A few hours later, he reined his horse to stop at the crest of a high hill and surveyed the prairie, searching long, but not a single buffalo came into view.

"It's hard enough just to live here," he said. "I hope the whites will honor this treaty and not lie like they have before."

Lean Bear, who hadn't spoken since they'd left the village, shook his head. "I don't have as much hope," he said. "It is no wonder so many of our young braves have gone north to fight with Roman Nose and his band."

Arriving in Denver five days later, Black Kettle stared at the floor in frustration when Governor John Evans strutted into the meeting alongside Colonel John M. Chivington, commander of the Third Colorado Volunteers. U.S. Army Major Wynkoop and several other officers followed the governor.

Black Kettle lifted his head to stand tall and proud when told to speak.

"All we ask is we have peace with the whites. We want to hold you by the hand. You are our father. We have been traveling through a cloud. The sky has been dark ever since your Blue-Gray war. My braves are willing to do what I say.

"We want to take good tidings home to our people that they may sleep in peace. I want you to give all these chiefs of soldiers here to understand, we are for peace. We have made peace so we are not mistaken by soldiers for enemies. I have not come here with a little wolf's bark, but I have come to talk plain with you."

Black Kettle had been a great warrior in his youth. The southern Cheyenne recognized him as Chief. He and Lean Bear, who stood by his side, had been to Washington to shake hands with the Great Father, Lincoln, who presented them pretty medals to wear. Lincoln also presented to them papers stating they were good friends of the United States.

Black Kettle gazed into the eyes of Colonel Chivington, speaking without hesitation. "Although your troops have struck us, we throw it behind and are glad to meet you in peace and friendship. What you have come for and what the president has sent you for, I don't object to. I say yes to it. The white people can go wherever they please. We will not disturb them and I want you to let them know.

"We were friends with the whites, but you nudged us out of the way by your intrigues." He gazed into Colonel Chivington's eyes. "Why don't you talk straight and let all be well?"

In September 1868, the gallant Roman Nose died in battle; his death caused many Cheyenne to lose heart. The young warriors in the Dog Soldiers, a Cheyenne military society, turned south. In November 1868, they asked to join Black Kettle's tribe. He welcomed their return, giving them a warm reception in his camps.

"I am glad you have come home. I have returned from Fort Cobb where I met with General Hazen. He promised me our village will not be attacked," Black Kettle said.

He had signed the Medicine Lodge Treaty a year before, in 1867. However, after settling on their reservation, they seldom received the provisions the treaty promised. He moved his tribe farther south, beside the Washita, to avoid problems with other Kansas tribes while expecting to receive provisions the treaty promised.

~~~~~~~

Rowdy found a small detachment of soldiers at the nearby remount station, which consisted of a fair-sized cave in the bend of the riverbank. It served as a holding area for supplies when the wagons arrived.

Rowdy's friend, Jake Johnson, was part of that detachment. The troopers primary duty was to patrol the area to prevent raids by the Cheyenne on nearby farms and ranches. They also guarded the supply wagons delivering goods to the Cheyenne.

Jake urged the supply contractor to hire Rowdy as a teamster, and then send him to the remount station. This job allowed him the opportunity to talk with Pretty Girl Sleeps.

"I told you I'd get you a job down here," Jake said. "Come on," he added, "I wanna introduce you to Sergeant Corley, the man in charge of this outfit."

Sergeant Corley had just come in off patrol, leaving him in an ugly mood. He was a tall, heavy-set man with a ragged drinker's cough.

"Sergeant Corley," Jake said. "This is Rowdy Hawkins, the new man. He just got hired on as a driver for the supply wagon."

"Don't look like much of a man to me," Corley said, with a frown.

"Well, he is," Jake said.

After Corley spun on a heel to stomp away, Rowdy shook his head. "That's one mean son of a gun, if I ever saw one."

Jake grew up in the small town of Warrensburg, Missouri. He joined the army after the War Between the States ended. The Army sent his unit to Oklahoma during the Indian uprising. While the two young men joshed with each other, Jake sat on the bank of the Washita to clean his Army issued revolver, anxious for action.

Rowdy leaned against the trunk of a fallen tree watching the supply wagon, loaded with the meager provisions promised to the Indians, as it wound its way along the rough, rocky trail toward the remount station for its regular delivery.

"The Army food out here ain't much, is it?" he said, glancing at Jake.

"No, it ain't," Jake said. "The troops gripe about it all the time, but it don't do no good."

"At least it's more than the Indians get from what I've seen," Rowdy said.

"That's army life."

"I'm glad I didn't join the army during the war. I might not have gotten as much as I have."

"You'd have made a good soldier, Rowdy," Jake said, with a laugh. "Gripin' about the food like you do."

"Another reason I'm glad I didn't join the army before the war ended was I didn't want to kill Americans."

"I didn't want to kill Americans, either," Jake said. "But I wouldn't mind killin' Indians."

"Indians are Americans."

"They ain't Americans," Jake said. "They're Indians."

"Yeah, they're Indians, but they lived here before any white man came to this country. That makes them more Americans than anyone who came here from somewhere else."

"My folks came here from somewhere else," Jake said. "And they're Americans, by damn."

"They're not born Americans," Rowdy said. "They're just Americans 'cause someone gave 'em a piece of paper sayin' they are."

"Aw, you're just sayin' that 'cause you're sweet on that little Indian girl." Jake smacked Rowdy's arm while giving a big laugh. "Hell, that's what's wrong with you."

Rowdy and Jake transferred the transported goods to their rickety wagon for delivery to the Cheyenne village, and tomorrow they'd do the same for the Arapaho village. Rowdy drove the team downstream toward the Indian camp while Jake rode guard to prevent trouble when they distributed the provisions.

Black Kettle's family had learned the white man's language years earlier and spoke it well. During Rowdy's first visit, he struck a friendship with Black Kettle's nephew Little Wolf. At the same time, he became smitten with the chief's granddaughter, Pretty Girl Sleeps.

"Why do they call you Little Wolf?" Rowdy asked, while unloading the provisions.

"When I was a boy, my grandfather found a wolf cub. He tamed it to become my companion," Little Wolf said, grabbing crates to unload the provisions.

"Still got him?"

"No, the soldiers shot him at Sand Creek." His face grew somber just mentioning the name.

"What happened at Sand Creek?" Rowdy asked.

"My uncle said the soldiers came during a snow storm, killing almost everyone," he said. "They killed and then scalped my parents that day. I wasn't there when it happened," he added. "Black Kettle had sent me to Bent's Big Timbers

Trading Post for supplies. I returned to find the dead and wounded."

"That's crazy," Rowdy said. "How old are you?"

"I'll be twenty in December, if I live that long," Little Wolf said."

Rowdy jerked away in surprise. "Why wouldn't you live that long?"

"Many of my people didn't."

"What do you mean? What happened to them?"

"Where are you from?" Little Wolf asked, drawing away from Rowdy as if he chewed locoweed.

"I grew up in south Texas during the war."

"Didn't you hear stories about the attack on Black Kettle at Sand Creek?" Little Wolf asked.

"In 1864, we paid more attention to the War Between the States than the Cheyenne."

"Like I said, the Colorado Militia killed hundreds of our people at Sand Creek."

"Why didn't Black Kettle fight back?"

"He had returned from Denver where the Governor promised peace if we stopped our raids."

"Why did the militia attack if the Governor promised peace?" Rowdy asked.

"We ask that question every day," Little Wolf replied.

Rowdy stopped working before he nodded his head toward the beautiful maiden who always stood nearby, pretending to groom her horse while he unloaded the wagon.

"How old is Pretty Girl Sleeps?"

Little Wolf laughed. "Why don't you ask her those questions? Are you afraid?"

"I ain't afraid," Rowdy said. "It's just that I respect her and don't want to intrude on her privacy, if you know what I mean."

Little Wolf laughed again. "You may as well talk to her because every time you leave, she begs me to tell her everything you said."

"You don't tell her, do you?"

"Yes, I do," Little Wolf said, still grinning.

Rowdy wheeled around to him. "How could you do that?"

"Because she always asks what we talked about."

"Damn it," Rowdy said, pretending to draw his revolver.

"You wouldn't shoot me." Little Wolf shined a wide grin.

"What all have you told her?"

"Everything," Little Wolf said.

"What do you mean by everything?"

Little Wolf kept grinning. "I told her you said she was the most beautiful girl you'd ever seen. I told her you said you wished you could kiss her. I also told her you said you wanted to marry her. And, I told her . . ."

Rowdy held up his hand. "You didn't tell her all that did you?"

"Yes, I did," the young Cheyenne answered, with an even bigger laugh.

Rowdy's face turned a deep shade of red.

"I swear, Little Wolf," he said. "Why did you do that?"

"I had too much fun watching the two of you gawk at each other," Little Wolf said. "Look how much time you have wasted."

"Well, I ain't wastin' no more."

Rowdy hopped from the wagon, striding straight toward Pretty Girl Sleeps.

She whirled around to groom the horse that she had tied to a small bush.

"Can I help. I'm a pretty good groomer," he said with a smile.

She smiled and nodded. "If you want to," she said."

"I do," he said. "And I'd like to say something, if you wouldn't mind."

"Go on and say it," she said.

"I've got something to tell you, Pretty Girl, if you don't mind me calling you that. I find it hard to say in front of you. All this time, I wanted to talk to you but I worried you wouldn't like me."

She hesitated before speaking. "I don't mind," she said. "You have been kind to Little Wolf and to my grandfather, Soldier Boy, if you don't mind me calling you that."

"I don't mind, either," he said. "But I'll tell you one thing. You ain't gonna find another guy like me."

"I know," she whispered. "The first time I saw you, you worked as a cowboy and now you're a teamster, but I didn't think you noticed me."

"Oh, I noticed you," he said. "And I've thought about you ever since that first day."

"When Little Wolf told me you said you wished you could kiss me, I remember seeing you a year ago when you drove cattle by here and I wished I could kiss you, too."

"Dang," he said. "I didn't know Indians girls …."

"What?" she said, with a shy smile. "That we like to kiss?"

"I mean," Rowdy stammered. "I didn't know what all your people do. I mean, I just know I wanted to …."

Pretty Girl Sleeps lifted her eyebrows. "Then why don't you stop talking so much?"

With a mere nod, he reached his arms around her waist, pulling her close. Holding her as tight as he could, he dreaded the answer he might get.

"I know this sounds crazy," he managed. "But just as I am right now, I offer you all my love. I don't have anything else. I love you, Pretty Girl."

Tears filled her eyes. "I love you too, Soldier Boy."

"I must tell you true," he said. "I'm runnin' from the law, but I fought in self defense."

"I believe you," she said. "But it doesn't make any difference because I still love you."

The moon was in its third quarter, water from the beautiful little creek flowed over and around rocks, and birds sang in the tall trees, creating a calm and peaceful moment for Rowdy and Pretty Girl, who stood holding each other.

"Can you come to the village tomorrow?" she asked. "I'd like you to meet my grandfather."

"It would be a major honor," Rowdy said. "I've wanted to meet him for a long time."

The next morning the sun rose on a beautiful day, even though there was a chill in the air. Rowdy rode into the Cheyenne camp before he stepped down from his horse. Pretty Girl waited for him, and then took him by the hand, leading him into Black Kettle's teepee.

"Grandfather," she said, nodding. "This is Rowdy Hawkins, the man I told you about."

Black Kettle nodded for him to sit across the fire pit while Pretty Girl took her place beside her grandfather.

"I've always been interested in the Cheyenne," Rowdy began. "I've wondered why you keep going to peace treaty meetings if the whites lie every time?"

Black Kettle looked at Rowdy for a moment. "There are too many whites, so we must learn to live with each other. I believe the Army is always late sending the provisions they promised in order to force the Cheyenne to move north to the Kansas border."

"Would that be so bad if provisions started arriving on time?" Rowdy asked.

"The Kansas Indian tribes hate the Cheyenne. They attacked settlers and wagon trains to trick the army into blaming the raids on the Cheyenne," the chief said. "It is why I moved my tribe south to Washita Creek. But now they tell us to go back to Kansas, to live among our enemies."

Rowdy had no explanation so he sat in silence for several minutes before speaking.

"Black Kettle," he said. "I promise to do everything I can to help you and your tribe. I told Pretty Girl Sleeps the same thing."

"She believes you are a man of your word," Black Kettle said, solemnly. "So I will also believe it."

During the rest of the summer, Rowdy slipped away from the remount station to meet her at the water's edge. The summer sped by in a whirl when, all too soon, winter chilled the air. Every night after the troopers fell into their beds, he slipped through the brush toward the village.

Pretty Girl Sleeps greeted him with a smile when he stepped into the clearing.

"It's so good to see you," she said, running into his arms. "How do you work on the wagons every day and then spend every night here with me?"

Rowdy returned her smile. "It was a little tough at first, but I don't work on the wagons every day now, because the supplies aren't arriving as regularly as they were supposed to. When Black Kettle asked me why they aren't, I didn't have a good answer for him."

Pretty Girl was an absolute romantic, unless you counted the one sorrow she carried in her heart: the cholera death spread by whites at her parents' village. "I miss you each day," she said, as she wrapped her arms around his waist, pressing her head against his chest.

Rowdy buried his face in her soft, silky hair, shaking his head. "I'm just in love with you, that's all," he said. "Sergeant Corley can't do nothin' to me. The freight company I work for has problems hiring men to work with the Indians. They want me to stay here."

"I just don't want you to get in trouble," she said.

Rowdy held her close. "Did Black Kettle ever tell you what the problem was when he attended the Medicine Lodge Treaty up at Ft. Larned, Kansas?"

"Yes," she answered. "Grandfather said the Cheyenne chiefs thought they would have a reservation along the Arkansas River in southeast Colorado, not one along the Arkansas River in southeast Kansas and northern Oklahoma."

"I don't understand why the government did that," he said.

"I don't either," she said. "But something I do understand is, I like Jake, but I don't like Sergeant Corley. He acts like a mean man."

"He is mean," Rowdy said. "Don't let him mess around with you."

Her voice trembled. "What do you mean?"

"What I mean is, don't let him hang around you or try to talk to you. I've seen him in action—he's a bad one."

"I would never have anything to do with him," she replied, in a soft whisper.

"I know you wouldn't, but be careful," Rowdy said. "He told some of the troops he'd like to catch you off by yourself. I can't do anything about it because he's in charge of the detachment and I'm just a civilian, so please be alert when you're away from camp."

"There's not much hope for us, is there?"

"Oh, no, Pretty Girl," Rowdy said. "There's lots of hope because I'll be leaving here sooner than you think. And when I do, I'm headed for Texas without lookin' back."

"Headed for Texas without looking back?" Her eyes opened wide as her hand touched her lips.

"Yeah," Rowdy said. "And I'd take you with me, if you'd come."

"I would ... but the sooner, the better."

A covey of quail spooked from their nesting place. Rowdy flinched as if he'd been slapped. "Someone's coming," he whispered.

Sergeant Corley erupted from the bushes. "There you are. I'm responsible for you civilian workers and you're acting like a traitor, sneaking out of camp at night. That Indians girl just leads you on, so she's on my list to take later."

Sergeant Corley yanked the pistol from his flapped holster, "I'm marching you back to camp. You're damn lucky you ain't in the army—I'd have you before a court martial."

Sergeant Corley carried out another loud harangue outside Rowdy's tent. He ended it by saying, "I'll tell the night guard to shoot you if they catch you away from your tent after lights out."

"I figured you'd get caught one of these nights," Jake whispered when he entered the tent.

Rowdy closed his eyes while sucking a deep breath. "It'll be alright," he said. "All he can do is put me on report for leaving camp. I ain't no soldier."

Next morning, the iron wheels on the old supply wagon clanked across slick river rocks. The noise stirred Rowdy to his senses, causing him to rush from his tent.

Sergeant Corley drove the wagon toward a column of dust signaling the supply train's arrival.

Rowdy mounted a horse to chase after the wagon.

"Sergeant Corley," he yelled. "They hired me to meet the supply wagon. It's my job to deliver the provisions down to the Indians."

"Well, you ain't been doin' your job," Corley said. "But, now that you're here, load this wagon. I'm sending Jake on patrol. It's high time he acted like a real soldier."

While they confronted one another, the wind blew the dust aside to reveal several columns of mounted troopers. Lieutenant Colonel George Armstrong Custer appeared unannounced, leading four columns, comprising eight companies of cavalry troops.

They represented a force of over five-hundred men riding from Fort Supply one-hundred-twenty miles northwest. Once at the remount station, Custer announced he carried orders to relocate the Cheyenne and Arapaho to their reservation on the Kansas border.

A junior officer issued orders for the remount station to patrol to the northeast. Custer's Osage scouts had reported that a band of Indians had attacked a nearby ranch, stealing a few head of cattle.

With senior officers arriving, Sergeant Corley turned the wagon around to hurry back to the remount station. Rowdy rode into the camp at the same time Custer's columns arrived.

Sergeant Corley called his detachment, including Jake, aside after he reached camp. "Saddle your mounts and get your gear ready. We've been ordered to ride with the patrol."

~~~~~~

The next morning, in dawn's first light, a hard, cold north wind blew flakes of snow. A patrol of twenty men angled to the northeast at a fast steady pace. Rowdy watched Jake depart with a worried brow.

By late morning, the sky brightened for a while and by sheer force of will, the patrol rode on hour after hour. After a frigid night that left the men drained, they shifted direction to the southwest, heading toward the relay station in the sporadic snow.

~~~~~~

Rowdy noticed the camp's unusual activities after Jake's patrol returned to the remount station. Soldiers hurried about, preparing their weapons and gear, and packing ammunition and grub into their saddlebags. Thinking this action might distract the guards for a while, he tried to slip away to visit Pretty Girl Sleeps, but Sergeant Corley spotted him.

"Hawkins," he yelled. "You're restricted to the camp. Orders are to seal the camp until the column departs."

"What's goin' on?" Rowdy asked.

"Don't ask," Corley said. "Just do as you're told."

"Platoon Sergeant Corley, report," Custer's Aide-de-Camp, called.

~~~~~~

"Sir," Corley said before he loped his horse to the head of the column to salute Custer.

"We're going to attack that Indian village downstream," Custer said. "I'm tired of ordering patrols into the countryside to catch a few runaway Indians. It's time they were taught a lesson, if you know what I mean."

"Yes, Sir," Corley answered. "I know what you mean."

"Given what you reported to your company's captain about Hawkins and that Indian girl, I don't want him to warn them," Custer added. "So, while columns get into position, place him under guard at the remount station."

"Yes, Sir," Sergeant Corley responded with a snappy salute, followed by a big grin.

Sergeant Corley returned to his platoon, and then led Jake aside.

"I'm ordering you to guard Hawkins," he said, jabbing a finger on Jake's chest. "I know you're anxious to see battle, but it's important that Hawkins doesn't leave the camp. Shoot him if you have to, but don't let him leave the camp."

"Shoot him?" Jake said, his mouth as wide as the Missouri River.

"Yes, and if you shoot him dead while we're away, I'll let you go second on that young Indian girl he's so sweet on."

Jakes eyes grew wide, "I ain't never …"

"You'll learn to love them young ones." Sergeant Corley said. "We're gonna teach them redskins a lesson they won't forget."

Corley mounted his horse to join the column, leaving Jake and Rowdy behind.

The soldiers rode forward in four separate columns during a light snowstorm. They planned to attack the Cheyenne village along the Washita River, Black Kettle's village. Custer ordered his troops to attack at dawn.

~~~~~~~

Rowdy didn't understand why Jake pointed a rifle at him. "What's got into you?"

"Sergeant Corley ordered me to shoot you if you try to leave the camp." Jake jabbed his rifle at Rowdy, pushing him into the storage cave. "Custer's gonna teach them Indians a lesson about followin' orders, just like I'm gonna teach you."

Rowdy shook his head. At first, he failed to comprehend the grand scheme of events, but as if a bell rang inside his head, he got it—*Custer planned a sneak attack.*

His mind raced with possibilities. His life, his love, hung in the balance—he needed to act and act right now. Somehow, he had to trick Jake into letting him leave the camp.

Rowdy canted his head aside, making a loud click between cheek and jowl. "Sergeant Corley has you all wrong," he said. "He thinks you're a coward and you wouldn't shoot Indians. He didn't want you to embarrass his detachment by freezin' in battle, and it sure worked." Rowdy shook his head. "You swallowed his 'guard Hawkins' story, hook, line, and sinker."

"What are you talking about? He told me to shoot you once the attack began."

"Yeah, well, he wanted you to believe it. I bet he even told you what he asked you to do was mighty important, didn't he?"

"How did you know?" Jake's eyebrows bunched with the question.

"You notice he don't send you on patrol when they figure they'll meet warriors?"

"Yeah, and I've complained about it, too."

"Like I said, he thinks you're a coward. This fight would have been a good chance to prove him wrong, but you're stuck in this cave with me while the rest of the men become heroes."

"Damn it, I wanted to collect some scalps. I heard some of the soldiers bragging about it."

"Aw, you're not the kind to shoot poor, defenseless Indians are you?" Rowdy said.

"Damn right I am," Jake said. "Just gimme the chance. I'll show Corley."

"Alright then, let's ride out there together," Rowdy said. "If anyone sees us, you can tell 'em I escaped and you chased me. But, once you're out there, join the fight, and collect a few scalps. I'll be long gone. Corley won't ever know what happened to me. Come on, let's get saddled. Show 'em you ain't no coward. Join the fight. Don't get left behind again." Rowdy nodded at the remaining horses in the corral.

Jake raised an eyebrow. "We're gonna attack together?"

"Hey, quit stallin'. You ain't afraid, are you?" Rowdy asked.

"Hell, no, I ain't afraid," Jake said. "And you're right. Let's get mounted."

"I'll ride out first so it'll look like you're chasing me," Rowdy said, as he swung into the saddle, racing from the camp.

Moments later, Jake followed, whooping a loud cry.

A half-hour later, at the sound of a single gunshot, Rowdy charged from the trees along the Washita. A few moments later, a volley of shots rang across the prairie and, bullets whizzed past his head. He reined in, glancing toward the village.

Little Wolf burst into a clearing, guiding several women and children to escape from Custer's first charge. A squad of soldiers rode behind them, shooting every Indian they saw. Little Wolf, running with a small child in his arms, tumbled forward when a bullet struck him in the back. Another trooper shot him on the ground, killing him.

Rowdy drew a sharp breath.

"No," he yelled, spurring his horse into a run toward the village.

Sergeant Corley splashed across the Washita with Jake riding at his side, along with others, shooting at Black Kettle.

A heavy volley of weapon fire covered the entire area in smoke as Black Kettle jumped on his horse, lifted his wife up behind him, trying to escape the village.

The Cheyenne Chief and his wife fell beside the riverbank, riddled with bullets.

"This is why I joined the army," Jake yelled, at the top of his voice. A cheap copper cartridge jammed in his Springfield rifle, forcing him to grab a Colt revolver from a holster hanging from his saddle to keep firing.

Rowdy charged into the burning village, where he noticed Corley and Jake. Pretty Girl Sleeps ran toward the trees as Sergeant Corley spurred his horse after her. Jake followed close behind, his revolver blazing, while Rowdy angled behind the teepees to catch them.

165

"No, Sergeant Corley," he yelled. "Don't shoot her." He galloped alongside Corley.

Corley swung his heavy revolver around, striking Rowdy in the face, the blow almost knocking him from the saddle. Corley fired a pistol round with deliberate aim, the bullet lodged in the meaty part of Rowdy's thigh.

Rowdy raised his rifle to shoot; his 44-caliber lead slug tore through Corley's heart. The bullet's force knocked him from the saddle. He bounced once, skidding across the ground.

Jake kept riding and shooting, trying to catch Pretty Girl Sleeps before she escaped into the brush.

Rowdy jacked another round in his Henry rifle while he spurred his horse beside Jake, grabbing his arm.

"Don't shoot her, Jake," he yelled.

A few strides behind Pretty Girl Sleeps, Jake yanked loose from Rowdy's grip to fire at her.

The bullet nicked the side of her head, knocking her from her feet. Blood welled from the gash above her ear. She glanced behind at the riders, her eyes wide in terror.

Jake slid his horse to a stop, aimed his revolver at her upturned face. He cocked the hammer. "I ain't no coward," he yelled.

Rowdy shoved his rifle's muzzle against Jake's ribs before pulling the trigger. The blast knocked him from his horse, sending his body tumbling end over end down a steep, rocky embankment.

"Come on, Pretty Girl," he yelled. Lifting her up behind him, he spurred his horse away from the village as fast as the tired horse could carry them.

A young trooper spotted them racing across the smoke-filled valley. He raised his rifle, firing at them. He missed, but reloaded to fire again, only to miss a second time.

Pretty Girl slumped forward while Rowdy rode hard, holding on to her as best he could until they cleared the battle area. Cresting a ridge that placed them out of sight, he reined his winded horse to a stop before he jumped from the saddle.

He held her in his arms to wipe blood from her face as he splashed canteen water on her wound.

"I'm sorry about your grandfather," he said. "I hate the men who did this to your people. I love you, Pretty Girl."

"I love you, too, Soldier Boy," she managed to say. Those few words left her breathless.

After bandaging her wound, he wrapped her in a heavy coat. He helped her stand beside the tired, heaving horse. Glancing over his shoulder, he gazed toward the rattle of small-arms fire coming from the village before heaving a deep sigh as he closed his eyes.

Rowdy slipped the wanted poster from his shirt pocket before impaling it on a dry twig. Then he mounted his horse, lifting Pretty Girl Sleeps up behind him. He headed for Texas without looking back.

The End

From the Author:

Thanks for taking time from your already hectic schedule to read my story, **"Headed for Texas Without Lookin' Back."** I hope you'll leave a review on Amazon and visit my WEB page and leave a comment or a question. This story was inspired by the character in my **Billy Howard Western Series**.

Cowboy lives began with the darkness to darkness struggle of ordinary men to survive in a world that had little to offer after the Civil War. Change in the frontiers of our country came very slowly and the rugged men of the west, both good and bad, changed even more slowly. So it is that this colorful era of our country still lives in the stories of their descendants whose lives have mirrored their fathers … and without western writers, may soon escape our grasp and be lost forever.

I've always been interested in the Old West. I grew up on the ranches in the Texas panhandle where my grandfather Cliff White (1885-1983) and my dad Alton Robertson (1911-1991) were cowboys. I followed in their footsteps as all three of us at different times, starting from 1920 to 1956, worked at the same place, the famous Coon/Culbertson Ranch where they had the world's largest herd of Hereford's and the second largest herd of Brahma's.

I've roped wild cattle, stayed in cowboy camps, slept on the ground, rode good horses and rough horses, drove herds, and learned cowboy life by actually doing it. I've been a rancher, rodeo contestant, auctioneer, private pilot, song writer (songs recorded by Chris LeDoux,) Texas and Oklahoma Real Estate Broker, skydiver, and US army veteran.

I was born and raised in the panhandle town of Dalhart, Texas. I'm now retired and living in Hooker, Oklahoma where I'm pumping wells, working at a feedlot, and team roping. I've had numerous stories, poems, and articles published in news papers and magazines, and have published ten books which include:

Tall Tales and Short Stories: a *Robertson family legacy.*

I'll Be Seeing You: a b*attle with cancer.*

POW/MIA: America's Missing Men: *the men we left behind in Vietnam.*

Killin' Time: *a collection of short stories.*

Mortal Secrets: *a mystery novel.*

Rodeo Stories: *a collection of true cowboy tales.*

https://www.amazon.com/RODEO-STORIES-Collection-Cowboy-Tales/dp/1496943163/

Rodeo Stories II: A collection of true cowboy tales.

Billy Howard and the Buckskin: *a western novel.*

https://www.amazon.com/Billy-Howard-Buckskin-Chimp-Robertson/dp/1522828761/

Billy Howard and the Palomino: *a western novel.*

Billy Howard and the Appaloosa: *a western novel.*

Visit Chimp's Author's Central page:

https://www.amazon.com/Chimp-Robertson/e/B004S7GVRC/

Visit my WEB page: www.chimprobertson.com

Biography

Chimp Robertson is a former rodeo contestant, author, private pilot, artist, auctioneer, rancher, song writer (songs recorded by Chris LeDoux) army veteran, and sky diver. He has had many articles and stories published in various magazines and news papers, and is the author of ten books.

Born and raised in the panhandle town of Dalhart, Texas, he is retired and currently living in Hooker, Oklahoma where he is pumping wells, working at a feedlot, and team roping.

THE SAVAGE POSSE
JS Stroud

The March winds blew across the open spaces of the West Texas desert in 1868 at a pace that picked up sand, driving it into a person's flesh with the sting of hot needles. I had been here before, how many times I had forgotten. I was an outcast, cursed at birth with the blood of two races flowing through my veins. The Apache and the white-man hated me equally, even before I was born.

The wind blew as the clouds overhead turned black. They hid the light from the stars and the moon. The storm circled high above tearing at the sky in its fury as rain funneled down in a stream.

I shouted at my horse as we topped the last ridge. "Looks like ice and hail coming; if we don't find shelter soon we are going to be in real trouble." The pony turned its tail to the storm as it headed south, but I knew the move came too late. Lightning flashed across the sky in a long arch, striking the ground in jagged bolts, igniting fire after fire as it touched dry patches of desert grass and piles of rolling brush. Flashes of light shot from the ashes as the fires consumed them before dying in seconds as the rain cascaded down in rivers. A string of dark clouds slammed together, spinning as the strength of the winds drove them across the open spaces of the sky. Wild animals cowered in their holes as thunder shattered the stillness of the night.

When the first of the storm hit, I pulled the brim of my hat down. The chilly rain was cold as ice as wind drove it under my heavy leather slicker. It soaked me to the skin with every blast of the wind and every movement of the horse.

"The Miller's farm is somewhere near here," I yelled. "If we can make it there, we can spend the night in their barn."

The rain turned from sheets of icy water to hail as the storm raged in its fury. I pushed the strength of the horse to his limit while the winds tried to drive us into the flat lands of the valley. The chunks of ice grew larger and heavier. Each strike was like the blow of hammers that had no end. The chunks of ice, half the size of a man's fist, grew larger. This kind of storm could beat a man to death in seconds, or a horse to death in minutes.

I had bruises and cuts with blood running from my arms and back in more than a dozen places. I didn't know how much longer we could survive out in the open spaces of the desert. If we didn't find cover soon, the steady pounding of ice would beat us to death.

Yanking the reins, I turned west while sand-filled ditches became raging rivers. At the top of a long ridge, I glimpsed the lights of the Miller farm on the mesa. I knew we could be there in under an hour, if we survived the battles of the journey.

I squeezed my knees tighter against the horse I called "Nightshade." He was a little buckskin with a few patches of black and gray across the chest and shoulders, a good horse but still half-wild.

Nudging him forward, I fought him with the reins at the same time. He didn't like where we headed, showing me with every move and every turn we made.

"Come on," I growled. "We can't stay here all night. If we do—we're dead." We headed into the worst of the storm; Nightshade knew it as well.

He had lived his life in the desert; he knew the outcomes of such storms. Black clouds twisted in the sky above us, the wind screaming its fury as it ripped small trees and brush from the ground by their roots. I tied Nightshade under a rock overhang as the storm built its strength, moving to the southeast.

It looked as if we would all live through the night as the storm passed by the cliff, and then passed the lights of the Miller farm. I glanced at the animal, yelling over the fading roar of the storm, "If you don't want to freeze to death, we had best be going."

Nightshade stumbled in the wind as we came from under the protection of the cliff. "That pilgrim Miller may not be too happy to see us," I hollered," but that will be his problem. Right now, we have bigger things to worry about."

We skirted around small rivers and swollen streams, then waded through mud holes as deep as the horse's belly, filling my boots with heavy, oozing mud. The alternative was the raging rivers in the valley—there was no crossing them.

I complained to the horse as we forged the first swollen river. "I told that stupid Miller, when he first came into this country, he couldn't make a living on the mesa. It was nothing but rocks, sage brush, and rattlesnakes." Nightshade hadn't listened to me any more than Miller had.

Well this storm ought to teach him no man can stand against nature, I thought. The horse staggered, falling to its knees as its iron shoes contacted the mesa's slick, wet stones. For a second, I feared he may have broken his leg, but he rose with a quick step. Slipping from the saddle, I took the reins, leading him on foot towards the Miller home and their small wooden barn.

"It's going to be pitch dark when we get there," I shouted over the last gasp of the howling storm. "We'll head straight for the barn. I'll put some grain in the stall for you before giving you a rub-down. Lord knows you've earned it." I struggled along the trail toward the top of the mesa.

"I'll pay Miller for some hay and grain in the morning. After that, we'll move on," I murmured aloud. "Word has it Santana is hiring gunhands along the Mexican border. I could use the money."

A faint glow bloomed to the west, carrying the scent of burning juniper, cactus, and sage in the air.

"Looks like Miller is burning off the south side of the mesa," I said, as my eyebrows furrowed, not reckoning why he let it burn in the night.

"If he is planning on putting that land to the plow, he is a bigger idiot than I thought he was. I have told him before, this is cattle country—it's rough and hard. The only thing it's good for is cattle, or maybe sheep or goats, but only an idiot would try farming this place."

Flames spread for over a mile across the mesa's top. The fire raced southeast in the same direction as the storm. I wasn't worried about the flames or the storm returning; they would follow the wind, heading southeast. Whenever a bad storm hit this area, it almost always traveled in a southeast direction.

I knew John Miller; he was a strong man with a will of iron. I figured he knew what he was doing most of the time, but this time, I figured he had bitten off more than he could chew.

The Miller place wasn't much, even by Apache standards. He made the home from pine logs drug from the valley below, notching them into place with two small windows and a stone fireplace. From the same pine logs, he built a barn with a blacksmith bellows inside. The barn held two stalls for his horses. Nearby, he fashioned a rope corral beside a hay meadow that lay dry most of the year.

Jessie, John Miller's wife, was a small dark-haired woman in her late twenties with dark-brown eyes. Jessie Miller looked even older than her age from years of the hard work she had been doing, accompanied by the stress of raising three children on top of a rock mesa filled with rattlesnakes and scorpions.

It was a hard lonely life. This was no place to raise a family, not a white family anyway. This was Apache land; it always had been Apache land and always would be. A few tribes from the Comanche nation rode across the blistering sands of the desert and the mesa. On occasion, Mexican bandits, or cavalry deserters, came this way, but even they knew what would happen if caught by the Apache.

The night winds changed directions. For the first time, I got a good whiff of the smoke. More than juniper, cactus, and sage burned. The smoke carried the sickly sweet odor of burning leather, hair, and flesh.

Sliding the rifle from its scabbard, I levered the weapon, letting a brass shell slide under the cocked hammer. The barn collapsed to nothing but a pile of ash as I rode atop the mesa. The house fared no better as it lay smoldering.

The waning moon cast dark shadows, but I glimpsed the impression of a body lying in the front yard. I slipped from the saddle, treading softly towards the Miller home while images of what happened raced through my mind.

I stood with my weapon in my hand, gazing at the shape of a man twisted and broken with four arrows buried deep in his chest. His scalp was gone and his face bashed beyond recognition. I knew it was John Miller from the size of the body and the width of his shoulders.

"I should have put a bullet in you the first time we met," I scolded. "Maybe then your family would still be alive."

I trudged to Nightshade, seeking a small shovel tied behind the saddle.

"It doesn't look like you were doing much farming up here," I said. "Dealing with Apache will get you killed quick." I spit on the ground before scouting around once more, just in case someone lurked in the darkness.

"I'll dig you a grave tonight," I said. "Tomorrow I'll dig four more. That is, if I can find your wife and the children."

The West Texas mesa consisted of nothing more than hardpan caliche and rock. It was hard slow digging. The morning sun rose over the horizon, burning most of the clouds away. Before finishing the first grave, my hands became bloody and sore while my back hurt. I wanted to kill John Miller all over again, for what he had done.

"You played hell bringing your family out here," I bellowed, staring at the butchered corpse of what had once been a man with all the hate and anger I had in my soul. "Now, I am the one stuck digging the graves."

I knelt to pull the arrows from his chest. I slung a slipknot around John Miller's feet before I looped the loose end around Nightshade's pommel. The blood stained rope reminded me just how fast a man could die on the mesa. This was a hard land—it called for hard men.

I let Nightshade drag Miller's body to the gravesite, where I gave his body a shove with the heel of my boot, watching it slide into the shallow hole.

"It's only right that I dig the next grave large enough to hold your wife and kids," I said aloud. "I think they should be buried together, but, as for you, you can sleep alone.

"You are the one who dragged them up here. Their deaths are on your hands. It was you who made the decisions for them in this life," I said. "I sure ain't gonna let you lead them in the next."

Anger for the man still filled my heart as I threw the first shovelful of dirt into the hole. I was happy to see his dead eyes covered with dirt. I no longer wanted to look at his face. A shallow grave, often dug up by critters, was a lot more than he deserved. It was all I had dug, a shallow grave.

Smoke lingered over the ashes of the house when I started digging the next grave. It had to be large enough to hold one woman and three children. If I could find a doll, I would place it in the grave with the children. If not, I would make one to place in the hands of the smallest child. I pounded hardpan caliche and rock for the next nine hours before being satisfied with the resting place for the wife and children. They had done nothing to deserve the life they had been given or the death they received.

I sunk the burial hole four-feet wide, five-feet deep, and almost six-feet long. It was all I could do for her and the children, but it was enough. Now came the part I dreaded, finding the small charred remains of the mother and children. The timbers were still hot to the touch, burning my hands as I pushed aside red and gray embers. I rummaged through layers of smoking gray ash and charred wood.

The first body lay just inside the home where the front door once had been; it was Jessie Miller. The savages had scalped her. The fire left her eyes as empty sockets. Water-filled blisters covered most of her face and body. Her clothing was nothing more than ashes that fell apart as I touched her.

I grabbed her wrists to pull her body from the carnage, only to have her flesh tear loose from under my grasp. Blood and water poured from the wound. I staggered back as the stench hit me. This was something I hadn't expected. It forced me to hold back tears.

People weren't meant to die like this. I found a new hate for John Miller.

"I wish I could dig you up to kill you all over again," I hollered. My words echoed from the canyon wall. Sure, it was stupid. If the killers were anywhere near, they would know someone was still alive, but I could not help myself. I had a hate that boiled over into my soul as my heart held a rage only another death would cure.

John Miller may have brought his family up here, but others had done the killing. I wanted to see them laid out in their own graves. I wanted to see them suffer and die like the young woman before me.

Stomping to Nightshade, I removed the rope from the saddle. I tied the rope to Jessie's arms just above the elbow. Nightshade slowly pulled her from the ashes towards the open gravesite, where I placed Jessie in the center of the deep grave, face-up with her arms out stretched.

"I will place the young children in your arms, that way they can rest with you forever."

I draped one of my blankets over her body before I plodded to the ashes of the home, rooting around in the ash for what was left of the children.

The bodies of two small children lay under the shell of a wooden bed, their frail arms still clamped around each other in death, as they had been in life. I struggled to pull them apart. I didn't care who had done this, white-man, red-man, or slave, I pledged to make them pay.

I laid each child beside their mother; one on her left side and the other on her right. I intended to lay the youngest child on her lap with a doll cradled in her hands. That way, I could wrap Jessie's long slender arms forever around the children she loved so much.

I never found the last child.

Four hours of searching the ashes brought only blisters and burns. The youngest child had vanished without a trace.

Nothing remained to show she had ever lived.

The sky grew as black as my soul as I tossed the first shovelful of dirt in the grave, slowly covering a mother, her children, and the dreams they shared. A new storm blew in from the northwest. With it came sheets of rain, but I was glad for it. It would wash away the blood, the filth, and maybe, a little of the rage and anger burning in my heart. The shovel held nothing but rock and mud while I struggled to fill in the grave.

The clouds that rolled across the mesa blocked the light from the already dark heavens.

Rivers ran in what once had been dry washes, while the mountainsides slowly washed away. Even the wolves and the mountain lions hid from the fury of nature as a new storm swept across the land, giving life to a few while killing others.

I was soaked to the skin when I placed the last shovelful of mud and rock on top of the grave. It had been a hard day and a hard night of burying. Despite my rage and my exhaustion, I refused to sleep beside the humped graves of this family.

Taking Nightshade's reins in my hand, I led him away from the Miller farm. Tomorrow, I would circle the mesa top, searching for tracks hidden in the surface of the sand. With luck, I would know who had killed the Miller family and why they had taken their lives.

This high country, where hardly nothing lived except rattlesnakes and scorpions, held a few stands of trees, struggling to survive. They were scattered, offering little shelter. I found a tall rock with a flat surface on the southern side where I reined up against it to escape the wind. After securing Nightshade with a rawhide strap, I took the saddle from his back, along with my rifle and blanket. Coffee would have been nice along with some hard tack biscuits, but I didn't have either. There was no way I was going to build a fire on the top of the mesa, where its flames would be a signal seen for miles.

It made little difference if the Millers had been killed by whites, blacks, or Indians. None of them would let me live if they knew I rested there, so I settled for a piece of dry jerky and a few sips of water. In the morning, I could fill the canteen from almost any stream or wash swollen with water after the rain. I gave Nightshade the last few drops of water from the bottom of the canteen before I laid it beside the saddle.

I would scout the mesa top for any kind of sign with the sun tomorrow. The arrows in John's chest had crow feathers on their shafts and red flint tips cut from a single stone. These were the markings of the Navaho tribe, but they would never travel this far east; they were blood enemies of the Apache. They hated the Apache, but they feared them, too. No warrior from the Navaho tribe would set foot on Apache land. This was Apache land, bought and paid for with their blood and with their tears. It ran from the banks of the Arkansas River south to the last speck of sand along the banks of the Rio Grande River. Besides, the Navaho had no reason to kill the Millers, and they had no reason to steal a child.

I used my boot to smooth the sand after pitching the larger rocks aside to lay down the saddle and blanket. I had seen a thousand nights just like this, with the stars gleaming overhead accompanied by the howls of coyotes or wolves. In the distance, long-nose bats fluttered from one stand of cactus to another, searching for the desert flowers' sweet nectar.

Somewhere in the darkness, a small child struggled to survive. If alone, wolves followed her footsteps. If not alone, it meant the same savages who burned the Miller farm had taken her. The same savages had mutilated her father and scalped her mother and sisters. I ached to scream into the darkness that I was there for her, but only death would follow my words. If the murderers knew I searched for them, they might kill the child out-of-hand, leaving her body for the night scavengers, or hang her from a tree for me to find—for me to bury.

Sleep came with a cost; a child terrified and alone filled my dreams. In one, she wandered the desert while wolves followed her footsteps. In another, the blade of a knife held the little girl's scalp; she cried in pain as the blade pierced her flesh.

The heavy rains that fell during the night weren't what disturbed my sleep while I shivered from the icy touch of the water soaking my wool blanket. I woke to a morning no better than the night; it was gray and dismal. The rains had eased, but now, a cold fog drifted across the valleys to the mountaintops.

After I saddled Nightshade without a word, I returned to the Miller home. There was little, if any, chance I would find any sign of the men who had killed the family, but I was going to try. It was a cold and lonely life living on a mountaintop. With the children's death, it became even lonelier. They were as close to family as I ever had.

Life in the desert comes with the rains; flowers were in bloom. I gathered several cactus roses for the mother along with a handful of wild flowers for the children. I carried a powerful hate for the man who brought them here. He would be lucky if I bothered to carve his name or a date on a wooden cross. I placed the wild flowers and cactus roses at the foot of the family grave before offering a silent prayer ending with a promise.

"I'll find your daughter," I whispered. "If I can, I'll find her a good home. If not, I'll find the men who took her, listening to them scream as I fill their graves."

While circling the mesa top, I searched for any sign of the killers, but I didn't expect to find any. It came as no surprise when I didn't. Torrential rains had washed away any traces of the men. I did find three steep trails leading from the mesa. One led north, one led south, and one led west. To the west lay nothing but more desert, rattlesnakes, and scorpions. A man would have a hard time surviving the heat or finding water, this time of year; it was suicide to go west. A few settlements lay to the north, small towns and villages, but nothing large enough to interest the kind of men capable of killing an entire family.

I eased Nightshade down the trail south. This led to Apache land. If a white man were caught there, it meant certain death. But I had no fear of the Apache—my veins held the same blood as theirs. Sure, it was mixed with a white-man's blood, but my skin was almost as dark as the Apache, my blood was just as red.

My mother was born into the Apache tribe, but as a child, she had been stolen by the Crow, who raised her as one of their own. In her travels, my mother learned the ways of the Crow, the Apache, and the white man, which she taught me well.

My father was an Irish immigrant working a trap line in the high country of Colorado in the days of the Mountain Man. For a while, he trapped beaver and muskrat in the freezing cold waters of the Rocky Mountains. He killed buffalo on the open plains of Nebraska and Kansas. He learned how to kill; he was good at it.

In the winter of 1853, he had taken my mother as a wife—why I didn't know; maybe he had wanted a son to carry on his name. While my mother wanted a girl child to carry on a family, it looked as if neither would have their way. My father died ten years after my birth; he never saw the son he had wanted and my mother never saw a little girl playing with dolls. I grew up in life tramping along trap lines beside my father. I learned to kill and I loved it. Father died during the War Between the States, fighting as he had lived—with a gun in his hand.

After his death, my mother and I had traveled south across the prairie to live with her people, the Apache. I never learned to fit in. I was an outcast, a half-breed. They never let me forget it. A hate filled me that tore at my heart and burned in my soul. I had killed as a child—buffalo, elk, bear, and even once, a mountain lion.

The first time I killed a man, I was thirteen years old; it happened before I even understood what I was doing. One minute, I stood alone beside the river, watching the sun sink into the horizon while listening to the birds as they sang to each other; in the next, blood covered my hands as a dead man lay at my feet.

He had come at me from the shadows with his hands outstretched, grabbing and pawing. I crushed his head with a stone. I was already an outcast; the blood of an Irishman tainted my Apache blood. My hair was dark brown and long, hanging to the small of my back, with streaks of red in the summer, instead of the coal black hair of younger Apache women.

My eyes were green with flakes of yellow that showed up in the night like the eyes of a cat. Only the rims showed the dark black color of the Apache. Maybe that was why he had wanted me; I was different. My mother once told me that one day the braves would see me as a beautiful woman. When that day came, I could have my choice of whom I would marry. But by now, I had learned to stand on my own, and I did—bashing his head with a rock.

The tribe respected the warrior. For over seven winters, he killed buffalo, elk, and deer for the tribe. I feared what would happen if anyone found out what I had done. I tied the warrior's hands to a fallen log before I pushed him into the rushing waters of the Arkansas River. His body floated downstream, farther along its banks. Within minutes, the strength of the rapids claimed his body as he vanished into the river's rushing water as I stood watching.

At fifteen, I killed another man after he stole my horse, leaving me to die in the desert. I walked for almost thirty miles in the heat of the day, and most of the night, to find him snuggled against a cliff face. The fire he built reflected the heat from the rocks against his body. The light movement of his chest as he breathed showed he lived, for the moment. In the early hours of the morning, I crept upon the sleeping figure. He must have been warm and comfortable rolled in the blanket like a caterpillar in a cocoon.

I took my time, aiming carefully before slowly pulling the trigger. The slug struck the back of his head. The rifle may have been old, and a little rusty, but it had always been a good gun. It shot straight; the soft lead bullet mushroomed on impact. The man's face disappeared under the force of the spreading lead. Blood soaked his blankets as he went from sleep into death without knowing his life had already ended.

After I stripped his clothes from his body, I left him lying naked in the sand. It more than satisfied my anger to let the scavengers devour what was left of the body, which is why I left him naked, face down in the sand.

Once, I crippled a warrior in a fit of rage. I hurt others out-of–hand, not caring if they lived or died. My careless actions caused the medicine man to ask me to leave, not for my own good, but for the good of the tribe.

My hate ran too deep and I had no control over it. Over the years, I learned to control my rage, but the hate within my heart still burned bright. Its heat warmed my chest while I searched the ground for the body of a small child.

I had wanted to kill men before but not like I wanted to kill these men. These were the cold-hearted men; they would torture or mutilate a child, then scalp her while she still lived, just for a handful of pennies or for a few paper dollars. These were the scalp hunters for the lords and ladies of England. I wanted to see their blood run in rivers before the blade of my knife ended their suffering.

Through the years, I trained Nightshade well; we hunted together many times, but this hunt was different and he knew it. He slipped among the shadows, silent as a ghost, stepping over rocks with the ease of a cat, searching with his eyes to find the soft pools of sand to silence his steps before he moved forward, even breathing shallow. He had become as much of the hunt as I.

Hour after hour, Nightshade lifted his head into the wind, following a blood scent I failed to detect. He returned to the wild animal he had once been. He was the kind of animal I needed to track down a nest of killers.

The heat of the desert wind no longer held a meaning for me; the sun no longer burned at my flesh. I became a part of the desert, like the rocks and the sand. I needed little or nothing to survive. I only needed the hate burning in my heart, the weapons at my side, and the knife in my belt.

On the second morning, I cut thorns away from a cactus rose to let the cool nectar run down my throat as the sun climbed high to shine above a lake of sand. I sat in the saddle with the rifle in my hand when a soft tinkling signaled the movement of people. Far to my right, they plodded along, more than a mile away, moving slowly. The rattle of pots and pans when they banged together alerted me. Moments later, a dog barked, followed by the tittering voices of children. I bumped Nightshade with my boot heels, moving towards their noise.

I knew what I would find; a line of horses stretching across the desert with tent poles tied to the flanks of half-wild horses without brands or shoes, horses loaded with the possessions of its owner. Pots and pans would dangle from the poles while the smaller children, unable to walk any distance, would ride on deerskin rugs.

They carried mounds of buffalo hides rolled into bundles and tied securely with rawhide straps. Half-starved dogs would be nipping at the horse's hooves while small children, stripped to their waists, would be running wild. I witnessed this scene many times, both as a child running beside the horses and as an adult, riding guard around the column. I guided Nightshade from a gully into an open stretch of sand. The outriders would see me soon. I wanted them to know who I was and what I was doing.

This might be the tribe of my mother's people, and maybe not. It made little difference to the Apache what tribe you were, as long as your veins held Apache blood. The blood in my veins ran deep from my mother's mother to a thousand others, so I sat in the open with my rifle on my thighs, waiting to learn who would be the first to see Nightshade and its savage rider. I didn't have long to wait before I spotted a change in their movement, even from that distance.

A young warrior found me. He held his head and his spear high as he charged forward, yelling and screaming into the wind, while I sat on my horse in silence, waiting for him to draw closer. He had painted his face and arms for war, imitating the Apache he had seen going to battle, but he had never been there, and I knew it. At fifty yards, I called for the first time.

"I am Venom," I shouted, "from the tribe of the Snake. Do not make me kill you." The Snake tribe feared my name, but I did not know if this warrior had ever heard my name, or if he even knew the meaning of fear, but he lowered his spear before his horse slowed to a stop.

"I have heard of you," he yelled. "You are the one who kills red-man and white alike. Your spear carries the blood of warriors on its shaft while your hate runs deeper than your heart." The young warrior painted his face for war, but his eyes held fear.

"I have come to tell your chief I have outgrown my hate," I declared. "I wish to pass by in peace. I have no wish to carry the blood of the Apache or their brothers on the tip of my spear."

The warrior rode away leaving me to wonder if my name still meant anything to the Apache, or if I needed to take more lives before the day ended. Nightshade shifted from side to side, as we stood in the desert sun, waiting for the warrior's return. Large flies circled around before eating hunks of meat from our flesh, seeking the liquid beneath. They were hard, vicious bites from the swarm of flies that followed the caravan day and night, living off the scraps of food left behind, and from the flesh of the living.

Small spots of blood dripped from the bites on Nightshade's back and sides as we waited for the warrior. Their caravan stopped while the sun stood overhead. The clouds had rolled away, letting the crystal grains of sand glisten in the light. A half-dozen warriors, each with a painted face, rode one beside the other, as they raced across the desert toward us. Eagle feathers decorated the tips of their spears while the bright red feathers of the black bird rode upon the shaft of their arrows in their quivers. I sat in silence with the rifle in my hand while they ride closer.

If they wanted a battle, that is what I would give them. I raised my rifle barrel, centering its sights on the first warrior's chest before I lowered it three inches. It would cause a slow death, if they wanted to battle.

The warriors drew within yards, waiting to see if I would open fire, but I had no wish to kill without reason. I lowered my weapon to gaze at the warriors.

"Can I ride through in peace?" I asked.

The lead warrior nodded his head. "Red Cloud, Chief of the River tribe, says you may ride through in peace, but you are not welcome in the tribe or around the children."

I laid the rifle across my thighs before I patted the left side Nightshade's neck. We lived alone too long; he hated the smell of people, any people.

I spoke to the warriors in a quiet voice, "I am on a hard journey that could take many days. I could use food and a small canteen of water. I have gold coins to trade for them."

The warrior shook his head. "We will give you food and water for three days, but we have no use for gold."

It was evident the name of Venom still brought fear to the younger warriors while stirring hate from the older ones. Young women and children unloaded the provisions from the tent poles when we rode into camp. The married women and braves raised poles for their tents while the elders started the fires. Dark shadows floated across the camp as the sun fell. The tents would be up soon and the camp would be swarming with the laughter of children and the sounds of music.

The Apache had no use for gold, but I managed to trade a Green River steel knife for a strong bow made from a hedge tree limb and a dozen arrows carved from the same wood. The bright-yellow arrow shafts carried dark red feathers from the wings of a black bird on one end while the other end held black flint tips. I draped the bowstring across the saddle horn while sliding the arrows into a ratty, worn quiver a child threw at me when I left the village. The laughter of children echoed across the desert while the scent of cooking food carried from their fires.

I missed the joy of children's laughter, but I was not welcome. They still called me Venom. I was an outcast from the Apache people, and would be for as long as the tip of my spear still held the stains of a red man's blood.

Nightshade moved in silence with his ears pricked forward through the camp of the Apache. True, they were not his enemy, but they were not friends. The buzzing of a Western Diamondback rattler caught my ear as we threaded through a long line of buffalo hide tents. I needed the snake for more than just a meal. Groups of children, some playing with dolls made from cornhusks, moved out of my way after I dismounted to search between the tents, seeking the deadly snake.

I confronted an old woman with streaks of gray in her hair as she headed towards the cooking pots. She held the snake's head in one hand while its body wrapped itself around her arm.

"I will give you two pieces of gold for the snake," I offered.

She stared at me for several moments before she spoke in a low guttural rasp. "What does Venom woman want with a snake?"

To lie would do no good, so I told her the truth.

"I will use it to kill bad men," I told her. "How many, I don't know."

"Who are they?"

"I don't know that either," I answered. "They are scalp hunters. I believe they have stolen a child from the Miller ranch. I hope to kill them before they kill her."

The old woman handed me the snake. "How will you kill them with this?"

"I will milk the venom onto rags before rubbing the venom into the arrow shafts. After that, I will tie the rags behind the head of the arrows. Even if the poison doesn't kill them, it will make them sick enough for me to walk up to them, slitting their throats. With that done, we will see what will happen." I slipped two gold coins from my pocket to hand them to the old woman.

"Keep them," she snarled, waving my hand away. "Scalp hunters deserve no better than a slow death. If I could, I would join you," she shot back, "but I am old." She turned toward the fire before I strode away with the snake.

We returned to the hunt with Nightshade leading the way.

There was no sign I could follow, and no trail I could see, so I had to trust Nightshade followed a blood trail drifting in the air. The burning sand of the desert drifted in waves as we moved from shadow to shadow looking for whatever shade we could find. After three days without rain, the water from the Apache's hadn't lasted long. We needed fresh water, the same as the men we hunted.

It wasn't deep impressions of hoof prints in the sand or the long, slender tracks of a wagon that alerted me that we drew close to the scalp hunters. The stench of rotting flesh drifted in the air; it made me want to stop and vomit. Their rancid stench signaled the wagons were full; the scalp hunters were heading home. It wouldn't be long before any child with them would be tortured and raped. Afterwards, they would scalp the children, leaving them to die. The fragments of her scalp would carry the story of her life and death; with the selling of her hair, the scalp would carry on her story.

I sensed a shadow behind me; it moved with the clouds, drifting in the wind. Someone followed me, they were little more than specks of sand shifting with the breeze, but I knew they were there—they tread upon my soul.

This was no land for pilgrims or for the weak. The men following slipped between the shadows; they moved as silently as a sidewinder across sand. They were Apache; they were as deadly as the venom riding on the shaft of my arrows.

"You keep going," I whispered to Nightshade, "I have to get off." I slipped from the saddle into the shadows. This was a game I had played as many times as the sun had risen and as many times as it had fallen; it was a game I was good at and I loved. Like the Apache, this was the game I was born for. I slid from shadow to shadow with the poison-tipped arrows in my grasp. The voices of young men whispered in the dark like the soft fluttering of bat wings.

"Why do we follow a woman into battle?" one of them asked.

Another growled the answer. "Because Buffalo Calf told us to," he said, "If we don't, we will be in big trouble with her."

The name of Buffalo Calf had come to me before. Her legend claimed she walked the Trail of Tears as a child and survived. Her legend also claimed she knocked yellow hair from his horse at the Battle of Washita. She stepped out from a tent behind Custer, striking him with a coup-stick. His troopers rallied to him, which stalled Custer's attack long enough for the Arapaho and Comanche to gather, preventing the complete annihilation of the Cheyenne after his troopers killed Black Kettle. Young braves stood in silence at her counsel. She became a legend in her own time; a woman feared and respected.

I stepped from the shadows with the poisoned arrows in my hand.

"Why would Buffalo Calf want you to ride with me?" I snarled, "I am called Venom, a woman of two bloods. I am the enemy of the white man and the red. Why do you follow me?"

Three young braves stood in silence, not believing a half-breed sneaked into their counsel to threaten their lives. The youngest one spoke first.

"I am called Bright Eyes. My grandmother gave you the snake for the poison. She gazed into your eyes. She recognized the same pain in your eyes she suffered throughout her own life. She said you are a good person but life has put a fire in your heart, in your soul, that you cannot quench. 'You are the warrior most braves strive to become but will never be' were her words. She ordered us to go find you so that you may teach us the ways of life and of death."

I stared at three children who had never seen battle; to refuse them was impossible. It would bring the wrath of Buffalo Calf and the Apache Nation with it. I was stuck with children I did not need or want.

"You are my posse," I whispered. "If you live through the next few days you will become warriors. If not, I will fill in your graves."

Four savages with the blood of the Apache in their veins rode as one. We were a posse, not in the eyes of the white man's laws, but in our own laws; and with us, would come true justice.

Bright Eyes was the youngest, Stands Still was next, and then, Never Runs.

"Gather your horses," I instructed, "then follow me. The stench of the scalp hunters is in the air. We will catch up with their wagons before the moon crests over the top of the mountains."

Three Apache children rode behind me; this was a game to them—they had never taken a life. They never felt the cold blade of steel cutting through their flesh and bone, or reeled under the sledgehammer blow of a bullet striking their body. This was new to them, but to the men we followed, it was an everyday thing.

The scalp hunters lived on the edge of death; it was their closest companion, their mother, and their child. They lived for the kill of an elk, a buffalo, or a man.

I left the young warriors in a dry wash, while I climbed to the top of a hill to scout the area. Below me, a string of tired horses dragged three wagons through cactus, brambles, and sand dunes. Pile upon pile of buffalo hides and human hair rode upon wagons, drenched in blood. Behind one of the wagons, a string of children followed, tied together with rawhide straps and ropes made from human hair.

A few of the children were as young as three years while others were close to nine. They were a part of the stench we followed for so many miles. I learned to hate the odor. Tonight, while they slept, we would take our revenge for the lives the scalp hunters' had taken. Bright Eyes sneaked close beside me.

"How are we going to do this?" he asked. "If we attack in daylight, they will kill the children, taking their scalps for the money."

"We will avoid a direct fight," I replied. "Tonight, I will sneak in to take the children away first, setting fire to the camp as I leave." I pointed to where we expected to leave the children.

"Do not let any of the hunters survive," I growled. "If you do, I will have to hunt them later to finish what we started. If even one of them escapes, he will bring others in vengeance. Your village will be destroyed along with your loved ones."

Bright Eyes slipped a steel blade from his belt, cutting the thorns from a desert rose. He rubbed the blood-red flower across his chest in the shape of a star.

"White man's justice," he snarled. "Today, the scalp hunters will meet theirs." One by one, the young Apaches moved the bleeding red flower across their chests. They had become my posse. I didn't know if this was a good day to die, but they were ready to die at my orders.

"Gather brush to start the fire," I ordered. "When the moon is hidden behind the clouds, I will move forward to steal the children back from the white savages." I showed the others the dry arroyo where I planned to hide the children. "Once they are safely hidden, we will kill these animals who find pleasure in hunting and torturing children." I shifted to my cache, planning to offer poison tipped arrows, but the young men shook their heads.

They pointed to the belts around their waists; they wore new belts made from the skin of snakes.

"We're not stupid." Never Runs laughed. "We have learned. Buffalo Calf told us about the snake, how you used the venom. We figure if it's good medicine for you, it's good medicine for us. It's time the scalp hunters receive what they give."

The men before me may have been young, but they were smart as well. I had no doubt they had laced their arrows with the snake's deadly venom.

The golden rays of a dying sun reflected orange and red against the grains of sand along the desert floor as it dropped behind the bulk of the mountains. The bright, red flames from their campfire dwindled into the darkness of the night, leaving only ashes.

While we watched, the last of the scalp hunters curled into buffalo-hide blankets. Within minutes, they fell asleep, leaving only the guards awake. Bright Eyes stood with a steel-blade knife in his hands. Stands Still and Never Runs held the poison-tipped arrows. The last of the camp's lights faded while the howl of a prowling wolf fell silent.

"The moon will rise soon," I whispered. "We have to make this quick." I drew my thumb across my throat. "Kill the guards in silence with your blades. Then meet me on top of the ridge. If they are able to fight back, that is where we will make our stand."

Without a word, three novice warriors slipped into the darkness. They were less than shadows drifting with the wind; tonight they were the souls and hearts of a thousand dead Apache warriors—they were on the hunt.

The fires of my own blood ran cold as I crept towards the dying embers of the fire, seeking the children tied behind the wagon.

"Hush," I whispered as I drew close to the line of children. "We came to free you." The blade of my knife cut through the thin strips of leather before I gathered the children around me. Soft layers of sand muffled our steps, as we slunk away from the wagons into the shadows of the night.

"Keep walking," I whispered as I pointed to the arroyo. "Wait for us there," I said before I turned to leave, "I have one last task to do."

I sneaked into their camp, setting the blade of my knife against a guard's throat. My hand covered his mouth as I whispered in his ear, "You kill women and children, you torture the innocent, and you rape for money. You enjoy the death of others. Now, enjoy your own death." I sliced the blade across his throat, enjoying the warm, sticky blood as it ran across my hand to drip on the ground. His death had been silent, so I laid his body on the ground before I ran into the main camp with the poisoned arrows in my hand, jabbing one into each sleeping man. They would learn soon enough that they were already dead.

I glimpsed Never Runs, Bright Eyes, and Stands Still running towards the sleeping men with poisoned arrows in their hands. They followed the ways of the warrior, showing no mercy to the hunters of children as they drove the arrows deep into the hunters, letting the poison flow as the blood soaked the poisoned rags. The cries of the dying would become the silence of the dead.

Three hours later, we laid the bodies of the scalpers under the wagons before we set fire to the camp; their bodies burned with the hides and hair.

My name would grow with the telling of the story. I would become known as Venom, a half-breed of the Apache tribe, an outcast to her people. I carried the blood of two nations in my veins, and I was the leader of a savage posse.

The End

From the Author:

Thank you for reading Jim's story, The Savage Posse. Jim writes stories the old-fashioned way—taking pages from his and his family's life stories. Jim's stories have been honed by telling these tales to his children and now his grandchildren. The Oral tradition dates back to man's earliest times. If you liked the Jim's story, please leave a review, so other will know this a path well worth walking.

We hope you enjoyed reading Jim's story. Please look for Jim's stories on Amazon.

Biography

At twenty-six, Sherlene and I became husband and wife
and it's been a great life. We have three
children, ten grandchildren and now two
great-grandchildren. Together we've
worked logging timber everywhere from
the hot humid swamps of Louisiana to the
frozen snow covered mountains of Canada.

I write about how it feels to have the
cold blade of steel cut through flesh and
muscle and how it sounds as it grinds
across bone. I write about the sledgehammer like blows from
the soft lead of a bullet shattering bone and cartilage, seeking
to take a life. I write about these things because I have lived
through them. I never learned to write in a school or classroom,
life has been my teacher, and that is how I write.

Here is a list of his books:

"The Old Rider, Death of an Outlaw"
"Nightmare at Saint Francis"
"When Dragons Wake"
"Nosferatu, Bird of Death"
https://www.amazon.com/SILENCE-DRUMS-JS-
Stroud/dp/1482794624

https://www.amazon.com/Hard-Ride-JS-
Stroud/dp/1523844302

TO SET A THIEF
Chuck Tyrell

There I stood, leaning on the bar, enjoying a cool beer in the Monarch saloon when the Apache County Sheriff, J.B. Hubbell, stormed through the swinging doors. He held a 10-gauge Greener, its hammers cocked. The dark sheen of the double-barrels matched Hubbell's dark scowl.

"A little bird told me I'd find Mort Eggertson drinkin' in the Monarch, and, sure enough, I did. I'd purely appreciate if you shed that there Remington Army. Step away from the Winchester ya got leaning against the wall."

I raised my hands, a hard thing for a man like me. But I put them up, keeping them away from the Remington Army revolver in a cross-draw belly holster. I didn't let 'em stray toward the One-of-One-Thousand Winchester '73, the most accurate rifle that company makes.

"What're ya hassling me for, Sheriff?" I called in a louder voice than necessary. "What for? I ain't done nothing but have a beer."

"I got a flyer on you, Eggertson. Says you shot a man in Holbrook. Shot him when he never had a gun. Shot him even though he wasn't outta diapers for mor'n a few years. Yeah,

Eggertson, you never shoulda shot Ronny James. I'll just put you into my hoosegow until Marshal Meade can come to fetch you."

"He'll have to be awful quick, Sheriff, 'cuz Garland Wilkins's got business with me. He's not gonna stand for me being shut up like some kinda criminal."

"Shut up, Eggertson. Nobody never broke outta my jail. Nobody. Come on."

"You want me to leave my irons laying where they can get rusty? You oughta be civil enough to carry 'em to jail with me. Oughtn't you?"

"George," Sheriff Hubbell said to a deputy who hid behind him, hoping I might not notice him. "George, you step around here. Go relieve Mr. Eggertson of his weapons, ya hear?"

"Aw, Sheriff. Mort Eggertson killed a boy in Holbrook. Don't want that he should kill me. I'm too young to die, I surely am."

I raised my voice again. "George, my friend, you can gather these guns a mine, but be right careful with them. I'd hate to have any damage done to 'em. I'll need them to work right when I get 'em back. Come on, boy."

George sidled around the sheriff and his big shotgun. He grabbed my Winchester before fishing my Remington from its holster. I made no move to stop him. Woulda done me no good if I had of. "You all watch out. When Garland Wilkins and his men come to get me outta jail, you'll be sorry if ya don't take good care of me."

During my loud speechifying, I kept an eye on the men drinking in the Monarch. A feller never can tell if the Wilkins gang is nearby. Like as not, someone connected with Wilkins stood close enough to listen. They'd learn from him if he wanted me busted out.

A bridge across the Little Colorado put Saint Johns on the map, the only crossing this side of Grant's Crossing. Mexicans lived in the bottoms while Mormons lived on the heights where they tended their fields, watered by ditches running from an upstream dam. In between, the Saint Johns' Ring ruled the town. If not the ringleader, Hubbell sounded the bell for the Ringers.

Sheriff Hubbell marched me from the Monarch fifty yards along Commerce Street to the jail, right in the middle of town. Another fifty yards'd take me to the town limits. "You open the door, Eggertson. It ain't locked."

I did, while observing nobody occupied any of the three cells.

"You take the middle one, Eggertson. Don't want you close to a window."

"Why's that, Sheriff? Figure someone'll bust me out?" I laughed at my own lame joke.

Hubbell spat out the door. "Somethin' like that," he said. He never had a sense of humor.

"Well, I can tell you. Garland's coming. He surely is. You'd better get ready for hard times, Sheriff."

Hubbell ignored me while he grabbed a ring of keys from the wall. He unlocked the barred iron door on the center cell.

I sauntered inside. The door clanked shut behind me.

"George, you git on home. Git some shuteye," the Sheriff said. "Come relieve me at midnight. You'll watch Eggertson until morning."

"Yes, sir." George stacked my Winchester in the gun rack before he hung my gun rig holding the Remington on a nail in the wall. He squinted at me, pulling the corners of his fat-lipped mouth into a frown. He shook a fat finger at me. "I'll be back."

"Maybe I won't be here, George. Maybe Gar Wilkins'll a broke me out by then. Better hope you ain't here when he comes. I'd hate to see ya mess your pants."

George slammed the door on his way outside.

Hubbell sat at his desk, reading by the light of a coal oil lamp, and writing in his tally book. After a while, he stood, clomping to my cell in his high-heeled riding boots, not that he'd ever roped a steer. "I'm gonna go do my rounds, Eggertson. You'll stay put if ya have a brain in your head."

"Yeah. If Garland comes along with his strong-arms, you'll be sorry you ever put me up in this poor excuse of a jailhouse."

"You stay put, hear?"

I didn't favor him with an answer. I plopped on the iron bunk that hung from the wall by quarter-inch chains. Hubbell turned the lamp low before he snugged the door shut behind him. The clatter of his high-heeled boots along the boardwalk toward the Barth Hotel faded. Tired, I lay on the bunk, covered my face with my hat, and waited for Garland Wilkins's boys to spring me.

"Hey. Eggertson. Hey. You awake?" a voice called in from the alley-side window.

"Don't holler," I said. "You'll wake the whole town."

"Stand back. We're gonna blow the Hell outta this jail's wall."

"Don't waste your powder. Sheriff's gone on rounds. If you hurry, you can walk right in, unlock the cell door, and get me outta here."

"Huh? Just walk in? That ain't no fun." The voice whined like a kid learning there'd be no fireworks on the Fourth of July.

"Come on. Never know when Hubbell's gonna get back."

Two dark forms sneaked through the door. "Hey. Where's the keys?"

"Hanging on a peg behind the desk."

"Oh. Yeah, I see 'em."

The keys tinkled before footsteps scuffed across the board floor in the dark. Whoever came to my cell hadn't bathed in a month or so, given his fragrance. A key clanked in the lock.

"Shit. Ain't the right one," Stinky said.

"Only three, man. Try another," I said.

The key clicked. The cell door opened, setting me free.

"Thanks." I shook Stinky's hand. "Let's get outta here. I got news for Garland Wilkins." I pulled my Winchester from the rifle rack before grabbing my gun belt on the way out.

"Horses 're behind the jail," Stinky said, a short, slight shadow of a man. "Let's move."

"Lead on." I followed Stinky around the jailhouse. Standing a might over six feet, I weigh in the neighborhood of one-ninety. Most of it in my chest and shoulders, which means I need a hefty horse. These owlhoots planned ahead, bringing me a sorrel gelding, standing more than sixteen hands at the withers. They said their names while I adjusted my stirrups.

"I'm Cy Gibson," Stinky said, "an' he's Jesse Simmons."

I nodded. "Cy, Jesse." Then we forked them cayuses and lit a shuck. No one fired a shot. Cy and Jesse seemed glad to get away without gunplay.

"Where we going?" I asked while we rode away from Saint Johns, heading south.

"Heading east through Alpine," Cy said. "Then around the Escudilla before moving south to Alma. Gar'll be waitin' there. Says y'all 're bringing word of a herd comin' down the Trail."

"Yep," I said, "but I'll talk about that to Garland. Meantime, we'd better push it. From all I hear about Hubbell, he'll be after us with a dozen riders soon as he finds you busted me out. Lead on."

Cy took the lead, heading up an arroyo toward Mormon Road. The waters that carved the gulch left only rocks, making the trail a rough one. About halfway, Cy's squat paint horse stepped into a hidden crevasse in those rocks, and broke its leg. We had no choice but to end the poor critter's misery. They ain't no way to fix a horse's broken leg. We cut its throat, not wanting to risk a gunshot.

"Hubbell's a coming, boys," I said. "Cy, cache your saddle and tack behind the rocks. Ride double with Jess. Is there anywhere close we can get another horse?"

"Gib Brewer's place along Sycamore Canyon," Cy said. "He's always ready with a cayuse."

"Sounds good. If we're gonna beat Hubbell's posse, we can't have ya ridin' double," I said.

After caching Cy's gear, we slow-walked the horses through the arroyo to top out above Valle Rondo. Sunrise lit the sky from behind the ridge over toward New Mexico.

Daylight brought the aroma of frying bacon. "Smell that?" I said.

"What?" Cy asked.

"Bacon, I reckon." I pulled in a deep lungful of mountain air. "Yep. Bacon. Let's go have a look-see."

We eased off the Mormon Road into Sycamore Canyon, walking our horses in the soft grass and making as little noise as possible. Maybe fifty yards away from whoever cooked that bacon, I dismounted the sorrel, pulling my One-of-One-Thousand Winchester from its saddle scabbard. Through the sunrise haze, a little girl stood at the cook-fire. A woman, maybe, but as short as a schoolgirl. When she finished cooking, she swiped a hot biscuit in the bacon grease in the pan. The paint mare in the holding pen whickered, spoiling the moment. The girl reached for her rifle.

"Lay the rifle on the ground real slow, little lady," I said. "Real slow." I eared back the hammer of that almighty accurate Winchester.

She dropped the rifle like a hot poker, then stumbled back like her knees might be shaking.

"That's a good girl. That grub you've fixed smells right fine. Got enough for visitors?"

"Quit lollygagging around, Mort. All we need is her mare," Cy said.

The girl dipped her head before pivoting to face us.

My neck jerked stiff while my jaw dropped. *Cuter than a bug's ear* flew into my mind.

"Your mounts look like they need a rest and time to graze," she said. "I can feed the three of you while those poor horses are eating, too."

We musta been a sight. Three bad men who'd not seen a razor for at least three days. All with cocked guns in hand.

The girl shrugged. "From what he said, you must be Mort Eggertson."

"I am," I said.

"My brother told me you was in jail. How come?"

"Killed a man," I answered, frowning.

Her face grew just as hard as mine. "Then you deserved jail."

"Ah, but he'd of killed me if I'd been a hair slower with my Remington. They say he wasn't heeled, but he had a hideout Derringer." I waved the Winchester a bit, but not far enough for her to get any ideas about going for the rifle again.

"Come on, Mort. That posse of Hubbell's cain't be all that far behind us. Let's git."

"I could whip up a bit more bacon and biscuits if you want," she said.

I reckon she thought to stall us to let the posse catch up.

She wore a six-gun, but unbuckled the rig to lay it by the rifle. "Just to keep you from getting the wrong idea and shooting me. Ain't got no hideout, neither."

"You don't seem all that scared of us, Missy," I said.

"Mr. Eggertson, you give me the feel of a better man than you carry on. If you were all that bad, I'd be dead. I reckon you don't like killing. Maybe you've rode with a posse your own self." She talked big, but a little tremble hid in her voice.

I smiled. Women say I'm good looking, but I never gave it a thought 'til she smiled at me.

She took the biscuit and bacon from the frying pan, placing it on the grub box. Then she built another sandwich from what remained. She handed it to me, but I gave it to Jess Simmons. He took a big ol' bite. He hadn't eaten in nearly a day, and it showed.

"Go ahead, Missy. Fix some grub." I held the Remington on her. No sense taking chances.

She stirred more biscuit dough. Quicker than you can say whodunnit, she made biscuit and bacon sandwiches for us. While we ate, she went to setting a coffeepot on the fire. Always did like good coffee.

When it steamed, she filled a cup, handing it to me. "Only got one tin cup. The other men'll have to wait on you."

I took the cup, tasting her coffee. "Strong enough to melt horseshoes," I said. "Just my style." I slugged it down before I returned the cup. She filled it, giving it to me; I passed it to Cy.

"What's your name, Missy?" I asked.

"Kimberly," she said, "but everyone calls me Kid."

"Kid what?"

"Kid McCullough."

I couldn't help taking half a step back from her. "You kin to the McCulloughs south of Alpine?"

"Family," she said. "You been around here long, you'd know 'em. They're my brothers. There's Kane and Kenigan. Then there's Kris. I bring up the rear. Oh, yeah, my pa's Kieran McCullough."

"Mustangers," I said.

"Among other pursuits."

"Well, Kid," I said. "We're gonna have to borrow your paint mare."

She didn't say anything, but anyone looking at the set of her jaw and her squinting eye, knew her pot steamed.

"I'm not going to die," I said, "when I've done nothing wrong."

She just stared at me.

"If I didn't kill that man, I'd of been killed myself. A man has a right to protect himself."

"Come on, Mort. The kid don't make no never mind. If we got this much time, might be good to go a round with this here girl." Cy, a runt of a man, stood a couple inches taller than the kid, but he held a full-sized Smith & Wesson Russian in his hand.

"No need for fireworks, Cy," I said. "We don't do little girls. No real man does that. Put your hogleg away. Go saddle that paint mare. Jess can stay on the bay. I'll ride the sorrel."

Jesse's big-eyed face said he'd like to go a round with Kimberly, too. I may be a killer, but my mother brought me up to respect women, even little ones like her.

When I told Cy to saddle her mare, the Kid's face grew red and her nostrils flared.

"I'll get the paint." She didn't want us in with her half-broke black filly, that's for sure. At the gate, she pursed her lips to whistle. The paint trotted to the kid, nice as you please. She slipped a bridle on the paint mare to led her from the pen.

"Nice filly," I said, studying the black in the holding pen. "Really nice. Cy, grab the lady's saddle to plop on the mare. Let's get outta here. Jess, see what she's got in the way of stores."

"Bacon, beans, coffee, flour," Jesse called. He hoisted the gunnysack with the kid's stores in it, tying the sack behind the cantle of his saddle.

"Okay," I said. "Kimberly, those goods'll keep us going for a while. Sorry to take your stuff, but with it we might stay out of that posse's way. We'll hit the badlands if we have to, and make a run for the Rio. Now, if you'd please turn around, placing your hands behind your back ...."

With three six-guns staring her in the face, there wasn't much Kimberly McCullough could do but turn around. After tying her hands behind her back with a piggin' string, I made her lie on the ground. I rolled her onto her side, tied her ankles, and looped them to her wrists. She couldn't get up. I had her trussed like a dogie calf ready for branding.

"Kimberly," I said.

She glared Bowie knives at me.

"We didn't take your black filly, and we never hurt you. Remember that, Kid."

"Time to get outta here," I said before I forked the big sorrel. We left at a trot, headed toward Sheep's Crossing. From there, we could go south to Alpine, around Escudilla Mountain, and on to Alma across the New Mexico border.

Kimberly McCullough lay on her side, all tied up. She might be smart enough to work her way outta those piggin' string knots, but she'd not be telling anybody about us for a long time. Even when she gets loose, it'll take her a while to get the black filly trained enough to ride from the plateau to her daddy's place below Alpine. Of course, I left her the camp knife she used to slice bacon. I left it sticking in the log where she'd put it after slicing hog belly for breakfast. Yeah, she had more than an even chance of getting clean away. That's the way I planned it. I'm not about to kill a woman, especially not one as young and fetching as Kimberly McCullough.

The early morning sun lifted into the sky, bringing the day's heat. The paint mare Kimberly called Patches made a good mount for the runty Cy. Jess stayed atop the mountain-bred bay that rode from Saint Johns. I liked the tough sorrel gelding Cy and Jess had brought for me. For a horse of more than sixteen hands, he rode easy, even while stepping around rocks and dodging cactus and Manzanita. The three fine mounts left us sitting pretty. We held a steady pace across the New Mexico line to Alma. When the sun hit the western horizon, it plastered the sky with the gold and orange of a true Arizona mountain sunset. I found this high country to my liking. It got me to thinking once I finished the job at hand, I'd pay it another visit. I promised myself to do that, returning for my own piece of land in the high country, and a chance to call on that kid called Kimberly McCullough. If I could just pull this job off with Garland Wilkins ....

With nary a hint of trouble, we rode past Escudilla Mountain. Our back trail showed no dust signs of Sheriff Hubbell and his posse, but we didn't stop to camp. After resting the horses at a water hole, we grabbed pieces of bacon from what we took of Kimberly's stores. In the saddle, we chomped on bacon, riding through the night. The sky brightened before the sunrise when we caught sight of Alma, a town once called Mogollon. If my luck still held, Garland Wilkins waited for news of a cattle herd coming south along the Outlaw Trail.

Cy Gibson gigged the spurs to Patches, making her bolt like a scared rabbit. 'Twas all Jess and me could do to keep him in sight. By the time we rode along the main drag, Patches stood hipshot in front of the Red Hen, leaving no doubt Cy had gone inside.

The sun had yet to crack the horizon, but the Red Hen already smelled of breakfast—coffee and biscuits, bacon and eggs, and even those breakfast T-bones. Reining in, Jess and me lined our cayuses alongside Patches, looping the reins a turn on the hitching rack before following the aroma of frying food flowing from the Red Hen.

"'Bout time y'all got yer cracker asses in here," Cy hollered. "Come on, the coffee's good and the eats is better."

Jess and me grabbed chairs at Cy's table, nodding at the heavy-set waitress when she asked if we wanted coffee. "Tell me, ya got hen fruit and sowbelly?" I asked.

"We do. All you can eat, this time of the morning. What'll it be?"

"Three aigs, over easy, half a dozen slices of sow belly, fried up crinkly and crisp, and four biscuits," I said. "Butter'd be nice, too."

"No butter," she said, "but I can dip yer biscuits in bacon grease."

"That'll do," I said.

"Gimme the same as him," Jesse said before gulping a big mouthful of coffee. His bright-eyed smile said the coffee tasted better than okay. I'd hardly gulped a mouthful of my coffee, when a broad-shouldered, square-jawed man pushed the door open before stepping inside the Red Hen.

Cy and Jess jumped to their feet when the newcomer strode across the room to our table. "Cy," he said, nodding at them. "Jess. This here Mort Eggertson?"

I sat still. "I'm Mort Eggertson," I said. "Lately of J.B. Hubbell's jailhouse."

"This here's the boss," Cy said. "Garland Wilkins. What he says, goes."

I stood to stick out my hand. "Pleased," I said, but he ignored my hand.

"Tell me about the herd," he said.

"Yeah, well, there ain't too many, maybe a hundred head, coming from north of Moab, down the Trail. Should be here in a couple of days. You mix them with yours, keep half the payoff. I'll take the other half of the cash up the Trail to Isom Dart. He'll deliver it to where it's supposed to go."

"That right? Well. We'll see when those cows get here." He shifted around to leave.

Cy gawked at Jess. Jess raised an eyebrow at Cy. They shrugged.

"Looks like we'll see," Jess said.

"Garland Wilkins's the hard man folks say he is," I said. "But I got cows coming along the Trail. Bet you a silver dollar, they're prime. You wait and see."

"Plan to. Plan to." Cy said, going back to eating.

I drank another gulp of Red Hen's good coffee.

"So you're gonna take cash back up the Trail? Gonna pay someone up there?" Jesse's eyes'd gone all hard on me.

"Look," I said. "A herd like that starts with a few cows up the Trail, maybe all the way up to Rustler's Roost. An outfit starts them cows down the Trail, taking them forty or fifty miles, and another outfit shows up with a few more cows. Adds a few more all the way down here. I reckon MS-Bar men'll be trailing the herd when it gets here. Maybe a hundred cows, all different brands. My job's to set the herd up with Garland Wilkins so he can sell 'em for a good price. He takes his share and I pass the rest on up the Trail to Isom Dart. You know of him, people call him the Outlaw Mail. That way, people who supplied the cows'll get what they're owed. See?"

Jesse nodded and sat down.

The herd moseyed south from Mexican Hat, through Navajo Spring before following along the Little Colorado. It skirted Saint Johns and J.B. Hubbell to arrive outside Alma three days after I rode in with Cy and Jess. Moving a herd of a hundred cows, you're lucky to get fifteen miles a day, twenty on a good one, but beeves needed feed, so where they found grazing grass, the cows moved slower.

Garland Wilkins found me at the Lone Pine, the only drinking place in Alma I found decent.

"Eggertson," he hollered when he came in the door. "That herd you bragged about? It's about two days out. Looks like WS-Bar cowboys are pushing it along."

"They'll do it right," I said. "You can use them to go on to Mexico or wherever, or you can use your own cowboys." Learning the herd arrived made my day.

"Reckon I'll ride out to have a look. Be good if you'd come along."

"Sure thing," I said.

"Let's go," Wilkins barked at me.

Wilkins smiled after checking the herd's cows. "We'll take 'em," he told the WS-Bar foreman, a man called Beardsley.

"We'll hold 'em here 'til yer boys get here," Beardsley said.

Garland Wilkins and his gang, me included, took over from the WS-Bar hands.

"We've got about this many cows on the other side of Alma," Wilkins said. "Be best to run 'em all together. It'll be a long trail down through Canyon Diablo, but we've done it lots of times. Won't be worse with more cows, won't at all." He doffed his hat to scratch his head. "Mort ... " First time he ever called me that ... "I'd like you to ride along with us, help with them cows."

"I can do that," I said. "Got to get the pay for them cows back to Isom Dart, might as well start at the beginning."

Wilkins spoke the words I'd been waiting to hear. That night, before we rode away from Alma, I wrote a letter to my girl, Cynthia, in Charleston, Arizona. I didn't tell her all that much, only that I planned to drive cattle. I promised to find a pretty rock for her collection when I rode through Canyon Diablo. I sealed the note, sending it by Wells Fargo. Hoped she'd get it all right.

After a week, I'd grew more than a little saddle weary. I pulled nightrider two times on the way toward Mexico. The camp cook's grub rated the worst I ever ate—no big surprise.

The big surprise happened in the middle of Diablo Canyon. Texas John Slaughter and his posse waited for us in the narrowest section of the canyon. They lined up across the canyon about halfway mark to Mexico. Slaughter shut the door behind us with another line of sworn-in posse.

Texas John lived up to his reputation as a hard-as-nails lawman. He captured ever one of them rustlers, me included, without having to kill a one. Then he took us to the county jail in Bisbee. Ten cells for twenty rustlers. After he locked us in, he jangled the keys and showed a wolfish grin. "Sure good to have you rustlers under lock and key," he said. "Ranchers from here all the way to Moab have complained and complained about missing cows, but no one could ever catch the rustlers. Till now, anyway. I reckon you all know what us western folk do to rustlers, don't you? I expect the judge'll order the gallows built any day now."

Whispers passed as chatter between inmates at Cochise County jail. Someone started pounding on wood outside, around the corner where none of us inmates could see. A scaffold? A hanging tree? The noise stopped whispers.

Texas John came stomping to the cells, two deputies behind him, armed with double-barreled sawed-off shotguns. "Which one a you rustlers is Mort Eggertson?"

Half the rustlers pointed their fingers at me.

"Why?" I asked. "What do you want with me?"

"Ain't me what wants you, Eggertson. It's Marshal Meade. U.S. Marshal Meade. Seems you've left a string of dead men behind you all the way from Fort Benton on the Missouri. You're bigger than anything this county sheriff can handle. I gotta turn you over to Marshal Meade. No two-ways about it."

"Boys," he said to the two deputies, "You keep them scatterguns on them rustlers. If any makes an unseemly move, blast 'em." He unlocked the door to our cell, jerking his head at me to step out. I did. "Stick you hands out, Eggertson." I did. He cuffed me before he slammed the door, and then locked it.

"Tell your friends, adios. You won't see them again," he said to me. "Come on. Marshal Meade's a waiting." Enough to make a man sweat.

Slaughter led me from the cell as the Wilkins gang murmured, "Tough luck, Mort. Keep yer chin high."

I kept my chin high.

Big John and his two deputies marched me to the new county courthouse, the one with the spire-like cupola on its roof, before entering its front door. Once inside, out of sight from the street, Slaughter removed the cuffs to shake my hand. "I give you Pinkerton agents credit. That's a long time to ride with a bunch like that and come out alive. Your horses are out back, and you're free to go. We'll take care of the Wilkins Gang, never you worry. And thanks. Thanks for sending that letter to Charleston. It came through just fine. If it's all right, I'd admire to know your name."

"Russell Taklin," I said.

He shook my hand again, touching the brim of his hat. "One more thing, Russ," he said. He pulled an envelope from an inside vest pocket. "This here's a bank draft to the Hashknife Outfit up in Holbrook. They furnished most of the cows. Their owner, Burt Mossman, will make sure the moola gets to the right people. Can you do that for me?"

I touched my hat brim. "You bet."

I rode away on the sorrel; I figured I'd earned him. I also led Patches, because I'd promised to return her to Kimberly; at least, I promised myself.

More than a month later, I delivered Slaughter's bank draft to Mossman. That job completed, I resigned from Pinkerton's. I carried a bank draft of my own. Reward money for setting up the capture of Wilkins's gang and other funds I saved during my undercover service. I'm not much of a drinker. The Great Missouri Steamship Race of 1870 showed me not to wager money.

Riding my tall-shouldered sorrel, armed with the bank draft, I figured myself ready to find a place in the White Mountains. The sorrel, Patches, and me rode across the meadow towards the McCullough place.

As I remember, it happened on May first. Typical of Arizona, the sun shone bright in azure skies. A man could fall in love with this country, easy.

Ahead, Old Man McCullough sat on the porch while I walked the horses along the valley. Kimberly stuck her head around the corner to gawk at the visitor. When she saw me, she made a beeline for the house, bolting from the front door holding a Winchester. She jacked a shell into the chamber, cocking the hammer.

I raised my hands, but I let the horses keep on going.

"Put the rifle down, Kid," Old Man McCullough said when I came closer.

Kimberly glared at her pa, all but snorting fire. "That's the man who tied me up and left me to rot in Sycamore Canyon." She kept the rifle to her shoulder.

Kimberly's pa spoke a little more conviction. "Do what I say, girl."

She lowered the rifle, but left it cocked.

I stopped Red, my name for the sorrel, about twenty-five feet from the house. "Morning, Mr. McCullough." I think I sounded respectful, because I wanted his respect. Everyone I know who knows Kieran McCullough respected him.

"Howdy, Russ," he said, "ain't seen you since Fort Lancaster. Never did thank you for what you did."

"Russ?" Kimberly screamed. "That's not Russ. That's Mort Eggertson. A thief and a killer."

I crossed my hands on top of my saddle horn. I spoke straight to that riled-up woman. "I apologize for what we did up on the mountain, Kimberly. My name is Russell Taklin. I worked for the Pinkerton Agency. You know the saying, 'you gotta set a thief to catch a thief'? We set up the Saint Johns jailbreak. The Wilkins gang accepted me as an outlaw. I got in good with a bunch of rustlers working out of Alma, New Mexico." I took off my hat and ran my fingers through my hair, which had grown a little long for a man figuring to go a-courting.

"I learned they smuggled cattle through Canyon Diablo into Mexico. I sent word to Sheriff Slaughter in Cochise County in a letter. Texas John and his men caught that gang of rustlers this side of the Mexican border. Ranchers in Arizona and New Mexico and even Utah and Colorado won't have to worry about the Wilkins gang no more."

I offered her the lead rope to the paint mare. "Here is Patches. I brought her back to you."

Kimberly scowled.

"Kimberly, listen. You, too, if you please, Mr. McCullough. This Arizona high country has got under my skin. I've got my eye on a couple of sections up on Big Diamond Creek. I'm going to buy them, figuring to build me a home up there. Kimberly, I hope you won't mind if I come here to visit once in a while."

She turned bright red.

"You'd be welcome, Russ," Kieran McCullough said.

"How do you know him? When did he become Russ?" she asked, with hands on her hips.

"Ten years ago, your brother Kenigan got framed by a crooked sheriff. They had the trial before I found out what happened." Her pa eased from the chair to stand against a post. "Turns out Wells Fargo hired Pinkerton after several gold shipments disappeared in that crooked sheriff's county. Russ slipped in undercover to catch the sheriff red-handed. While undercover, he found evidence that the sheriff framed Kenigan. The governor pardoned him after Russ and Pinkerton's appealed his conviction. Russ saved Kenigan from hanging."

"Nobody ever tells me nothing." Frustrated, Kimberly swung atop her black filly.

I dug into my pocket for a gold eagle. I tossed it to her. "Rent for borrowing your horse."

She tossed the coin back to me. "Keep it. Or, if you want to double it, put it down on me and Big Enough. We're set on winning the Fourth of July race in Holbrook this year."

I gave her my best smile, and raised an eyebrow. "You're going to win that big race with your little filly?"

"She's plenty big enough," Kimberly said, "and so am I." She spurred the black horse across the valley at a dead run.

I watched her ride away. I couldn't help gauging the speed of that little filly. She was nothing, if not fast.

"You come visit any time, Russ. Any time, hear?"

I promised myself I would. Kimberly's pa and I watched her race her black filly over the spring grass on McCullough's White Mountain meadow.

The End

Biography

Charles T. Whipple is a native of Arizona who resides in Chiba, Japan. Whipple writes fiction and nonfiction. His  articles have appeared in many magazines, including Time, Newsweek, Honolulu magazine, Tokyo Journal, Cruising World, Boating New Zealand, Sport Diver, and more. His nonfiction books include Seeing Japan, Inspired Shapes, and several in Japanese.

He writes western novels under the pen name of Chuck Tyrell for Black Horse Westerns, Edition Bärenclau, Piccadilly Publishing, Sundown Press, and contributed short stories to the Express Western anthologies Where Legends Ride and A Fistful of Legends, and Western Fictioneer anthologies.

He is part of the Ford Fargo persona that writes the Wolf Creek series from Western Fictioneers. He has won prizes for both advertising and journalism, and received the first-place Agave Award in the Oaxaca International Literature Competition in 2010. His novel, The Snake Den, won the 2011 Global eBook Award in the western fiction category. Whipple was a lifetime member of the now-defunct National Association for Outlaw and Lawman History. He is a current member of Western Writers of America, Asian-

American Journalists Association, Society of Writers, Editors, and Translators (SWET), Tauranga Writers Inc., and, of course, Western Fictioneers. Whipple is married, has one wife, two sons, four daughters, and 19 grandchildren. He is fluent in spoken and written Japanese, and understands many forms of English.

If you have questions or comments, contact me at: chucktyrell@gmail.com

https://www.amazon.com/Snake-Den-Chuck-Tyrell/dp/1535584122

https://www.amazon.com/Return-Silver-Creek-Chuck-Tyrell/dp/1535584106/

https://www.amazon.com/Pitchfork-Justice-Chuck-Tyrell/dp/1535583266

TIBBY'S HIDEOUT
Frank Kelso

Tibby Newcomb stormed from the farmhouse to slam his wide-brimmed straw hat on the barnyard before plopping down beside it. "I ain't going." The eight-year old sat cross-legged, cupping his chin in a hand while his elbow rested on a knee.

Behind him, Ma scurried chickens away from her baggage next to the freight wagon. She tousled his hair when she passed him.

"Yer pose reminds me of yer Pa, dark-haired, skinny, and danged stubborn," Ma said.

"This here's *my* home. It ain't right for ya to take us an' run off," Tibby said.

Ma yanked him from the ground with a fistful of his shaggy black hair. "Thibodoux Thaddeus Newcomb, get in that there wagon. Sass me one more time, an' I'll snatch ya bald-headed." She lifted him onto the open freight wagon. "Ride or walk, makes me no never mind, but ya understand this: Yer going to New Mexico with me and Isaiah. Not. One. More. Word." Ma stepped to the front of the wagon, placing one foot on the front hub to climb aboard.

"Please let me stay with Grandpa Anschutz. He needs my help on the farm." He swiped a hand across his cheeks, smearing the tears on his dirty face.

After he spoke, he glimpsed Ma shaking clinched fists above her head.

She twisted around. "Arrgg, Tibby," she said, stomping to the wagon's tail.

"Baby, baby. These here folks ain't yer real—" Ma hugged him, but he pushed her away.

"I ain't no baby. Grandpa Anschutz might not be my real grandpa, but he's my onlyest Opa." Tibby yanked a pillow from under Isaiah, his little brother. "Why not marry a German fella from Comfort? The fellers who came calling have right good farms. Why leave to marry Joe Junior?"

From the corner of his eye, he studied Ma, who straightened, turning her head to scan the well-tended farm. Karl and Gerta Anschutz adopted his family after Ma carried home their son's body. Wil Anschutz died in the same Kiowa attack that killed his Pa and Uncle Thaddeus. He didn't have a true memory of those events, just listened to what Ma reported from those days.

"They's good folks. Us'ns will say prayers for Karl and Gerta," Ma said. "I feared ya boys might not've survived if'n they hadn't took us in. How some ever, that danged War of Rebellion is long over—it's time for us to move on." She tied on her homemade straw hat.

Ma favored wide brimmed hats to the cloth bonnets most women wore on the open prairie. Grandma Anschutz had trimmed Ma's mousy brown, straight hair into what Oma called a "Dutch boy." After a family breakfast that morning, Oma and Ma agreed the Anschutz family would wait inside 'til we rolled away, since folks waiting outside made parting all the harder.

"If we're gonna sit here, can I go to the outhouse?" Isaiah said, climbing from the wagon.

"Come back here soon as you're done," Ma called. "And wipe clean."

She leaned her face close. "Child, this here land has got too many bad memories. These danged Texans kilt my Pax. I ain't never forgivin' them." Ma puckered her lips like she'd spit, then scrubbed her face with both hands before shifting her head to gaze around the farm again.

The sheen of new grass camouflaged the arid realities of the upland plateau in late spring. In another month, the sun would rule. Soaring temperatures would wither the grass, turning it brown and lifeless. The constant heat would change the springs and creeks into dry pockets.

"Joe's people have lived in New Mexico an' the west for thirty years. The Robidoux brothers trapped fur an' traded in old Santa Fe an' Taos before the Mexican War. He owns him a general store in Las Vegas, New Mexico, and a sheep ranch in the nearby mountains. He's a good man. He makes me happy. He's come to take us home." She wrapped an arm around Tibby's shoulder.

"Ain't there somebody else, Ma?" he whispered.

Ma pulled his face away to gaze into his eyes. "He done sump'n to hurt ya ... or Isaiah?"

"No, Ma. This ain't nothing like that ... awww, ya wouldn't understand."

"Are ya scart he ain't honest? Or he's a swindler?" She tousled his hair, but he smoothed down his cowlick. "He sure ain't marrying me for my money." Ma shined a dimpled smile.

"That's for dang sure," he mumbled, but she rewarded his 'dang' with a knuckle pop on top of his head. Rubbing the spot, he glanced up, letting his eyes droop while forcing a sad smile. He pasted on what Ma called his sad-eyed, puppy face.

"Why are ya marrying anyhow? Ya used to say ya didn't wanted no other man but Pa. What changed?"

Ma hugged him to her chest for long minutes. "Tired of being alone at night. I miss sitting on the porch in the dark, talking, and snuggling. Turned twenty-two last month—I'm still young. Way too young to dress me in widow's black more than six years." She held him at arm's length, smiling. "Listen to me yapping out my heartstrings to my eight-year-old."

Ma placed a finger on his nose. "Joe Junior makes me alive again. He's come here to move us to New Mexico. I'm a-getting' married in his church with his family a-watchin'. Get that into yer blockhead, *dummkopt*, as Opa likes to tease ya." She grabbed him in a headlock, knuckle-scrubbing his hair, while he squealed in mock pain.

Seven-year old Isaiah climbed into the wagon. When he passed by, he flipped off Tibby's hat. Isaiah looked like him, with Pa's straight, black hair, and every bit as lean and lanky.

"I'm tired of yer horseplay. Isaiah, sit up front on the wagon seat between me and Carlos. He's a-driving the wagon." After settling on the wagon seat, she placed a double-barrel shotgun across her lap. Ma called, "Joe Junior, I'm 'bout as ready as I'm gonna git."

That spring day in 1867, Joseph Robidoux, Junior, signaled to roll the freight wagon from the German immigrant's farm near Comfort, Texas. It joined another three wagons carrying freight west on the military road to Pope's Crossing on the PecosRiver, then the wagons planned to head north, following the river to Las Vegas, New Mexico.

Tibby sat on the last wagon's tail, picking feathers at random from the pillow beneath him. He mumbled, complaining under his breath, soft enough it'd not carry to Ma.

"Nobody understands, not even Opa. I'll just hav'ta run away. Wait a few nights, so she thinks I'm going along, then

I'll scat." He nodded with a sharp bob, as if he agreed to a bargain.

"Once they're underway, Joe Junior ain't gonna turn all these wagons around to search for me. I'll hide out for a few days, an' walk back here to Comfort—it ain't *that* far."

Tibby no sooner decided, than Joe Junior reined in his big gelding, dismounting. He strode alongside the rolling wagon. A slight hawk-nose, hinting at Indian blood, filled the man's square, sun-browned face.

"Ya always ride that big sorrel?" Tibby asked.

"Rusty's an easy riding horse, mighty comfortable. I let him rest every other day, so I don't wear him out." Joe Junior slapped the end of the reins in his gloved palm twice while he spoke. "Bess said you want folks to call you Tibby. Said you thought saying Thibodoux makes folks sound like they lisp. Alright if I call you Tibby?" Joe raised an eyebrow.

"Sure." Tibby shrugged. Joe stood well over six-feet, about as tall as Pa, Ma told him. Joe's baritone reminded Tibby of a bullfrog's croak—deep and booming. He held no memory of Pa's voice. Ma said Pa wore a beard, but Joe sported a bushy black mustache hanging past the corners of his mouth. It matched his long, dark hair, combed straight into a pigtail held in a leather cuff.

"You know how to ride?" Joe jerked a thumb at Rusty.

Tibby shot him a lip-curling snarl at the insult.

"Sorry. Dumb question to ask a Texan." He scratched the back of his neck before he nodded his head at the gelding. "Like to ride my horse while we're talking?"

"Sure." Tibby hopped from the wagon.

Joe lifted him onto the saddle. "I don't like riding on a wagon—hurts my butt. A saddle's easier on the butt, don't you think?" He eyed Tibby's height. "You 'bout tall as your Ma?"

"I'm not her five-two, but I'm heavier. Ma's like a bird; her bones don't weigh nothing."

"I ordered a saddle made to fit her. Do you reckon she'd let you use it when she isn't riding?"

"It don't make no never mind. We ain't got no horse," Tibby said.

"Tomorrow, we'll join the rest of my supply wagons at Fort McKavett. There'll be more men and stock for the trail west. I bought Bess a little buckskin mare for a surprise—don't tell her."

"Ma'll like that. *Opa* and *Oma* didn't like her riding—they feared she might get hurt."

"Bess told me you don't want to leave them. Sometimes friends can be more dear than kin."

"All I know is I like them, and I like living here. I ain't in no hurry to move away. Ma carries bad memories of how we came to Comfort, but I don't. All I remember is the good times."

"We all should be so lucky," Joe Junior said.

Man and boy followed the wagon without interrupting each other's thoughts for a spell. The soft rolling hills of central Texas rippled before them, a lush green in the late spring.

"Ma told me ya got a sheep ranch in the mountains. Are them mountains close by? How tall are they? Ya ever climb clear to the top?"

Joe chuckled at his rapid-fire questions. "The ranch sits in the Sangre de Cristo foothills. The peaks're over two miles high. I often hunt elk up there, but never considered hiking to the top."

"Ain't never seen tall mountains. Folks carry on like they're a wonder, all snowy and pointy on top. Ain't never seen snow, neither. What kind'a moniker is that 'San grey' you called them?"

"It's Spanish—Sangre de Cristo. It means Blood of Christ."

Tibby waved his hands, signaling to keep-away. "Lordy, I struggled to learn Opa's German. Now you come along a-talking Spanish. No, thanks. Done learned enough of strange tongues."

"I'm impressed you learned German. It's hard to say the proper pronunciations."

"Opa forgets to talk in English when we're working on the farm. I understand him good, but he don't understand me so good. Do all the folks talk that Spanish where you live?"

"The Mexicans do, but few *Yankees* do. The people who work for me are Mexican, so we speak Spanish most of the time, unless we're with Yankee customers. When a lad of your age, I spoke French with the old mountain men and fur trappers, but they've died or gone away."

"If ya got ya a general store, why ya need a sheep ranch?"

"Our family came from French Canada. Trade has been the family's business since my great-grandfather Joseph's day. My parents named me Joseph Junior to honor him. He built the family's first trading post in the wilderness. Later, the town of St. Joseph, Missouri, grew around his post. He named its streets after his children. Trade in pelts and hides dwindled after people moved west, which led us to owning herds for wool and mutton. Sheep make a tidy profit."

"If ya got all that, and family up north, why'd ya come down here to steal my Ma away?"

Joe kicked a rock in the road. "And I thought we were getting along?"

The next day, they rolled from Fort McKavett. Joe gave Ma the mare and saddle the night before. Tibby'd never seen Ma this happy. She didn't need him no more. It's time to run away.

To his surprise that evening, Ma gathered Isaiah and him beside the campfire. "I asked Joe Junior to carry us across to visit yer Pa's land. I wanted to say goodbye to Pax and Uncle Thad. Ya boys ought'a visit the land where yer Pa fought and died before we leave Texas behind."

"We taking the wagons across the ford Uncle Thad and Wil Anschutz built?" Isaiah asked.

"No, child. Miguel and the men will keep the wagons rolling toward Head of Concho. We'll ride across to the farm on horseback; a half a day there, an' a day's ride on to Head of Concho."

"Are the dead Kiowa still laying there?" Tibby asked, jumping up. "Remember how ya learned us to watch out for them Kiowa. They're more sneaky than them ol' Comanche." He glanced at Joe Junior. "In our family, we yell 'Kiowa' to warn of danger."

Isaiah punched Tibby's arm, which forced Ma to move Isaiah on her other side.

Joe coughed, clearing his throat before he answered. "Their people would've given them a proper ceremony. They don't bury their dead like Christians do. They wrap the body in buffalo hides before laying the remains on a wood altar to return to the land."

"You gonna tell us the battle story again, so we can see where it happened?" Isaiah asked.

Ma's head dropped to her chest. "I only wanted to visit where Pax and yer uncle Thad are at rest. Done told ya. I drug their bodies inside before I set fire to the cabin with them inside. 'Twas all I could do by myself. Why do ya keep asking the same ol' questions?"

"Opa told me in his country, that's a warrior's funeral, an honorable tribute." Tibby said.

"This ride won't delay us none," Ma said. "The weather's clear, so we'll camp overnight at the old farm before we ride west the next morning. I want ya two to behave, and mind Joe."

Ma placed a hand under each of their chins. "I mean it. Ya two gotta stop the mischief."

A moment later, Isaiah mumbled a reply before Tibby said, "Yes, Ma." This will make it easier for him to sneak away. Yeah, he'd slip away tomorrow night. Be long gone by sun up.

The next morning, after Tibby rose to dress, Joe told the boys, for this short distance, they'd ride double, one each behind Bess and him. The family reached the Concho in three hours.

"Ma, the ford's like you told us in the story." Tibby hollered, pointing at the limestone shelf where the Middle Concho formed a wide waterfall. He and Isaiah slid from the horses to run toward the water.

A quail whistled a mating call. Smaller winged darts flitted among the brush alongside the Concho. The horses' movements spooked a pair of wood ducks into flight from the deep pool at the fall's base. The flowing water fed the thick brush, which sheltered the local wildlife.

"You can wade across the upper shelf. Be careful around the drop-offs," Joe called.

While Ma and Joe Junior rode the horses across the rock-bottomed ford, Tibby glanced at Isaiah. "Ma's riding slower and slower, like she don't want to visit the old place a-tall."

It didn't surprise Tibby none when Ma insisted the boys stay close to her. "There's still wild Comanche out here an' who knows what kinds of riff-raff. Stay within sight, ya hear?"

Tibby slapped Isaiah's arm. They laughed together where Ma couldn't catch their antics.

"It's easy to see why Pax picked this," Joe called. "The small springs seeping in these hills making it greener here than to the west. The Middle Concho nourishes the whole valley."

At the top of the ridge-line, Joe gave Isaiah and him permission to run ahead as long as they didn't get out of sight. Joe rode with a Winchester "Yellow Boy" rifle in the crook of his arm.

Once they arrived at the cabin's ruins, Ma and Joe dismounted. He stood close behind Ma.

"There ain't nothin' here, but a mound of rock and weeds." Tibby's shoulders sagged when he gazed at a pile of rocks forming the highest point. He figured it must'a been the fireplace.

Isaiah chimed in. "This don't look like no cabin and barn to me."

"It burnt to the ground ... an' it's been six years." Ma twisted around, burying her face against Joe's chest, releasing a low moan. "Didn't expect it'd take me like this."

Joe wrapped his arms around Ma, kissing the top of her head. "You're doing what your family needs, Bess. Let it all out. Tell them goodbye. Then, you can ride west without regrets."

"I guess Ma don't need me to care for her no more," Tibby said, nudging Isaiah.

Above the cabin's ruins, Joe set up an open camp at the edge of pin-oaks next to a lush meadow, the remains of Pax's fields. After tying a canvas tarp between two bushes, Joe pointed to the thicket, "That's the privy. No poison-ivy in there." He handed Ma a green-striped towel. "When you see her towel on the bushes, you know your Ma's in there—you stay away—got it?"

Ma stared at the ruins below for a long time before she eased down the slope. She stood near the ruins before covering her face with the towel. Tibby watched from above while her shoulders shook in rhythm with her sobs.

"Give her some time alone, boys," Joe said. "Let her unburden her grief. She'll be her happy self again, once we ride west." He sent the Isaiah and him to gather firewood. "Gather dry, dead limbs like I taught you. We'll light a small fire with no smoke. No need to attract unwelcome visitors."

When we returned, each carried an armload of downed, dry branches.

Ma called from the ruins. "Field peas and pole beans are still a-growing in my garden."

Tibby and Isaiah rushed to join her. They placed fresh-picked vegetables on her towel.

Later, Ma escorted Isaiah and him into camp, carrying fresh-picked vegetables in her towel.

Crossing the camp, Ma slid the shotgun from her saddle scabbard.

"Whoa," Joe held out a hand to stop her." Where are you going with that?"

"There's a mess of rabbits in my garden. I reckon they'll make us a nice supper."

"They'll be better than the elk jerky and *refritos* Carlos sent along." Joe lifted a red cloth sack with Carlos's food. "Do I assume that's the shotgun you wielded when you lived here?"

Ma dipped her head as if his question embarrassed her. "No, I used an ol' muzzleloader back then. Papa Karl ordered this Bayard 12-gauge from Belgium. The breech breaks open to load ready-made shells." She flipped the lever behind the twin hammers to let the double-barrels drop forward. The open breech exposed the brass-bottomed shells.

"He whittled the stock to fit me. Next, he shortened the barrel by ten-inches to make it easier for me to handle." Before easing down to the garden again, she tied a skinning knife's scabbard on a belt, which carried her extra shotgun shells. She looped the belt across her shoulder.

While Ma hunted rabbits near the ruins, Tibby sneaked from Joe's camp to scout the next rise north to find a possible hideout.

~~~~~~

After a half hour, the shotgun boomed. Isaiah spun around to run toward the ruins.

"Wait," Joe called. "She's not done. Don't go down there. She'll return when she's done."

After glancing around, Joe asked, "Where did Tibby run off to?"

"He's playing like he's a scout out looking for Injuns. Said he'd be back in a bit," Isaiah said.

"You think we should help him find some?"

"Nah. He's always going gallivanting. He drove Oma *verrückt*." Isaiah tapped his temple.

In Bess's absence, Joe and Isaiah played mumblety-peg with the camp knife.

Bess fired her shotgun two more times over the next hour.

~~~~~~

Tibby returned the camp a few minutes before Ma tromped in with three rabbits. She'd skinned and gutted them, making them ready for the fire on green cottonwood sticks.

"Where'd ya learn to skin rabbits?" Tibby asked.

"Foolish boy. I larned to trap and skin rabbits 'fore I gained yer age." She patted his arm. "I didn't larn healing sitting in the house all day. Healers tromp the woods to find herbs and roots for their potions. When you're a bit older, you can join me when I go collecting."

"Ma can do anything," Isaiah said, blatting his wet tongue at Tibby.

The family settled around Joe's warm fire. Before long, they enjoyed roasted rabbit with fresh, raw peas and beans. Joe let the fire burn down after sunset. Tibby watched Joe toss on a shovel of dirt to bank the coals.

Laying on his bedroll, Tibby listened to his Ma and Joe talk. In a while, they snuggled together. He reckoned they'd sleep good in a bit. He planned to slip away after they slept.

Tibby woke with a start—he had fallen asleep. He'd be later sneaking away than he intended. Gathering his gear, he rolled his blanket before grabbing his water and a sack of food. Yesterday, while he scouted north across the ridge, he spotted a tall, rocky bluff on the valley's far side. He figured to find a decent cave in among them rocks to hide 'til Ma left with Joe Junior.

A waning moon lit his way. He toted Joe's red gunny sack with elk jerky and cold *refritos*.

Opa taught Tibby to carry water, if leaving the farm. In his German way, Opa fashioned a water skin from a sheep's stomach. For Tibby's waterskin, he carved a goat horn, shaping it into a stopper

The sky brightened in false dawn while Tibby crossed a small creek in the valley's middle. He quickened his pace, intending to cross the open grassland before full daylight. It would not do for Joe Junior to see him crossing here if he expected to hide out.

Stunted pin-oak trees littered the bluff's west slope. Tibby climbed up the rocky bluff. Viewed from the south side, the slope appeared to continue rising, unbroken, to the top.

Tibby jerked back in surprise when he wandered to a drop-offs edge. A spring-fed waterfall had created a hidden box canyon alongside the bluff. He shifted direction to follow the rising terrain but stopped again after a few minutes. The lowing of cows rose from the box canyon.

"That's dumb. With all the grass in the valley, why pen them cows in here?" he said aloud.

A heavy blow between his shoulders sent Tibby tumbling into the box canyon.

Tibby lay where he stopped rolling.

In a while, he stirred, wondering what the heck happened. "Dang," he croaked. "What did I trip over?"

He shifted to sit up but failed in his first attempt. Scratching around with one hand, he searched for his water skin, but couldn't find it. His thoughts came jumbled. He lay confused. Hidden in shadows of sunrise, now and then, came a strange noise he couldn't quite place.

"Hey, tadpole, if you're looking for your water, it's right here. This is a right good water skin. Think I'll claim it once we're done here."

For the first time in his life, Tibby knew to keep his mouth shut—covering it with one hand.

"It's a good thing you ain't a yappy pup," another voice said from behind him. A "zzzzit … zzzzit" irritated like a fingernail on slate.

Tibby recognized the annoying noise, the repeated "zzzzzit … zzzzzit" of long knife blade drawn across a sharpening stone. Knife-man leaned against a gnarled mesquite, while he continued his sharpening. *He ought to use that knife to shave.* Tall and slim, Knife-man wore Rebel gray britches with a yellow leg stripe. He hitched a pair of dirty gray galluses over a faded, red long-johns top with frayed cuffs at the wrist.

After he swiveled to the other side, Tibby sized up the first man. Water-man wore ragged, dirty blue bib overalls over a sail-cloth, laced-yoke shirt. He held Tibby's water skin in his left hand. The first finger of his right hand lay inside the trigger guard of a Spencer repeater. The rifle barrel rested on his knee with its muzzle pointed at Tibby.

Their scruffy appearance fit Opa's description of "scavenger trash." He wouldn't hire workers in misfit clothes accompanied by out-of-sort manners.

"You answer some questions right quick, I might let you live to watch the sun set today. You thirsty?" Water-man sloshed the skin around. "A drink for each answer."

Tibby nodded, running his tongue across dry lips.

"You live near here?" Water asked.

Tibby shook his head.

"How'd you get here?"

Tibby shook his head. "Water."

"Gonna be stubborn are you?"

"Your rules—water for each answer," Tibby croaked.

Knife-man guffawed. "He got you there. Give him a drink."

Water lifted the skin, squirting a long stream at Tibby's face. Not much went in his mouth, but it washed and cooled his face while wetting his dry lips.

Tibby wiped his face with a ragged shirtsleeve, drawing blood from his forehead.

"I asked where you come from?"

"Folks got a ranch on the Colorado's south bank." He pointed north over the tall bluff and away from Joe and Ma's camp. "My horse shied an' I fell off, like a *dummkopt*. Once I got my bearings, I figured the Concho water is closer, so I walked south. Looks like I found water."

"Couldn't get you talk—now I get a sermon." Water spat a gob of tobacco, but Tibby scooted his boots aside.

"I'm due a drink," Tibby said.

Water squirted at his face again, forcing Tibby to shift around to catch it in his mouth.

"Spunky pup. Reminds me of me at that age," Knife said.

"Shut up," Water said, pointing a finger at Knife. "Was you alone? Hard to think yer folks would let you ride out alone," he asked Tibby.

"If'n I rode with anybody, don't ya think we knew to mount doubled before headin' to Pa's ranch?" Tibby shook his head, piffling his disgust at the dumb questions.

"He got you again." Knife laughed, ducking as Water squirted him.

"Hey, that's my drink. Squirt it over here," Tibby hollered.

"To hell with you, tadpole." Water tossed Tibby the half-empty water skin. "Let Randy decide when he gets back from scouting around. Enjoy breathing while you can."

"A little rustling riles folks, but killing a kid will bring a posse," Knife said.

"We'll get hanged for rustling, anyway. They can't hang us twice." Water replied.

"Y'all point me north with a full water skin. It's a week's hike back to the ranch. In a week, y'all be long gone. Nobody will know where ya went with them cows," Tibby said.

"On the other hand, tadpole, I can slit your throat to achieve the same result," Water said. "Now that you yapped about the steers, you ain't giving me much choice but slitting your throat."

Tibby decided to shut his mouth for a while. He hoped Randy, whoever he was, didn't come across Ma or Joe while he scouted around the Middle Concho.

Clopping hoofs signaled a rider in the pin-oaks hiding the canyon's narrow mouth.

Randy rode into camp to slide from his dun mare before it stopped, like an old cowpuncher. Compared to Knife and Water, Randy dressed in clean, well-fitting clothes. He appeared to have bathed and shaved in the last week. Striding to the campfire, he poured a tin cup of coffee.

"I would've missed them if not for their whooping and calling this 'uns name. They called 'Tibby.' Is that right?" He cocked his head, displaying a lop-sided grin.

Tibby nodded once.

A hard smack on the back of his head knocked Tibby to the ground.

"You lied to me, tadpole." Water jerked his thumb across his throat. "Slit his throat. Hunker here 'til his folks quit nosing around. After they're gone, we sell them steers to that butcher fella in Austin like we planned."

Knife shook his head. "I joined you two 'cause I need the money to pay the Yankee's land tax. I didn't sign on for killing a family and kids. Let the kid catch their wagon after we leave."

"Ain't riding a wagon. They ride two fine saddle horses— worth two-hundred dollars each." Randy scratched his neck. "Let's sit tight for today. Wait to see what they do before we decide."

Tibby studied the men while they lazed around the camp through the morning. Water tied a rope around Tibby's neck before he tied the other end to a young poplar tree shading the camp.

Knife fixed the noon meal. He fed the leftovers to Tibby on a tin plate, but made him eat with his fingers. Like it was the first time Tibby had ever done that.

Randy spoke to Water. After some complaining, he stood, grabbing his Spencer rifle. Water climbed the limestone cliff behind the camp. Randy strolled to Knife, who cleaned the skillet after the meal. Knife scrubbed the skillet dry with sand before he set it aside, grabbing his rifle. He saddled his horse before walking it through the pin-oaks at the entrance.

Tibby watched the two men depart. *They're up to no good.*

The noonday sun chased shadows from the canyon.

Randy sauntered toward Tibby, smiling as if they just met. "If your folks stay south, we'll let them be. Don't want the problems you're bringing to mess up this deal. This thing's been working fine for three months ... then you stumbled in at first light this morning."

Randy untied the rope from the poplar tree. "Put your back against this tree, sit down, and stick your arms behind you. I'm tying you here so I can get some sleep without you running off."

When the sky changed colors with sunset, Tibby watched Randy dig a cast-iron Dutch oven from the coals. About then, Knife trotted his pony through the pin-oaks. He unsaddled his horse before he watered it, wiping it down afterwards. Loose gravel tumbled down the canyon's edge, signaling Water's return. Each man grabbed a tin plate and coffee cup before ladling on a beef stew from the Dutch oven. The stew's meaty aroma set Tibby's stomach to flipping somersaults.

The men sat together, but didn't speak loud enough for Tibby to catch what they said.

Thirty minutes later, Randy strode close carrying a plate of food and Tibby's water skin.

"Here's the deal, Tibby. I'll untie you, if you eat and listen." He continued once Tibby nodded. "We've done played out thieving cattle hereabouts without drawing a posse. We need a week to move these cows before we're gone. To make sure we get that week, we're gonna take your folks' horses, leaving you and your family on foot. You show me where your folks camped. I'll explain all this to them, then let you go. Is that a deal?"

"If I help, ya will let us go?" Tibby used the big-eyed puppy face he tried on Ma earlier. He hoped it worked better on Randy than it had on Ma. He wouldn't trust Randy to feed his dog.

"Sure, Tibby. You help me—I'll help you and your family." Randy shined that same lop-sided grin he shined this morning after he rode into camp.

"Okay, I'll lead you to our camp." Tibby nodded in mock sincerity.

"Not so quick. I ain't getting tricked into an armed camp. What guns do y'all carry?"

"Joe Junior wears a cap-n-ball Colt and uses a single shot Sharps Fifty-two. Ma carries an old twenty-gauge, single-barrel, muzzle-loader for rabbit hunting. Isaiah and me ain't got no guns."

"You call your Pa, Joe Junior?"

"My Pa died in the War. Joe Junior ain't married to my Ma yet."

"The War created lots of widow women. Where's your wagon? Hard to believe a family would be riding double without a home or a wagon nearby?"

"We're gonna meet a wagon train at Head of Concho. Supposed to get there tomorrow."

"Your folks early risers?"

"Ma's up at the first color shift before the dawn." Tibby nodded in pleasant agreement.

"Sleep tight, kid. You'll see your folks at first light." Randy retied the ropes.

~~~~~

Randy roused his crew early, ordering them mounted in the dark. He mounted Tibby in front of Water. "I told him to slit your throat if you call to them before we get there. You got that?"

Water tied a rope around Tibby's neck, cinching the rope to the saddle horn. "Don't fall off, tadpole. You'll hang yourself." Water cackled aloud. "I know you're gonna like this." He jabbed Tibby in the kidney with a stiff thumb as he spurred his horse past the pin oaks.

Randy led them across the shallow valley before he glanced at Tibby for more directions. They dismounted in the trees north of his Pa's former plowed field across from Joe's camp. In the false dawn light, figures moved around the camp's low fire. The camp held no horses.

Yanking the rope around his neck, Randy jerked Tibby close. "It looks like they're packing to leave. Why would your Pa go off an' leave you? What ain't you telling me?" he whispered.

The cold steel of Water's knife chilled Tibby's throat.

"I told you—he's not my Pa. Let him leave. Never liked him anyway." Tibby turned his back to Joe's camp. "Take me back to your camp. Do what you gotta do to me after they're gone."

"I don't trust you, kid," Randy looked at his men. "I want those horses. Let's get this done."

The men tied their horses in the scrub post oaks before Randy led them across the field along the brush line. Water held the rope on Tibby's neck in his left with the knife in his right hand.

From fifty-yards out in the meadow, Randy called, "Hello, the camp."

Shadowy figures in the camp dropped to the ground. The shout caused the early morning birds' chatter to fall silent.

"Hello. I found a boy. I'll make you a trade if you want him back. He's a mouthy rascal."

Joe stood before stepping to the camp's front. "I agree. He's kinda mouthy. Not any kind of a worker, either. I hope you ain't expecting much." Joe held his lever-action rifle across his chest.

"Damn. That's a new 'Yellow Boy' repeater. Shoot him," Randy hissed.

Tibby clamped his teeth onto Water's knife hand.

Water yowled, dropping the rope to smack Tibby's head.

"Kiowas," Tibby screamed while he ran for the brush line. "Kiowas," he yelled again, to warn his family.

Joe dived to the ground when Randy and Water fired their pistols.

In a crouch, Knife ran left, trying to flank the camp, while Randy sprinted to catch Tibby.

Rapid fire from Joe's repeater sent Randy and his crew diving for cover.

Tibby played rabbit, laying flat on the ground under a bush while holding his breath.

Across the field, Knife jumped from hiding to rush the camp in a headlong dive.

A shotgun's blast slammed him hard, as if he dived into a wall—a lead wall.

"It's a single-shot," Water shouted, rushing the camp. "Get her before she reloads."

The shotgun's second barrel roared, drowning Randy's warning, "The kid lied about their guns." Randy spun to run north along the field's brush line. "I'll get you for this, Tibby."

Joe struggled to his knees, firing four rapid shots. One of the repeater's slug's found its mark, dropping Randy. After watching the man fall, Joe collapsed, still gripping his Winchester.

"Joe. Joe," Ma screamed. "I won't let this place claim another of my men." She ran to where Joe lay with his clothes bloody.

Tibby ran into camp, rushing to his Ma when she reached Joe's body.

"Ma, I'm back." He ran to her, expecting a hug.

Ma slapped his face with an open-hand. "Ya foolish boy. Yer silliness done got my man kilt. Ya ain't safe to be let loose among common folk." She grabbed the rope hanging from his neck. "Them fellers knew ya to be a walking calamity looking for a place to happen."

"Woman, you make enough noise to wake the dead," Joe said. He laughed his deep baritone bullfrog croak. "God, it even hurts to laugh."

Ma let go of Tibby, dropping next to Joe, "Who are ya laughing at? Ya best not be laughing at me when I'm a-holding a loaded shotgun." She said angry words, but Tibby saw her smiling.

"I told Tibby riding a wagon made my butt sore. So what happens? I get butt shot."

Ma hugged Joe tight before kissing his mouth. "You ain't getting away that easy, Mr. Joseph Robidoux, Junior."

She ordered Tibby to use the hand ax to cut four tall saplings for her to build an Indian travois for Joe.

"If ya want back in my good graces, ya'll not chop off yer foot or Isaiah's hand with this."

Tibby and Isaiah chopped and trimmed oak saplings from the nearby grove.

~~~~~~~

Once the boys left the camp, Bess dropped Joe's britches. A bushwhacker's bullet tore a gash across Joe's right butt cheek while he dived for cover. When Joe dived for the ground, he ripped a long gash in his forearm, which accounted for the blood on his shirt, faces and hands. Relieved to find his wounds minor, she fetched her satchel of herbs and medicines.

"You told me you're a medicine woman, a healer, but I never expected to get trussed up by you so soon," Joe said.

"Ya can laugh an' joke all ya want. Wait 'til I git to stitching to see who laughs last."

Amid his squawks, she cleaned his gashes—top and bottom. "I larned potions and poultices from my granny when a girl not much older than Tibby." She wiped the wounds with a swatch soaked in carbolic acid from her medicine kit.

"Oww, that smarts. It smells like coal oil. What is it?"

"Carbolic from coal tar. It's better than Granny's poultices to prevent blood poisoning. I trust Granny's potions and poultices for common things, but not gunshot wounds. Nature didn't have no gunshots. Grit yer teeth, I'm gonna sew you tight."

She continued talking to allay her nervousness while she worked on her man. "Granny larned to use roots and herbs for healing from an old crone in the north Alabamy hills where we lived."

Joe jammed a pants leg in his mouth to stifle his agony while her needle pierced his skin.

"I larned to stitch cuts from a travelling doctor in Louisiana. Larned to mid-wife from birthing my boys." She finished the last stitch, wiping the sewn edge with carbolic again.

"'Fore ya sweet-talked yer way into my life, I reckoned I'd move to Fredericksburg or Boerne. I hold the Anschutz dear, but I needed my own place, to have my own life."

"That means you'll need a little place to set-up practice in Las Vegas." Joe nodded to her.

"I'd like that. Thank you." She kissed him on the lips. "Ya still trade with the Injuns?"

"Sure. The Navajo and the Utes still come around. The Comanche aren't so welcome."

"Ya think I could talk to their medicine women?" Bess tilted her head, raising an eyebrow.

Joe laughed. "You'll need to learn Spanish. Most of talk it or have one who does. I notice you left out the Comanche medicine woman. When will I learn their story?"

"That's a bedtime story. You'll have to wait until we're alone."

~~~~~

The boys waited together at the camp's edge, gawking at Ma's stitchery, fore and aft. She waved them into camp so they could help her pull a fresh pair of pants onto Joe.

Tibby help Ma cut pieces from Joe's lariat to lash short cross-sections to the longer poles. With the basic frame formed, Ma tied a blanket across the lower section. She tied the smaller ends of the long poles into each stirrup. The long poles straddled Joe's horse while the large-ends dragged along the ground behind.

After laying Joe on his left side in the travois, Ma gathered Isaiah and me in her arms.

"This is the second time I've cut an' run from here. I'm tired of leaving the dead, toting the survivors, and carrying all I hold dear. I ain't taking another step," Ma said, stamping her foot.

Ma grabbed Tibby by the shoulders to give him a good shaking.

"Tibby, for God's sake, look all that's happened. Joe's been shot. We fought an' kilt them no-good bushwhackers. Why can't ya tell me what's so terrible wrong that ya want to run away?"

Tibby stifled a sob. "Oh, Ma—"

"What? *What?* Tell me." She shook his shoulders again.

"You recollect what you said when you told us you wanted to marry Joe Junior?"

"Don't recall nothing special. Told ya boys Joe wanted to marry me; I said yes."

"Then you said after you married Joe, they'd call you Mrs. Robidoux," Tibby said.

"That's what happens when a woman marries; she takes her husband's name," Bess said.

Tibby sagged as if the weight of the world fell upon his shoulders.

"Oh, Ma. I cain't go through life with a moniker like **Thibodoux Robidoux**.

The End

From the Author:

I appreciate you taking your "quiet time" to read "Tibby's Hideout." I hope you enjoyed its humor. One question folks ask is how did you get story ideas. As a teenager, I lived near Liberty, MO, Jesse James' hometown. That's where Jesse invented drive-through banking; like many innovators, Jesse was ahead of his time—according to the sheriff.

On a recent visit to my siblings in the KCMO area, I suggested we drive to "Joe Town," as we called it, to visit the Pony Express Museum and other historic sites; an easy drive for a pleasant visit. The founder of St. Joseph, Missouri, Joseph Robidoux, a French trapper, named the main streets in downtown for his children and wife. I had just published "True to the Union," an award-winning short story on Amazon, with Thibodoux as a toddler nicknamed "Tibby." The rhyme of Thibodoux Robidoux stuck in my head. I outlined Tibby's Hideout on the return drive to KCMO.

As mentioned above, the Pony Express spread the word before telegraph put it out of business. If you liked "Tibby's Hideout," please tell your friends—the old Pony Express— word-of-mouth is the best advertisement. Amazon (and other readers) rates a book by the number of reviews; I'd appreciate a review, if you have the time.

A critique group member, John O. Woods and I are co-writing a western adventure series. "California Bound" follows Josh and Zach, two confederate survivors of a Yankee POW Camp. They promised if they survived, they'd go west to find their fortune in the California gold fields. The road to California isn't always a straight line. Look for it Fall of 2017.

Biography

Frank Kelso grew up around Kansas City, Missouri, the origin of the Santa Fe Trail. Historic sites, monuments, and statues abound highlighting the journey west, including the Wagons West, Pioneer Women, and the Indian Scout located on the bluffs overlooking the wide Missouri. Writing western  themed books fit with his upbringing. His parents considered storytelling a family tradition, and the taller the tale, the better, when sharing around the supper table. A biomedical research scientist in his day job, Frank writes short stories and novels to keep the family traditions alive.

Frank has several of his award winning short stories available on Amazon, which he uses to promote a following for his coming novels, "The Apprenticeship of Nigel Blackthorn" to be released in Fall of 2017 and "A Message to Santa Fe," to be released in Spring of 2018.

Please check my WEB http://frankkelsoauthor.com for my other novels and short stories. I offer followers free books and other prizes. Click over to my WEB page to sign-up with your e-mail. While you are clicking, give a "like" to www.facebook.com/AuthorFrankKelso/ If you'd like to browse my books and short stories, or read samples pages, stop by my Amazon Authors page:

https://www.amazon.com/Frank-Kelso/e/B00N990V3A/

If you have questions or comments, please contact me: frank@frankkelsoauthor.com

Links to my books:

https://www.amazon.com/True-Union-Frank-Kelso-ebook/dp/B00LYJOL3I

https://www.amazon.com/Flop-eared-Mule-Frank-Kelso-ebook/dp/B00M3IQXCG

https://www.amazon.com/Windmill-Frank-Kelso-ebook/dp/B00LWIU540

A MESSAGE FROM EE BURKE

Special thanks to Frank Kelso and the authors of *The Posse* for giving me a chance to read this fabulous collection of Western short stories, and for allowing me to include two chapters of my new book

E.E. Burke

Warm, witty... a little wild. That's what you'll find when you pick up a book by bestselling author E.E. Burke. Her chosen setting is the American West, and her latest series, *The Bride Train*, features a cast of unusual characters thrown together through a misguided bride lottery. *Maybe Baby* is her first Contemporary Romance, and features a handsome modern-day cowboy!

Other series include *Steam! Romance and Rails*, which follows the lives of dangerous men and daring women caught up in a cutthroat competition as the railroads advance across the frontier. Her novella, *Victoria, Bride of Kansas*, part of the unprecedented *American Mail-Order Brides* series, is a Kindle Top 100 Bestseller and a semifinalist in the 2016 Kindle Best Book Awards.

E.E., also known as Elisabeth, has earned accolades in regional and national contests, including the RWA's prestigious Golden Heart®. Over the years, she's been a disc jockey, a journalist and an advertising executive, before finally getting around to living the dream--writing stories readers can get lost in.

Steam! Romance and Rails, The Series Collection

Dangerous men and daring women are caught up in intrigue, mayhem, even murder, as the railroads advance across the Western frontier.

HER BODYGUARD: A woman embroiled in intrigue employs a bodyguard to protect her from a killer, unaware that he's an outlaw hired by her enemies to put a stop to her plans.

KATE'S OUTLAW: After a railroad heiress is abducted, one of her Indian captors inexplicably becomes her protector. On the run from danger, with enemies on both sides, they discover a love as powerful as it is forbidden.

A DANGEROUS PASSION: An inquisitive author sets out to expose a corrupt railroad baron and becomes ensnared in a deadly mystery and a dangerous passion.

FUGITIVE HEARTS: When a newly made widow tries to cover up the truth behind her husband's violent death, her plan backfires, sending her fleeing from a hardened lawman determined to bring her to justice.

This series collection reached #1 on Amazon's bestselling Westerns. If you're a fan of gritty historical detail woven with passion and suspense, this series is for you.

Visit my website to read excerpts and learn about new projects.
www.EEBurke.com
Follow EE Burke on:
https://www.facebook.com/authoreeburke
https://www.amazon.com/E.E.-Burke/e/B00EDYK9AU
https://twitter.com/author_eeburke (@author_eeburke)
https://www.goodreads.com/author/show/7215607.E_E_Burke
https://www.bookbub.com/authors/e-e-burke
And through the blog: http://getlostinastory.blogspot.com

The following excerpt is from:

HER BODYGUARD

Chapter 1

March 1, 1870
Former Cherokee Neutral Lands,
Southeast Kansas

Hell must be like this. Not lit with blazing fires, but cold and gray, barren as the dead prairie. Even the wind howled like a deranged demon, flinging bits of ice into Buck's face. He drew the blanket and oilskin tighter, although nothing warmed the persistent chill in his bones that'd gotten worse as he'd ridden north through Indian Territory. He was a walking dead man here in Kansas, so it seemed somehow fitting he'd entered the abode of the damned.

He patted Goliath's neck, glad for the company of his horse. He had few acquaintances, even fewer friends, and none who would risk their necks for another man's cause. Buck wouldn't have risked getting his neck stretched had the plea not come from his only remaining kinsman. Although at this point, freezing to death seemed more likely than being lynched.

The saddle creaked as he straightened. All around, he could see nothing but mounds of switch grass and stunted trees. No houses or barns, not even smoke from a chimney. He swore, his breath sending out a white cloud. The wind snatched it away. His plan had been to reach Girard before dark, buy a hot meal and a warm bed before meeting with his cousin to get details on the job he'd come to do. But he couldn't risk going on. He had to find shelter.

The fading daylight and worsening sleet made it difficult to see, but was that something just ahead? Buck touched his heels to his stallion's sides, moving closer to the mass taking shape. A buggy, slumped to one side. In front of it stood a single horse with its head down and a woman huddled in a cloak, removing the traces. What the hell was she doing out here all by herself?

Buck sat back in the saddle, uneasy. He'd made it a habit to avoid damsels in distress after being betrayed by one. However, he couldn't very well leave a woman out here on a lonely road in the middle of an ice storm. With a muttered curse, he kicked Goliath into a fast trot.

On his way to her, he passed the buggy's rear wheel, lying on its side in the brush like a wounded animal. Odd, he'd never seen a wheel fly off like that. Generally, the metal rim popped or a spoke snapped. Had the axle nut been loose when she started out? She was damn lucky the buggy hadn't rolled on top of her. He had seen *that* and it wasn't pretty.

His stallion whinnied, excited by the scent of the woman's horse. The mare threw its head and answered.

The lady hadn't noticed him because she was so focused on unhitching the fidgety bay. But now she whirled around. Her hood, drawn low over her face, shadowed her expression but it was clear by her startled response she hadn't expected anyone to come up on her. Rather than calling out for help, as he anticipated, she dashed toward the buggy's compartment.

The mare shied away from the sudden movement, then reared up, squealing. The buggy started to rock.

"Look out," Buck hollered.

The woman didn't move away from the danger. Instead, she dove into the compartment.

"Goddamn it!" The curse was lost in the wind. He came out of the saddle, dropped the reins on the ground. In a few long strides he'd reached her. "Get out of there."

What the hell was she doing? Trying to crawl beneath the buggy's seat?

The contraption tipped dangerously to one side. Buck snaked an arm around her middle and hauled her out of the death trap.

She twisted around, yowling like an enraged cat. "Get your hands off me."

Her horse squealed and tried to run. The lame buggy hopped.

"Stop screechin'. You're scaring the hors—" Something blistered Buck's cheekbone. "Ouch! What the devil?"

"Let me go!" She went for his face again with her claws.

"Stop that." He swatted her hands away, but managed to keep hold of her while he backed away from the buggy. "I'm just tryin' to—"

Her sharp teeth sank through the leather glove into his finger.

"Blazes!" He yanked his hand away and then grabbed a flailing arm, pinning her against him. Splaying his fingers over the side of her head, he smashed her cheek against his chest to prevent her from biting him again.

Furious screams became muffled growls. Her booted feet, dangling above the ground, lashed out to kick him. Thank God her skirts got in the way or she would've hammered his shins.

"Stop fighting, you loony woman." He sucked in a breath and checked his temper. Large as he was, and with her no bigger than a minute, he could easily break her.

As he adjusted his hold on her, the hood of her cloak fell back. His fingers slid through a silken mass of hair. In an instant, he became aware of the woman he held—her soft breasts and flaring hips, a delicate fragrance like wildflowers. Something hot and primitive coursed through him. His body responded before his brain could catch up.

She must've sensed his reaction because she started swinging her legs again.

He held her tighter. "Will you *listen?* I'm tryin' to help."

"Not...helping." She gasped the words. "You're...choking me."

Buck eased his hold. His physical reaction couldn't be helped, but he could sure as hell control his strength and keep from hurting her. "All right. I'm setting you down." He hesitated a moment before releasing her. "Don't fly at me with those nails."

She raised her eyes. The black centers swallowed the golden irises like an eclipse of the sun.

His gut clenched. He'd seen that look in the eyes of men he'd faced down, but not women he aided. He hadn't meant to frighten her. He frowned, more comfortable with being annoyed. "That horse about pulled the buggy over on top of you. That's why I grabbed you."

Her dark brows winged up. "You...you were *helping* me?"

"That was the plan."

She seemed further confused when he snatched his blanket off the ground where it had fallen during their tussle and flung it around her. Then he set off to retrieve her horse. That buggy wasn't going anywhere.

He approached the nervous mare with soft, shushing sounds and laid his hands on its quivering withers. The frightened creature stilled and let him remove the traces.

Sleet peppered the brim of his hat, although the worst of the storm seemed to have passed. He took a look around the bleak surroundings. They were still were in danger of freezing if he didn't find shelter soon.

After unhitching the harness, he brought the horse around. Thankfully, the woman hadn't run off. She'd inched over to the buggy compartment and was rummaging around again, maybe looking for something.

"Unless you've got an axle nut in there, we can't fix this buggy. Can you ride?

She whirled around with a tiny pistol clutched in her hands. "I'm not g-going anywhere with you."

Buck's pulse kicked up a notch. Her hands shook so hard he worried she might actually fire the damn thing before he could talk some sense into her. "You plan on staying here?"

Her chin came up. "I plan on taking *my* horse."

He bit back a curse. Did she think he was *stealing* the nag? Why was he even bothering to help her? He might as well head off down that road, leave her to her own devices. No one could blame him. Only ... he'd never abandon a woman. Not even one that was stark raving mad.

"Christ, I don't have time for this foolishness," he muttered.

He offered her the reins, but when she reached out to take them, he locked his fingers around her wrist and nabbed the gun. Then he hauled the reluctant damsel to where he'd left Goliath.

The stallion had remained, as trained, right where they'd stopped. He didn't dare put the woman on her horse. Frightened as she was, she'd probably race off and end up breaking her neck. He looped her mare's reins around his saddle horn.

"Wait!" she burst out. "I have m-money. I can p-pay you more."

"What are you clatterin' about? I don't want your money." Buck nearly added if he'd wanted to rob her, he'd have done it and been gone by now. "We got to find shelter before we freeze to death. You live nearby?"

The woman stared up at him, her eyes rounding. Was she so addled she couldn't understand what he was asking? Maybe the cold had gotten to her. He'd take her and head down that road, which he assumed led into Girard.

He lifted the woman onto Goliath and mounted behind her. There wasn't enough room in the saddle for two, especially with all those skirts, but somehow he managed to get her situated across his lap. Thank the saints she didn't go into conniptions.

The ends of her cloak snapped in the wind. She shuddered so hard it made *his* teeth rattle. He opened his greatcoat then wrapped them both in the blanket and oilskin.

She burrowed into his chest like a baby rabbit. Her vulnerability tugged at his heart. Wouldn't kill him to offer her comfort.

He curled his arm around her. "Warmer now?"

She nodded her head.

"Where do you live?"

"I...*we* have a farm...I'll see to it you're well compensated if you take me there."

So, she was married. No surprise. With so few women out here, even a crazy one would be snatched up, especially one smelling this sweet and with soft curves in all the right places.

"How far is it?"

"Up the road, just a little ways."

"A little ways? As in few minutes?"

"I...I'm not sure exactly."

Buck snorted in disbelief. She didn't know where she lived? "We can't wander around. It's getting dark."

"We could make Girard. It's maybe a half hour's ride."

256

Maybe? He turned the stallion and peered in the direction she'd indicated, gave a grumbling assent. He was going to Girard anyway. Although he wasn't sure they'd make it before night set in and the temperatures dropped even lower. "Anything else nearby?"

"Our farm…"

"That you can't find."

Shit.

Grudgingly, Buck nudged Goliath onto the road. According to his cousin's letter, thousands of settlers had poured into these former Indian lands. If so, where were they? Did they all live in town? Or was this strip of land reserved for the railroad's use? The exorbitant price they'd put on a godforsaken wilderness seemed ludicrous. Of course, why anyone would want to farm it was also a mystery. Didn't matter though. Sean had settled here, had worked the land, and now the railroad's owner—rich bastard—was trying to cheat him out of it.

Buck tilted his head down to keep the wind from snatching his hat. The woman turned her face into his vest like she was trying to warm her nose. He cradled her closer, felt her relax in his arms. Warmth spread through him, and not just from the heat of their bodies, it came from someplace deep inside, a part of him he'd thought was long dead.

He squelched a flare of alarm. Concern for another living creature, that's all it was. Nothing more. He didn't give a tinker's damn about anybody, save his family—what was left of it.

They'd gone only a few miles when something caught his eye. He straightened and peered at a shadow. Whatever it was, it was big. Then he sighed with relief. "There's a barn over there."

She peeked out from beneath her hood. "It's abandoned, and the house was burned down. We can't stop there."

The hell they couldn't. "So long as there's a roof, we're stopping."

* * *

The stranger wrestled the barn door open then dragged Amy off his horse. Before she could protest, her feet left the ground and he carried her into the dark interior, dumping her on a pile of hay before vanishing back into the night, taking his warmth with him.

The wind shrieked in a wild tantrum and the boards creaked and moaned, as the stranger rustled about getting the horses settled somewhere on the other side of the barn. Amy stared blindly into the darkness, hugging the blanket, shivering, both from cold and lingering fear.

It seemed her rescuer wasn't the mysterious assailant who'd been skulking around after her. When the towering stranger had come upon her out of nowhere, she'd feared the worst and had gone for her gun in the buggy. The first time, he'd pulled her away before she could find it. Then, once she'd retrieved her pistol, he'd disarmed her. That he'd done it so easily was beyond humiliating. The cold must've slowed her mind and her reflexes. Even after he assured her he meant no harm, she'd worried he might only be telling her that so he could take her somewhere and abuse her before killing her. But he hadn't done more than cuddle her close, as if he wished to comfort her. For some inexplicable reason, she'd let him.

She chewed her lip, her thoughts whirling. If the Land League hadn't sent this frighteningly large fellow after her, where had he come from? He didn't look like a farmer, not with that Henry repeater holstered by his saddle and those revolvers strapped to his hips. Not to mention the knife as long as her forearm, which she'd discovered while huddled close to him. On the other hand, he might've armed himself in light of the increased violence in these parts.

Was that why her typically protective suitor hadn't made it back to town to escort her? Had Fletcher been waylaid by thugs working for the Land League? Or had he, too, been caught unawares by the change in the weather? If she'd known a late winter storm was imminent, she would've found someplace to stay in town, despite the risk.

Her nerves jumped at the scrape of a match. Light flared. Amy blinked as the stranger approached with a lit taper. Not just well armed, but well prepared.

Her gaze traveled from his scuffed, square-toed boots up long legs encased in checkered gray trousers of the California style cowboys favored. A heavy greatcoat hung past his knees. Around his neck, he wore a faded bandana, its color indistinguishable. His hat looked older than his shoes and its brim shadowed his expression. Was he one of the countless drifters passing through, looking for work?

"At least we'll have some light." His spoke in a low drawl, raspy as gravel in a dry creek bed. Strangely enough, she found the sound soothing. After securing the candle to the underside of a bucket, he set it nearby. "Careful not to knock this over. I'd build a fire, but with all the hay this place would go up like a torch."

Why did he feel the need to explain as one would to a child or a very old person?

"My mental faculties aren't so deficient I'd set the barn on fire." She tried to adjust the blanket more securely, but her numb fingers wouldn't obey and it kept slipping off.

The stranger knelt, removing his hat. Flaxen hair fell in tangled waves past his collar, and the light revealed a ruggedly handsome face—in sore need of a shave. Brown whiskers bristled on lean cheeks and a tawny mustache nearly hid his mouth. But it was his eyes that captured her, their color, so unusual—somewhere between blue and gray, but pale as a washed-out sky.

"Give me your hands." He stripped off his gloves as he issued the command. Rather than waiting to see whether she'd obey, he began to chafe them between his calloused palms. "How come you're not wearing gloves?"

She bristled at the disapproving tone. He'd made it clear he believed she was a simpleton.

"I had need of my fingernails." She didn't explain the problem with the frozen harness strap, which had necessitated the removal of her gloves to pick away the ice. No doubt she'd dropped them during their struggle, and she'd been too flustered to retrieve her muff. Not that he would've let her go back to the buggy after she'd pulled a gun on him.

His wintery eyes narrowed. Along his cheekbone, a crusted line of dried blood marked a scratch she'd put there. Her insides coiled tighter. She shouldn't have made it sound as if she'd intended to hurt him. She didn't even remember doing it. All she recalled was the sheer terror that had overcome her when he grabbed her.

He released her hands and began to unbutton his vest and shirt.

Her heart fluttered with renewed fear. "What…what are you doing?"

"Ravishing your frozen fingers."

Capturing her hands, he threaded them through the opening in his shirt, then sandwiched her palms against his chest. His body radiated heat like a furnace, and soon her fingers began to burn. With a moan, she tried to pull away, but he held fast.

"It's good if you feel pain. That means you won't lose your fingers."

Lose her fingers? *God forbid.* She burrowed through crisp hair on his chest, seeking the warm skin beneath.

His eyes widened a split second before his features turned to stone.

The heat she'd taken from him went straight to her face. What was she *thinking* to touch him like that? She stilled her hands.

The muscles beneath her fingers flexed. Her skin tingled in response. The startling sensation spread up her arms and curled around the tips of her breasts. With a gasp, she yanked her hands away and tucked them under her arms.

Almighty. Was she *attracted* to him? She'd never been drawn to rough men like this one. It had to have something to do with the strangeness of the situation. She hugged the blanket as her teeth started chattering. He hadn't molested her, but that didn't mean he wouldn't if she kept touching him. Cold or not, she wasn't taking the chance.

He reached over and snatched away the blanket.

She squeaked in protest. "What are you doing?"

"We need to get you warmed up."

"If you t-take my blanket, how do you suggest I get warm?"

He grasped a handful of her damp cloak. "You won't, if you stay in those wet clothes."

He was right. Amy cursed another lapse in reason. Her fears had rendered her senseless. "I should've retrieved my valise. There is a dry outfit in there—"

"Fair to say it ain't dry any longer." He snagged his saddlebag. Thrusting his hand inside, he withdrew several items of clothing. "Here, put these on."

She wrinkled her nose. He didn't really believe she'd don his undergarments, did he?

He frowned at her and shook them. *Yes, he did.* And she'd be a fool to refuse dry clothes. Perhaps his shirt over her underclothes, just until her other things dried out.

Before she could act, he plopped down, yanked her foot into his lap and began to undo the laces on her boot. His touch set off another bout of shivers that had nothing to do with the temperature of the air.

"What are you doing?" She jerked her foot out of his hands.

"Taking off your wet clothes, since you seem too addled to take care of it."

"I am *not* addled." She scooted back. "I can tend to myself, if you would be so kind as to give me some privacy."

He stood, seemingly tall as a mountain, his eyes gleaming like polished silver. "Good to see you recall how to get undressed. I wasn't looking forward to doing it for you."

* * *

Buck strode to where he'd stabled his horse, anxious to get away from the all-too-appealing woman he'd rescued. He'd held her close enough to feel those sweet curves. Come to find out, her face was just as nice. Still, he hadn't been prepared for the surge of lust when she'd splayed her fingers over his chest.

She'd felt something, too. He'd seen it in her eyes. And for a half second, he'd considered taking her right there on the hay. Only, she was frightened…and *crazy*. Couldn't forget that.

Inside the stall, he scooped up a handful of straw and began to dry the remaining dampness from the stallion's smoky coat. Goliath pawed and snorted, preening for the mare in the adjacent stall.

"You better behave," Buck whispered. "If she's like her owner, she'll kick you into next Sunday for messing with her."

The stallion whinnied.

"You're right. Might be worth it. Still, better not take the chance. Besides, that woman's none of my business." Buck's hand stilled. He'd made her his business when he brought her in out of the cold.

He sighed, shaking his head. They were stuck here for the night, so he had to make the best of it. But once he got her safely to wherever it was she was going, he'd find his cousin and focus on the only business he cared about—getting justice for his family.

From the other side of the stall came the unmistakable shush of garments being shed.

Buck wrestled his conscience, but the temptation was too strong. Taking advantage of his height, he peeked over the wall, curious as a crow with a shiny object in sight.

She had her back to him and he couldn't see a thing below her neck because she'd pushed up a pile of hay and was hiding behind it. *Smart gal...*and not as crazy as he first thought.

Her green dress went over a rail, along with countless petticoats, each fancier than its neighbor. Lastly, she set aside a bedraggled headpiece too small to call a hat, but with plumes he was sure were peacock feathers.

He shook his head, more intrigued than ever. With those fancy clothes, she could've walked right off a fashion plate in one of those ladies' magazines he'd seen in his stepfather's mercantile. Who was she, and what was she doing out here, smack dab in the middle of former Indian land? This place was still wild, and based on what Sean had reported, it was getting a lot wilder since the settlers' dispute with the railroad had exploded into an all-out war. Was her husband involved? That might explain why she'd reacted with fear.

Buck's heart raced as he watched her lift her arms to shake out a glorious length of chestnut hair. The candle's light reflected off golden strands. He swallowed hard, his hands fisting. God, he would kill to run his fingers through those tresses.

His mind conjured an image of the voluptuous beauty stark naked, beckoning him to join her on his blanket. Sizzling heat shot straight to his groin. Biting back a tortured groan, he turned away before she caught him peeking at her.

He rested his arms on Goliath's withers. "Just my luck. I had to rescue a *Venus*," he muttered. "Why couldn't she be ugly and buck-toothed?"

"Sir?" Her voice drifted over, breathy and uncertain. "If you want to come back, I'm decent."

Decent? Sure she was. But those curves weren't, and no shirt of his was going to help. He'd lied through his teeth when he told her he wasn't looking forward to unwrapping her. Except, she'd claw his eyes out before he could see anything.

He touched the scratch across his cheekbone and winced. Should've announced his intentions before grabbing her, but he'd been so shocked to see a woman out alone in this weather, then when that buggy started rocking, well, he'd just leapt off his horse and raced to the rescue. A wry smile twisted his lips. That gal sure hadn't seen a white knight. Not that he was interested in being one.

Against his better judgment, he ventured back to where he'd left her, sitting on the hay next to the bucket that held the candle. She had her legs tucked up beneath her and that scratchy blanket wrapped clear to her neck and was clutching at it like she was afraid he might take it away. His conscience tweaked him. He'd all but threatened to strip her if she didn't undress. It'd been too long since he'd been in the company of decent women. This would be an uncomfortable night for both of them if he didn't at least try to ease her fears.

He unbuckled his gun belt, wrapped it around the guns and went down on one knee, carefully laying the revolvers within her reach. The Bowie knife went beside the holsters. Her eyes followed his every move. At last, her shoulders lowered and the tense expression softened. More than that, he could actually *feel* her distress draining.

Buck rocked back on his heels, bemused. Over the years, he'd honed his instincts, relying on gut-level intuition to stay alive. But this strange connection seemed to extend to an ability to pick up on the ebb and flow of her emotions, which tugged at his own like the current in a river.

She offered a slight smile. "Thank you for saving me, Mr.—?"

"O'Connor," he blurted, absurdly pleased by the gratitude shining in her eyes. On second thought, he should've given her an alias. Still, it was unlikely she'd ever heard of him. He wasn't as well known as his friend Cole Younger. "Couldn't let you turn into an icicle."

His breath clouded the air. Come to think of it, this ramshackle barn was damn frigid. It offered shelter from the sleet, but did little to keep the cold out. "Here, let me pile up some hay. It'll block the drafts and keep you warm."

"What about you? Are you warm enough?" She hugged the blanket, shivering.

"You want my coat?" His hands went to the buttons. Should've thought to offer it earlier.

Her eyes widened. "No, I wasn't implying that. I just thought *you* might be cold. We can share the hay."

For a moment, he was speechless. It'd been so long since anyone cared about his comfort, he hadn't expected it and didn't know how to respond. He shrugged to hide how much her concern touched him.

"Ah, don't worry about me. You hungry?" He rummaged through the saddlebag, finding the last piece of jerky. "It's not much, but it'll take the edge off."

"Thank you." She gifted him with a smile that snatched his breath.

He leaned back on one arm, trying his damnedest not to look like an infatuated schoolboy. Instead of sitting here mooning over her, he ought to find out what he could about the local situation. Whatever she knew might come in handy when he started searching for that railroad promoter.

"So, you live out here, Mrs., uh..."

"Langford," she finished.

He tried the name in his head. *Mrs. Langford.* Nope, he preferred Venus.

She bit off a small piece of jerky with perfect white teeth, chewed slowly and swallowed before continuing. "Yes, I live..." Her voice trailed off and her lashes lowered.

He leaned forward, worried. "Something wrong?"

She shook her head. "I'm sorry, Mr. O'Connor. I wasn't honest before. I don't live around here. I was headed for a friend's house before starting back to Fort Scott."

That she'd fibbed about where she lived didn't surprise him. She'd done it so he'd think her husband was nearby. But where she was going astonished him. "Fort Scott? That's another two days' ride."

"By rail it's only a couple hours. But the line hasn't reached Girard yet, so we have to go a few miles north to meet the workers' train."

"We?"

"I was traveling with an escort. He attended a meeting earlier today in Baxter Springs and didn't make it back. We'd arranged to stay overnight at a friend's farm, so I thought I'd meet him there."

"Your husband *abandoned* you in Girard?"

Irritation flickered across her face. "He's not my husband, and he didn't abandon me."

It was on the tip of Buck's tongue to ask why she was traveling with a man who wasn't her husband. But then, what did he care who she traveled with? He opted for a safer question. "Why were you there? From what I hear, it's not exactly a safe place for a woman."

She finished chewing the last bite before responding. "I had business in town."

"Business?"

Her lips sealed. Apparently, she didn't wish to elaborate.

Buck smoothed his mustache with his thumb and forefinger, mulling over her hesitation. Just what kind of business would a wealthy lady have with a bunch of rowdy settlers? When he'd come up on her, she'd been terrified, even after he told her he was trying to help. Had even offered him money. *More* money…

His scalp began to tingle, a sure sign something wasn't right. He leaned forward, draping an arm over his knee to appear casual. "I didn't mean to frighten you when I rode up. You must've been expecting trouble."

"Trouble is one way to put it…." She toyed with a curl at her cheek, not meeting his eyes. "You see, I thought you were going to kill me."

www.ingramcontent.com/pod-product-compliance
Lightning Source LLC
Chambersburg PA
CBHW020247180626
46810CB00006B/2409